About th

Maurice Jones, 67, is an award-winning journalist who first shot to infamy in 1977 with the shortest defection in history: three and a half weeks in East Germany, en route to the Soviet Union.

Jones spent 12 years working for the National Union of Mineworkers, including the tumultuous year of the 1984-85 strike when he edited the NUM paper, *The Miner*.

In 1991, two years after leaving the NUM, Jones won the coveted Newspaper Society Yorkshire Journalist of the Year award.

Jones, whose formal education ended at 15 when he joined the Merchant Navy, is a rarity among writers: a self-taught man who overcame huge personal obstacles to write this, his first novel, at a time when most people seek a quiet retirement.

A private pilot for over 20 years, he currently lives in Lancashire and spends part of the year on a small island in Finland, where he does much of his writing.

Jones has been married to his Finnish wife, Leena, for over 40 years. They have one daughter.

Praise for Maurice Jones's *Last Resort*

'With lashings of humour and great originality, Maurice Jones has got across one of the most challenging messages of our time: the old are not fodder for a throwaway society's ever-expanding scrapheap, but people in a different phase of life whose capacity for fun is not dead; just dormant, waiting for the right spark.

'To get the best out of this new quirky read, you need to approach it tongue firmly in cheek – for this is a cheeky book that translates novel ideas into the world of tomorrow. It is best appreciated by thinking, "this might actually happen!" – although I would not necessarily recommend it does!

'We may well have a new Tom Sharpe here.'

RT Hon David Blunkett MP

'The timing of this book could not be better. Society's gone to cock! Grandads, grandmas all shoved into care homes. It's an awful business. Thailand is supposed to be the land of smiles. What goes on underneath might be another thing … but it's certainly all smiles on top!'

June Brown (Dot Cotton, EastEnders)

'After reading this, no more fear. We've all got the green light to grow old disgracefully, and when your time's up, go with a huge smile on your face – like this book gave me.'

Jon Wise, *The People*

'What a truly fascinating and original idea … A damaged, crackpot local politician has a radical new plan to deal with our elderly care problem. Imagine a dark and anarchical *The Best Exotic Marigold Hotel*.'

Carmen Reid, Author

LAST RESORT

Maurice Jones

PEACH PUBLISHING

ISBN 978-1-78036-151-2

Cover art by Glyn Hayes

Published by
Peach Publishing

To British humour – our most enduring gift to the world.

And to my late mother, Leah, whose care-home treatment compelled this book.

‘This and no other is the root from which a tyrant springs; when he first appears he is a protector.’

Plato, circa 347 BCE

‘On the other hand, in April 2010, the *Times* reported that protector-supreme Harry Wieder, an American dwarf who campaigned for better public transport on behalf of disabled homosexual Jewish midgets, was knocked down and killed by a yellow cab while crossing a New York street on crutches. He’d just left a campaign meeting. Go figure!’

Maurice Jones, 2012

PART ONE

1

Titanic Refloats

Oddly for a rabble-rouser, Arnold Ratledge had been a late starter in the art of self-arousal – only really mastering masturbation in his early twenties.

After that, there was no stopping him as he tossed off an entire trade union and the wealth of a thriving local authority.

The union members could not have known what was coming. Wigburn Borough Council had no excuse.

'So you're trusting in cod, smelly geysers and a population marginally greater than Milton Keynes?' investment analyst Jack Dunsford had warned as Mayor Ratledge insisted on ploughing vast amounts of council cash into Iceland.

'Why not go the whole hog and use the last few quid to resurrect Viking rape and pillage raids?'

With his words still ringing in Ratledge's ears, Dunsford left Wigburn Town Hall forever with a request that his advice never be sought again.

Blinded by the promise of suspiciously high interest rates, Wigburn, in the heart of Lancashire, deposited more cash per head in Iceland than any other British or continental local authority.

And when the inevitable collapse came, 90 per cent of the authority's money had simply melted away.

The Ratledge plague had struck again: What his leadership did for organised labour in a disastrous strike decades ago, now infected an entire northern mill town.

Central government, obliged to save the borough from outright bankruptcy, stood ready to intervene. For Ratledge there could be no salvation as the media queued to bury him extra deep.

His grand plan to use the council as a route back to the national political stage was now as likely as an MP's under-claimed expense allowance.

Ratledge had not endeared himself to Wigburn right from the outset, attempting to tax prostitutes in a madcap bid to raise revenue.

The scheme centred on fitting girls with lightweight chastity belts that operated on a smart-card principle.

Working out of licensed brothels, the girls would, in effect, be electronically tagged, carnal access only granted to clients swiping a card – dubbed a 'hard card' – across the belt.

Payment was to be strictly in advance, punters billed instantaneously and automatically, according to the period swiped for. Getting rocks off and doing a runner – the bane of a prostitute's life – would be impossible.

At the end of the paid-for period, a 15-second warning buzzer would signal that the belt's jaws were about to snap shut, strongly discouraging any overrun.

A plastic prototype, incorporating ingenious sanitary features, had been built at Manchester University and there had been no shortage of student volunteers to do the testing.

But the whole project ended in disaster when the belt malfunctioned and a particularly adventurous student lost the tip of his tongue.

Wigburn Council was sued, the case dragging on for 18 months – not helped by lawyers having great difficulty understanding what the student was saying.

The council lost the case and the national media agreed that, without doubt, Arnold Ratledge was a delusional madman.

***

From an early age Ratledge had been a driven creature, convinced his natural role in life was that of leader. 'There are those born to lead and those born to be led,' he would tell confidantes – when the downtrodden masses were safely out of earshot.

An only child, in many ways he was the archetypal, pampered loner, inhabiting a make-believe world.

He stood out from the crowd by his sheer lack of anything that could make him stand out. No aptitude for music, painting, drawing, handicrafts, writing or even burying himself in a book; a critic's review would do, giving him just enough information to hold his own through low-level conversation, before steering the talk back to his favourite subject: Himself.

Some 5'5" of shapeless blubber, squeezed into garments that gave the illusion of manly form, housed this living vacuum.

None of this bothered Ratledge unduly. His unrivalled ability to fire up a crowd was all the compensation he desired for life's other shortcomings.

Ratledge's rhetoric enjoyed its first public airing in a modest 1950s courtroom and it gave the world a memorable taste of what was in store. A neighbour's Dalmatian had bitten him in the backside, ripping a hole in his new suit. He wanted it dead.

The court reporter had been semi dozing after a liquid lunch, listening with half an ear to the mundane details. Then Ratledge spoke and the reporter woke.

Mavis Ratledge, his wife of eight months, was being thrown to the wolves and it was her own husband doing the chucking.

Ratledge flashed her picture before the court, and she ticked all the wrong boxes of idealised womanhood: short, dumpy, thick glasses.

'This Dalmatian is dangerous and has severe mental health problems,' Ratledge confidently stated.

'Here is a picture of my wife – yet this animal gets an

erection whenever she walks by. Obviously this is a mad dog that needs to be put down.'

Two death sentences were sealed that day: the dog's and Ratledge's marriage.

Mavis Ratledge petitioned for divorce on the grounds that no woman could be expected to live with a man who'd provided the immortal headline:

WIFE-FANCYING DOG WAS
OBVIOUSLY MAD, SAYS HUSBAND

No one argued.

***

Ratledge's brain was in overdrive as he surveyed Wigburn's wrecked finances from behind his eight-foot, mock Georgian desk – a £500 'snip' that had proved highly profitable.

The story was that he had splashed £12,000 of public money on 'this shameful extravagance' as one regional newspaper described it.

The libel case added £20,000 in tax-free damages to Ratledge's bank balance – a nice little earner, and the idiot journalist he'd subtly encouraged to push the story never suspected a thing.

Yes, life could be good, but payback time now threatened as enemies queued to settle scores.

Dusting off old faithfuls, Ratledge blamed Wigburn's troubles on international capitalism, Wall St, media moguls – the usual suspects he rounded on at times of crisis.

It was and sounded stale, fooling no one as Wigburners scratched heads, marvelling at their own stupidity in electing him Mayor.

Ratledge was on course for another footnote in history; again, for all the wrong reasons. He was now at his darkest hour, desperate for any chink of light.

It dawned in a screaming headline that picked out in huge, underlined type, '£3bn.'

This colossal sum, dwarfing Wigburn's woes, was the estimated care-home cost for looking after Britain's elderly.

Alarmingly, it was expected to hit £6bn by 2020 and then go into the stratosphere. Ratledge devoured the report.

The whole care-home situation seemed to be in confusion, with politicians running around like headless chickens, laying eggs labelled inquiries, commissions, scrutiny bodies and anything else kickable into the long grass.

Three facts coalesced: Paid carers, many on the legal minimum wage, only had scant training for the job – no recognised qualification needed; annual care costs for a single old person could exceed £50,000; care-home profits, milked from the taxpayer and the elderly's means-tested assets, were astronomic for some companies.

With the baby-boomers approaching retirement, a mood of national desperation was setting in.

Alternative options included council-administered Personal Care Budgets that cut the elderly adrift with an annual pot of money, expecting them to fish for carers in shark-infested waters.

For Ratledge, a multi-millionaire, care of the elderly had been of little interest. His own future was assured and that's what mattered.

But the care issue was now generating widespread fear and chaos – twin midwives of political opportunity, and Ratledge's old friends.

Searching out a bottle of over-proof malt whisky from his hospitality cabinet, he poured two fingers, adding spring water to release the vapours. That's what sophisticated drinkers did, he'd read.

Wigburn's Mayor hated his uncouth image, indelibly established at a Labour Party fund-raising event decades ago.

Alongside the sausages on a stick, impaled cheesy bits,

silverskin onions, olives and savoury biscuits, a tempting bowl of exotic-looking 'nuts' beckoned.

Young Ratledge had ambled over to the bowl, grabbed a handful, popping a few in his mouth.

Failing to crunch them, he opted for lots of spit, calculating that even the hardest nut must eventually soften.

Only when he saw other guests putting hands to mouths and topping up the bowl did it dawn that he was trying to eat olive stones they had spat out.

With effort, he'd managed to keep the story out of the papers but was aware that time had not dimmed its appeal.

It was still good for a cheap knowing snigger whenever a dull dinner party needed livening up. It was never raised in his presence, but word always filtered back and the squirming embarrassment felt afresh.

As the whisky kicked in, Ratledge sat down, resting his feet on the desk. Head tipped back, his eyes gently closed as thoughts crowded in.

The buzzer he pressed was a direct line to Wigburn's Chief Financial Officer, Stanley Vincent. 'Stanley,' said Ratledge, 'can you pop up. I'd like a word.'

On that bitterly cold, windswept February day in Lancashire, Arnold Ratledge unknowingly set in motion a revolution of sorts.

Grey, lined and knackered they might be – more hip-replacement than hippy – but the Sixties generation were back in business, sowing the seeds of social upheaval.

***

Stanley Vincent paused at the foot of the office stairs, the throbbing in his left calf travelling up his thigh.

For a moment he hesitated, tempted by the swishing of the glass and chromium lift gliding between the floors of the Town Hall block.

But his doctor had been categorical: Exercise eased

a troublesome varicose vein, and so the seven floors to Ratledge's office would be taken the hard way.

Rejecting the easy path in life also stiffened the mental sinews, he told himself, and that sat well with his disciplined view of public finance – an approach drummed in as a child when every penny of pocket money had to be cherished or, preferably, earned.

All that had now been spat on by the reckless lunatic on floor seven; and he, Stanley Vincent, a byword for financial probity, would inevitably share both blame and shame.

Teeth-grinding resentment increased the tempo and strength of the throb. He paused, drawing deep breaths, struggling hard to stay focussed.

Was retirement not a few short years away; oblivion in which the disaster of the past two years could be buried.

Or could it? Doubts resurfaced. Would the media forever pursue him, seeking a comment whenever some council's financial inanity made the news?

He was, after all, a minor historic figure in his own right – a gatekeeper of the public purse who had failed miserably, especially in standing up to Ratledge.

The stain might well linger, like the memory of his father's bizarre breakdown in the 1950s.

Wigburn people still talked of Charles Vincent, the respected town policeman, who went on traffic duty one day, blind drunk.

For no fathomable reason, he decided not to allow any vehicle a right turn into Market Street, the main thoroughfare. A Morris Minor defied him and promptly had its pop-up, right-hand indicator ripped off by Vincent.

The driver bitterly complained to the desk sergeant at the police HQ, itself on Market Street.

'Eeeh, I was sitting here wondering why it had suddenly gone so quiet,' the local paper memorably quoted the sergeant saying. Charles Vincent agreed to alcohol aversion therapy, narrowly escaping instant dismissal.

Under controlled conditions, an electric shock was given whenever Vincent tried to raise a tumbler of whisky to his lips. The therapy worked for a short time, until at home one day he found he could beat the mental conditioning by pouring the whisky into a pint pot.

Kicked out the force in disgrace, the Vincent family endured both economic hardship and social ostracism, making Stanley more determined than ever to live a life of unimpeachable public service.

Now, all that had been compromised by the man whose office he was about to enter.

Not known for his physical strength, Vincent somehow twisted the brass knob on Ratledge's door so hard that a sharp crack echoed throughout the seventh floor.

'I'm not one to pull rank, Stanley, but isn't it customary to knock when you enter someone's office,' Ratledge said, dignity slighted. 'Tried to but something happened with your knob, your door knob. I think it's clapped out.'

Ratledge ignored the belligerence. 'Aye, there are those who think Wigburn itself is clapped out, or would like it to be,' Ratledge said, shooting Vincent a contemptuous stare.

'But then again, Stanley, there are those with a bit more faith. The people who believe this town isn't finished yet. And do you know who those people are?'

For Vincent, a man not noted for humour, the temptation was too great: 'Inmates of Farmleach?' Ratledge was not amused.

'OK, Stanley, I brought you up here for a serious discussion. If you're not up to it, we'll not bother.'

His boss's reaction surprised Vincent. Farmleach Mental Hospital/Unit for the Disadvantaged was often the butt of cynical comment by council employees. No one turned a hair except for a handful of politically correct nitpickers – Wigburn's 'authentic lunatics' in the opinion of many.

'I'm sorry to have wasted your time,' Ratledge said. 'I wanted to ask your advice – draw on your e-x-p-e-r-t-i-s-e – about an issue that might have the potential to turn this whole situation around.'

Emphasising the word 'expertise' opened a tiny fissure in Vincent's hostility. Maybe he was being too readily dismissive and should at least give his boss a few minutes. After all, what more harm could he possibly do?

'Ok, Arnie, it was just a joke. I'm a bit overwrought. So who are these "people" who believe Wigburn isn't finished?'

'Well, me for one.' Vincent's brief glimmer of hope evaporated and the disappointment showed.

'If you can break out of your pessimism for …'

'"Pessimism,"' Vincent interrupted. 'You call it "pessimism" when we have a situation where … staff don't know whether they'll be paid … bins are uncollected … schools are threatened … our old people, for God's sake, could face eviction from care homes … the prob …'

Ratledge cut in, rising from his chair. 'You know as well as I do that no government is going to let this or any other council go to the wall; they'll come up with emergency funding, or invoke their special powers, take control …'

'And confirm to the whole country that we aren't fit to run a Christmas club,' Vincent again interrupted.

'Ok, Stanley, enough. You either listen or leave.' For a few seconds that crackled with mutual loathing, neither man spoke.

Ratledge broke the silence, adopting a slightly softer tone. "Care homes … care homes, Stanley, you just mentioned the very subject I wanted to chat to you about.'

Vincent's jaw dropped as his imagination took fright: 'God, the maniac's now got his eyes on our old people.' Colour drained as Ratledge explained: 'Let me sketch in some background. This coalition Government's never going to last. I'll give 'em another year or so at the most.

'And what are the paper's full of much of the time? No, don't answer, I'll tell you. It's how are we going to take care of an ageing population, old farts like you and me in a few years.

'Did you know, Stanley, some care homes charge over £50,000 a year to look after one old person? You could have a 12-month fucking world cruise for that!' Vincent frowned at the 'f' word, but Ratledge was in full flow.

'Even the so-called cheaper homes at 29 to 36 grand a year have nothing to shout about. It costs less to send a kid to Eton. It's true, absolutely true.

'And I'll tell you something else. Unless we all book a one-way ticket to those Swiss topping-out joints, in a few years' time the situation's going to be impossible.

'We're drowning in old people and it's killing the nation – taxpayers, the NHS, and particularly us, the local authorities, the ones at the coal face, administering and helping to finance their care.'

Ratledge took a long swig from his glass. The thought of offering Vincent refreshment had not entered his head.

'We're all living too long, Stanley, and that's the top and bottom of it. There just aren't enough grafters – workers like you and me – to support the old buggers.'

Vincent's hackles were again rising. How this con artist could describe himself as a 'worker' was an affront to the nobility of labour.

Leg now throbbing intensely, Vincent glared at his boss and spoke from a sandpaper mouth.

'And what, Arnie, do you think I can do about that? Wipe out all our care home residents? I'm a finance officer, not a concentration camp commandant.' Ratledge kept his temper.

'What I want you to do, Stanley, is very simple. Get me the precise figures for Wigburn. I want to know how much we spend on the old in total: The care homes, home helps, what we're shelling out for transporting them around, the knock-on effects on other agencies, including taking up NHS beds long-term.

'I want to know every single penny we spend each year out of our total budget. And when you've done that, I want a full list of comparisons pro rata with other local authorities."

Vincent now took on a waxy appearance, common to chapel of rest 'clients' following cosmetic attention.

'Why do you want this information?' he asked, fearing the answer.

'At this stage I cannot tell you,' Ratledge said, almost managing a twinkle.

'I'm afraid that for now it all has to be confidential. Everyone's after my … errr … our guts and we must keep our powder dry. I can't risk any leaks, even though I trust you totally, of course.'

'Of course you do, Arnie,' Vincent sneered, adding, 'This will probably take weeks, and the vultures – bankers, lawyers, finance companies – are already breathing down our necks and I don't …' Ratledge cut in:

'You want the vultures to sod off? Do what I ask, but do it quickly. We might yet turn the tables on the lot of them and show that Wigburn needs help from no one.'

Vincent shuffled towards Ratledge's office door, much like the dole-queuing Wigburn men of old – despairing, without hope. Short of culling, there was no way care of the elderly could solve the town's huge problems, he told himself.

Mention of the Swiss euthanasia clinics had sent a shiver through Vincent, but surely not even someone as uncontrollable as Ratledge could be thinking along those lines.

Vincent softly closed the door, left the Town Hall, headed straight home and briefly toyed with the idea of resigning immediately.

He could not allow himself to be associated with any further Ratledge disasters. But again, the finishing line, his pension, intruded. He settled for a heart-to-heart with his long-suffering wife.

In reality, Ratledge had no cards to play; no more answers than Vincent himself. He was firing on pure adrenalin and animal instinct. It was an instinct that told him some game-changing opportunity was out there, somewhere.

And any serious answer he could come up with might work across Britain, maybe even the entire, demographically-challenged western world as governments, national and local, struggled to cope with the grey tsunami threatening all major economies.

The idea of him, eggshell bald, stemming the grey tide, forced a thin smile as he savoured the thought of playing protector. Yet again.

'Think outside the box, think, think outside the …' For the second time that day, he pushed a desk buzzer, this time summoning his much put-upon secretary, Eileen Faulkner.

There was a person he wanted tracking down. Someone who had once told him never to forget that 'every problem could be an opportunity …'

***

Seven thousand miles away and seven hours ahead of GMT, problems of a different nature were bubbling up on a still reasonably unspoilt part of Thailand's once tranquil island of Koh Samui.

At the resort of Nam Horm Ra-Kang, a Filipino guitarist yet again sang and strummed his stuff for the diners. The resort's owners were among the evening's guests, and Miguel was making an extra-special effort to impress his occasional employers.

Miguel felt happy to be in Thailand, and with good reason: Reputedly rich pickings from wealthy Thais and foreign tourists – and the inescapable fact that the Philippines was becoming a dangerous place for entertainers.

In 2009 six people had been shot dead as they belted out Sinatra's *My Way* on the karaoke machines that peppered the country. Miguel had been the warm-up man at a particularly rowdy bar in Manilla, getting drunken punters in the mood to warble their stuff.

For reasons that only the Filipino psyche could explain, friends and family members of the person at the mike – or even complete strangers – could turn maudlin, weepy, nasty and violent as verses heavy with allusion were belted out. Eye contact between singer and audience was particularly hazardous.

No offence whatever might be intended, but through the transformational magic of alcohol, murderous umbrage could be taken in the steamy, volatile clubs and pubs.

The clincher for Miguel was one poor chap who never got beyond the opening line, '*And now the end is near ...*'

A large man at a nearby table stood up, shouted 'Too fucking right, compadre,' pulled a pistol from his inside pocket and fired three bullets.

Those bullets changed two lives forever: Ending one and ensuring that Miguel would live out the remainder of his in a more placid land. And never, ever, sing *My Way*.

***

Wonderful Tonight, As Time Goes By – favourites of the Nam Horm owners – were now getting the full syrupy treatment from Miguel, but no-one was listening as family patriarch Visit Vatayanon spoke:

'We simply can't rely on foreign tourists, the bank's made it perfectly plain, Wanlaya. We either broaden out and cater for more of our own people, or the business is finished. That's the bottom line.'

For months Visit had sounded the alarm, warning of the direction the once flourishing business was now heading in.

Thailand's widely reported political upheavals and adverse

currency fluctuations had taken a heavy toll on the number of foreign arrivals in the 'Land of Smiles.'

Ominously, many of those were long-term visitors who normally returned year after year.

Wanlaya, the older of the two daughters who helped their parents run Nam Horm, cleared her throat. A business school graduate, combining financial acumen with a sensitivity rare in the hard world of commerce, she was given the nod to say her piece.

'Papa,' she began in a steady and confident voice that belied her tiny frame, 'I think if we do that, we risk losing many of our long-stay farangs.

'They come here, many from thousands of kilometres away, because it's peaceful and unspoilt. They tell me time and time again, if they wanted anything else, they'd be staying at Chaweng or Lamai; certainly not here.'

Sureerat, the younger sister, interrupted: 'But that's what we give them, normally, the peace and quiet. I know we've had a few problems recently, but they're exceptions. It's not usually like that.'

The recent 'problems' included drunken Thais damaging one of Nam Horm's pools, forcing its closure; hiring jet-skis from a nearby resort and terrifying swimmers with their recklessness; drunken karaoke sessions into the early hours; and door slamming that made sleep impossible.

The door problem had been particularly bad in the hospital-like, four-storey concrete and wooden block that formed the heart of the resort. Closed carelessly, the steel doors snapped shut, sending a metallic crash through the building.

Health workers – mainly auxiliaries, porters and cleaners (APCs) – seemed attracted to the block's hospital feel, and a 40-strong party on a combined vacation-study break – lectures in the day-time, mayhem in the evenings – had prompted the family crisis meeting.

The APCs' late-night karaoke efforts had stretched into the early hours, butchering well-loved tunes so comprehensively that two prized guests had almost checked out, Wanlaya reminded her family.

Donning only underpants, Englishman Ludo Scully had got up at 1am, strode to reception and delivered an ultimatum:

'You've got five minutes to stop this racket – or we leave in the morning.'

Reception staff were horrified. It had been no run-of-the-mill guest, but probably the most welcome regular customer on their books.

For two weeks Scully had stayed at Nam Horm in the steamy company of his beautiful, much younger partner, who to the outside world was his wife. A further 19 weeks lay ahead.

As in past years, rarely did the couple leave their little corner of paradise for five months, ordering lunch and candlelit dinners in their cosy and spacious beach-front bungalow, well away from the 'hospital block.'

Normally they turned in early, enjoying the best accommodation the resort could offer. And each other.

The unarguable downside was the karaoke machine siting – within metres of the beach bungalows.

'Mr. Ludo, we'll stop the singers immediately,' Thaworn Noibaht, the manager, had vowed.

'Singers! Singers!' thundered Scully, 'You call this lot singers! In my country there are sewing machines called Singers that have more tune.'

True to his word, Thaworn had immediately pulled the plug on the karaoke, cutting off one disgruntled practitioner in mid-verse.

Miguel, who had acted as MC during the evening, mumbled a prayer of thanks that this was happening in Thailand, not the Philippines.

The Vatayanon family discussions now grew more animated as Wanlaya stood up, her voice seemingly competing with Miguel's:

'But Papa, a resort, a hotel, it's like a restaurant. One bad experience and customers never come back …'

'*As time goes by …*'

'We'll lose these people forever …'

Silence fell from all quarters as the full impact of Wanlaya's words registered.

It was always bad form to raise voices in Thailand, but the 4'10" beauty with the impossibly large eyes knew they were at the crossroads and a wrong turn could be catastrophic.

The tourism industry was notoriously fickle: news of bad experiences spread like wildfire. Wanlaya's message had been unmistakeable: stick with the farangs – and only those domestic customers who could be expected to behave.

Miguel was relieved his song had come to an end. Time and words had gone by for him and Wanlaya seemingly in parallel, ending in a finale that could almost have been choreographed.

2

Don't Ring Us

Ludo Scully was weighing his options as he soaked up the sun on one of the few pristine beaches still within walking distance of Nam Horm.

To think clearly, he'd wanted to put some distance between himself and the place. Distance, in every sense, had become essential for perspective in his later years.

He accepted, as Lucy argued, that years of commitment to one resort was not something to be lightly discarded, but the worm of doubt was now nibbling: How could he be sure the recent mayhem would not be repeated.

Nearly half of each year was a sizeable chunk of life to risk under a specially discounted three-year agreement soon up for renewal.

Scully's journalist nose had sensed all was not well at Nam Horm, but was it really his business.

What mattered to him at this stage of life was to enjoy the fruits of his hard labour, much of it lived in circumstances that would have driven many people to an early exit. Now, at long last, he was modestly cash adequate, romantically content, but time poor.

He tried to sip his second cold beer of the day, but Lucy Milner – aka 'Mrs Scully' – had other ideas. She nudged him playfully as he fidgeted with his new, ill-fitting trunks. He'd not wanted them, but Lucy had told him they were sexy and so all discussion was immediately shut down.

He'd reasoned that when servicing a 'wife' 30 years his junior, a costume was not a matter to quibble about, even though it was too small and manifestly 'not him.'

Annoyingly, his trunks had created an angry red sunburn line at the border where a late middle-aged waist dissolves into the folds of the lower stomach.

Lucy saw and digested his discomfort and played the concerned little girl:

'I'm sorry, Ludo, I shouldn't have pushed you into buying that pair.' Pursed lips tried to a signal a pretend apology. 'But they are such a turn on.'

Scully's swimwear felt more over-crowded, as the irritation of the red stripe was now eclipsed by the more exquisite pain of a swelling groin.

Lucy caressed his freckled shoulders as she cooed her care. 'Be careful, darling, you know you burn easily.' She paused, letting the tension build.

'And I wouldn't want anything to go wrong with our vewwy, vewwy special evening.'

The deliberate mangling of the 'r' was an inseparable part of the build-up to their evening 'specials' when anything was possible; human imagination the only limiting factor.

The play-acting routine, with endless variations, had become a major feature of their six-year relationship, but the mutual excitement was still as powerful and fresh as the first time they'd indulged their cravings. Scully was certainly not going to wimp out over a bit of sunburn.

The child-like voice continued, accepting full blame for telling 'uncle' to buy the new swimwear 'because it gave me a tickly feeling right at the bottom of my tummy.'

All worries about Nam Horm turned to mush as Scully gave an intense shudder of expectation. At such times, he often wondered whether the coming night might be his last.

There can only be so much excitement an aged heart can take, he mused, before comforting himself with the thought that many actors and assorted celebs were still 'at it' into their 80s and beyond.

It was the word 'uncle' that was tipping him over the

edge; one of the triggers they used to uncork feelings of semi-forbidden fruit. It cooked up images that the mind police could not yet invade; they were still at liberty to think whatever took their fancy.

Scully was sure that one day some thought-reading machine would even bring that to an end, but in the meantime ...

'God, you really know which buttons to push, don't you,' Scully whispered through a dry mouth, heart beating furiously.

'I could die in your arms, right on this beach, here and now, and I would leave this life a happy man.'

His thoughts squeezed a sad smile out of Lucy. 'You always find the right words, Ludo, but that's not something I need to hear. I want as many years as possible with you. Even if you died, I'd have you embalmed, just so I could look at that deliciously ugly mug.'

Scully smiled his usual semi-distant smile which no one, not even his closest friends, ever quite penetrated. Lucy now frowned.

'Seriously, though, Ludo, I don't want you to get burnt. Melanoma is nothing to laugh at.' Scully put on a serious face for a moment and broke into tuneless song.

Hey, don't tell me you're not worth frying for ...

Lucy popped a middle finger into her mouth for a mock vomit. Both of them laughed the abandonment of a joined-at-the-hip couple – soul mates at every important level.

'You know, Ludo, you really do find the right words at the right moment, like pulling a rabbit out of a hat, but sometimes it's a dead rat.'

'It's not a rabbit I want to pull out at the moment,' he winked, allowing himself an uncharacteristic crude gesture.

For a few glorious minutes, all thoughts of resort troubles were banished to the land of minor irritants as Scully's relaxed mind journeyed back to his legendary 19-year marriage, contrasting it to life with Lucy.

Friend and foe alike had all predicted it would be life-long, the couple welded together by an unusual but not unknown matrimonial glue: mutual loathing. What was different about theirs was its strength and durability.

'Rock solid' was the usual term friends applied to the Ludo and Jenny marriage, likening it to the nuclear stand-off doctrine dubbed MAD (Mutually Assured Destruction), with one important difference: Ludo and Jenny raced each other to the apocalyptic red button daily.

In essence the marriage was a monumental mismatch, corrosive to the point that neither partner could live with the thought of the other finding happiness.

So they stayed together, originally 'for the sake of' their one child, Reginald, who at 16 headed for Canada with a heartfelt 'thanks, but no thanks' to any suggestion of continuing 'life' at home. Cynics speculated he would have found relative peace in Somalia.

The vacuum left by Reg's escape to a world of trapping, fishing and gold prospecting was filled by wider and deeper levels of antagonism at his erstwhile home.

Reasons great and small would be mined as pretexts for argument, followed by rows about how rows had started. Jenny's life-long hypochondria was now given fresh wings; only testicular problems escaping her inventory.

Mercifully, it all came to an abrupt end, courtesy of a Caribbean tree, an event that a vicar friend shamelessly described as an act of God.

'Even God must be fed up to the back teeth listening to you two,' Will Flather had once commented after a sherry too many in the Scully household.

True to form, Ludo and Jenny had argued bitterly over which coconut tree offered more shade on a blisteringly hot day in Cuba. So they each selected their own to lie under.

A sudden, exceptionally strong gust of wind, on what was otherwise a calm day, tore coconuts from their sinewy moorings. One nut, a three-kilo monster, had been directly positioned high above Jenny's head.

Friends of the couple turned up in surprisingly large numbers at the UK funeral four weeks later, some to pay their respects, others curious to see how Scully was taking his loss.

Flather, who had readily agreed to take the service, delivered a sermon heavy on the mysterious and merciful ways in which God moves. He exuded serenity. Scully exuded alcoholic fumes; coconut juice laced with Cuban rum.

'Penny for your thoughts,' Lucy inquired, snapping Scully out of his reverie. He ignored the question, returning to their banter.

'Speaking of rabbits, would you believe my ears feel like they're on fire – and it's not sunburn.'

'Well, someone's talking about you,' said Lucy teasingly, knowing that any reference to superstition or old wives' tales would niggle him.

Scully waved his hand dismissively as they both re-positioned themselves on the picture-perfect sands, taking great care to brush against each other suggestively, much as children, experiencing the first stirrings, 'accidentally' contrive to do.

Lucy was right. Scully's ears had good reason to burn.

***

It had been four days since Ratledge had asked his secretary to find Scully. He'd known for some years that he was still living in the north, running some PR agency. He'd also heard that he vacated Britain as often as he could, but his business still jogged along.

Cyberspace allowed him to sprinkle his stardust on client-pleasing press releases – wherever he was in the world – and when a publicity campaign went flat, he would invariably come up with some original idea; sometimes to the point of being revolutionary.

Inexplicably, the one person who brushed aside these gifts was Scully himself who lived down to his own peculiar take on the Marxist (Groucho) principle that any club accepting him as a member wasn't worth joining.

Ratledge now wanted some stardust sprinkling his way – and much else besides. But where was the 'bloody man' and for how long?

The two had not spoken to each other for many years following a working relationship that for a time had been awesomely effective.

The pair had wielded sufficient power to rock markets – even knocking a penny or two off the pound on some days, ultimately reducing it to the value of a single US dollar during a nine-month strike.

With the aid of Scully, Ratledge had captured the leadership of the mighty Federation of General Employees (FOGE) which brought together key workers from industry, the public services, transport and the communication sectors. Politicians of all colours readily bowed the knee to such concentrated union power.

Scully was Ratledge's Press Officer, a communist propagandist who applied his trade with zeal and utter belief.

The strike had, however, proved catastrophic and effectively killed FOGE. It also left both men bitterly divided, blaming each other for the outcome.

Ratledge later moved out of union politics and into local government, the hoped-for catapult back to national prominence.

Others had argued that the quickest and best route back to the national stage would be a Parliamentary seat, but Ratledge, instincts still intact, was unconvinced.

Over the years he'd witnessed far too many populist

ranters like himself have their wings clipped by party whips in Parliament.

The craftier tactic of jettisoning Parliament and becoming the powerful elected mayor of a local authority seemed more promising.

For Scully it looked like the end of his journalism career. The Conservatives had described him as 'the Goebells of the left' during the strike, a devastating put-down for a man whose hatred of the Nazis had shaped his politics.

Somehow, against the odds, Scully clawed his way back into general journalism – while still clinging to visions of utopian communism. He need not have bothered with either:

Political idealism crushed under the reality of gulags and self-serving Champagne socialists, his journalistic idealism soon followed suit as newspapers succumbed to a relentless dumbing down.

Rose-tinted specs smashed, he trod the well-worn path of the sell-out journalist: public relations.

It kept him afloat financially, but the price paid in self-loathing was high, promoting some companies and individuals he privately despised.

Occasionally, though, the old bones rebelled, and fees would be lowered or waived if some worthy cause grabbed his attention.

The world-weary cynicism was not quite shatter proof, but almost there.

***

Arms around each other's waist, fused together in affection, humour and a merciless lust, the 'Scullys' headed back to Nam Horm, dawdling along the water's edge.

Any excuse was seized to eke out the setting sun's final red and gold moments, a brief interlude in a crackpot world.

A jellyfish, the diameter of an outsize dinner plate, lay freshly beached on the water's edge. Scully, wanting a closer look, played God, using a twig to prevent it being washed back out to sea.

A passing fisherman intervened, and with precise hand placement gingerly lifted the creature, taking care that the weight of the body did not tear the flesh. The possibility of being stung did not seem to enter his head. Scully said nothing, giving way to superior knowledge and title.

Scully and Lucy watched as the fisherman waded out to sea, releasing the jellyfish only when judged to be safely away from both water's edge – and farangs uneducated in Nature's ways.

'What's wrong?' Lucy asked as Scully gazed at the fisherman, turning away, eyes downcast.

'Year after year we come here and what do we really know about these people?' He supplied his own answer. 'We know as much about them as I knew about that jellyfish.'

'You're too hard on yourself, Ludo. At least you notice what's around you. There are people who've been living in Britain for 40 years who know nothing about the place, not even bothering to learn the language.

'Anyway, you ate sashimi jellyfish the other night. Bloody hypocrite.'

Scully failed to stifle a smile before lapsing into a short silence as they walked the final few metres to Nam Horm's entrance.

'It's true what you say about making an effort in other lands, Lucy. I've known a few Thais in Britain and they seem to fit in perfectly – and I'm not just talking restaurants, I mean socially.'

Lucy thought it unwise to ask what sort of social contact he was talking about.

'I don't quite know what it is, maybe a handed-down serenity, but they just seem to have a way of connecting, whether it's with other people, creatures, the landscape or even the madhouse that's Bangkok. Everything seems...'

A shout from the Nam Horm reception cut Scully off in mid-sentence. 'Papa, Papa, come, please, there's a phone call for you from England.'

'Papa' was the affectionate term Thais used for their older, long-term guests and Scully always smiled, a little self-consciously, when it was addressed to him.

It was a measure of acceptance – and that he didn't mind, especially from Thais. Brushing the sand from his feet, Scully headed to reception as Lucy made her way to the bungalow, keen to turn up the air-conditioning to counter what she hoped would be a long, sticky night.

Scully picked up the phone. 'I'll bet you don't know who this is, Ludo?'

The short, flat northern vowels rang out, annoyingly distorted by a distinct bounce back. A faint tingling at the back of Scully's neck unsettled him.

His mind refused, point blank, to accept what his ears were telling him. He declined any guessing game, with a curt: 'Who is this speaking?'

'It's me, Arnie, Arnie Ratledge. Don't tell me you've gone senile, comrade, and can't even recognise my voice.'

Scully's immediate instinct was to slam the phone down, but for reasons he puzzled over endlessly that evening, he did not. Fear of appearing rude in front of his Thai hosts seemed the likeliest explanation.

After a few seconds Scully managed to choke out a barely audible 'What do you want?' to the man in Wigburn Town Hall.

'Nah then, nah then, lad.' Scully hated it when Ratledge switched to an exaggerated northern accent. 'That's no way to greet an old comrade after all these years.'

The only thing Scully loathed more than Ratledge's professional northerner 'act,' was his gratuitous use of the word 'comrade.' It still had serious meaning for him, comrades in struggle, comrades in arms against a common foe.

Having seen through Ratledge as a man who would have disguised himself as a woman to escape the Titanic – and then justify it as a gift to the world – 'comrade' was defiled when uttered through his puffy lips.

'Don't call me "comrade," Scully hissed, aware that his reception 'audience,' now including Visit and Wanlaya, were shooting him anxious glances.

Scully softened his approach slightly. 'Look, I'm in company right now...'

'I'll bet you're hooked up with one of those Thai crackers,' Ratledge interrupted.

Scully breathed in sharply. 'Actually I'm in a relationship, not that it's any of your business. Now tell me what you want and how you got my number here.'

Ratledge dropped the mateyness: 'Never mind how I got your number, I just want you to hear me out for a few minutes. I've stumbled on something so big that, if handled correctly, it has the potential to change British politics.'

Scully's sigh carried across the oceans.

'No, I'm serious. It could even re-structure western economies and deal a real blow to uncaring capitalism.'

Ratledge knew the buzz words that would gain the attention of his old 'comrade,' but was also aware that Scully had always been flatter-proof. He laid it on regardless:

'I'm not going to beat about the bush. Frankly, what I have in mind needs the aggression, the skill, the word-power and – above all – the lateral thinking of a Ludo Scully.'

Scully wanted to follow in the footsteps of his incommunicado son, Reg, and head for the hills; abandon himself to the warm embrace of the South China Sea; dive into some creature-infested thicket – anything but listen to a man he never wanted to hear about again, except in an obituary.

Ratledge's next words were a carefully crafted hook, not a game-changer, but designed to touch the rawest of nerves.

'I know this is still sensitive with you, Ludo, but I must raise it. I remember you telling me how your mother died terribly in a care home.'

'What the hell's that got to do with you?' Scully snarled, voice rising.

'There are many thousands, just like your mum, who face the same fate, Ludo – but it doesn't have to be that way. That's what I want to talk to you about, but not over the phone.'

'Yeah, well, you can write me a letter about it. Nothing will bring my mother back.'

'I know that, Ludo, and I'm sorry, but this might be a chance to avenge your mum – and help save other mums, and dads, from a similar fate. I'm sure it's what she would have wanted.'

'How the hell could you know what she would have wanted? You never even met her. Frankly, she couldn't stand you and always thought you sounded like Hitler on the telly.'

Scully had raised his voice. Nam Horm's owners and staff shifted position uncomfortably.

Ratledge fashioned a couple of top-drawer sighs, reserved for special occasions. 'Ludo … Ludo … when will you ever learn to judge me fairly.' Scully said nothing.

'Look, as an indication of how serious I am, I'm prepared to fly you home and back to Thailand, put you up in the best hotel, pay you a generous day rate – just so I can talk to you about it all for a few days. Nothing else – I promise – absolutely nothing else.'

Scully maintained his silence.

'It can't be done by letter or phone, it's all too sensitive. I'll ring you again in two days, at 5pm your time. This is the big one, Ludo, a final chance to do some lasting good.'

With that, Ratledge ended the call. Scully was left stupefied, the words 'lasting good' rattling around his head. The phone remained in his right hand, clenched so tightly it risked splintering.

'Papa, Papa, I am sorry, Papa, but could you please give the phone back to me,' the smiling, ever-courteous receptionist requested. Robot-like, Scully's right arm extended over the desk.

'Ha ha, Papa play joke,' the Thai laughed nervously as Scully's hand maintained its vice-like grip.

Mentally, Scully had Ratledge's windpipe in his hand as the much smaller girl's fingers gently tried to engineer the phone's release, prising away a digit at a time.

Finally the phone clattered free, marginally nudging Scully out of his trance-like state. He pointed his feet in the direction of 'home,' the bungalow that had promised an evening of sweet delight. Sex could not have been further from his mind.

Bemused eyes followed his progress as he shuffled off into the night air. Even the crickets seemed to grant his passage a period of silence as Scully, a life-long agnostic – 'give me proof, and I'll believe' was the line – cast his eyes heavenward and muttered about a deal with God that involved Ratledge's instant demise.

'Then I'll believe, Oh Lord, then I'll believe.'

A passing Australian couple took his prayer – the bits they could make out – as proof that the Poms couldn't really hold their liquor.

A cheery 'g'night, mate, mind how you go' snapped Scully out of his private communion; embarrassment returned some colour to his face.

The man makes one phone call and I'm already talking to myself, Scully noted with alarm. Desperately, he tried to put himself in the mood for love.

***

Lucy was aware of much of Scully's earlier life, but she knew when not to pry too deeply. The subject of Arnie Ratledge was normally taboo except when Scully was thoroughly plastered; then her partner's true word-power was unleashed.

Profanities she never knew existed filled a notable gap in her education.

Scully entered the bungalow and Lucy knew immediately something was wrong. Tonight she'd had a 'super' surprise in store, having squeezed herself into schoolgirl-size jodhpurs.

The effect was electric and disturbing: The illusion of an immature bottom, belonging to a highly precocious child, trying to assert its all-conquering authority prematurely. Flesh perfectly encased, every seam and centimetre of fabric combined to tempt all but the dead – and even that open to question.

The jodhpurs were topped by the tightest of basques, fitting like a second skin around waist and bust. Arms akimbo, a riding crop dangled from one hand and an exquisitely crafted eye mask graced Lucy's features with just the right degree of wickedness.

Brown calf-skin boots, ending just below the knee, provided the final touch.

In disbelief, Lucy watched Scully stand in the doorway without any discernible reaction.

'Cat got your tongue, uncle?' Lucy asked with the sort of casual freshness that could easily have come out of the mouth of a teenager, except that when spoken by her, the words dripped sensuality.

Use of the word 'tongue' was important. 'Waggers,' as they dubbed them, always played a highly active role at times of heat, painting salacious word pictures or paying longed-for visits to warm and wet regions; their private 'tropics.'

Scully slumped into the large teak armchair in which the cushions had already been thoughtfully plumped up for the evening ahead.

'Sit down, Lucy,' he requested, almost plaintively, and for a moment she hoped a new perverted twist to their usual games was being played out.

'Something bad's happened,' he blurted out before she'd even had time to park her bottom on the edge of the bed.

Lucy knew that at this stage in both their lives deeply satisfying sex ranked among the highest of priorities, with the power to bring out the best in both of them.

Simple, penetrative acts had never been enough for either, merely the modest pocketing of a single coin from an overflowing chest of waiting treasure that few discover and even fewer understand.

From the outset they had described graphically what each needed and both partners had readily obliged, overjoyed that they could discuss their anatomical details with not the faintest embarrassment. Nothing between them, they'd agreed, was taboo.

To ignore her – primed and on fire – something truly awful must have happened; one death, at the very least, would give reasonable grounds. Lucy placed an extremely high value on her sex appeal, and it was not to be brushed aside lightly.

'A phone call, a bloody phone call from your old boss,' she shrieked in disbelief as Scully started to explain.

'What's he threatened you with? Assassination, the rack, castration by a pack of rottweilers?'

Mention of castration stung as he gazed helplessly at his young partner.

'Look, he wants to ring me back in a couple of days. He mentioned care homes and my mother.'

'Your mother's been dead for over 20 years,' Lucy shouted, anger rising by the second.

'He wants to talk to me, over there, in Lancashire. It must be something important. Remember me telling you what a tight bastard he always was, well he's offered to pay the fare.'

Scully left out the bits about capitalism and western economies, knowing Lucy's aversion to politics. It would not have mattered if he'd included them. Lucy was now beyond boiling point.

'He might just as well have set those rottweilers on you,' she sobbed, the bed now bouncing under her rage.

'You've always told me how much you hate the man. You get one phone call from him, walk in here like a zombie, ignore me and suddenly there's talk of flights to Britain. Ignore him! What hold has he fucking well got over you?'

Lucy now felt foolish in her sex toys. She tore the mask off, revealing her tear-stained cheeks, and threw the crop vaguely in Scully's direction. It was as though the very heart of her femininity had been ripped out.

Scully again absorbed the truism about the unparalleled fury of a woman scorned. With this woman that could be magnified many times over. The sobs, now great and heaving, told him she'd passed the point of no return for the evening.

A gentle arm around her shoulders was brushed away as he tried to apologise for denying her the attention she'd longed and planned for so meticulously.

As in the old days, Ratledge was back in business, shredding chunks of Ludo Scully's life.

***

'They say smoking while pregnant reduces the baby's weight. They must be fucking joking. Our Roxanne was 13 lbs when she was born. If I'd not smoked, it would have taken a bleedin' crane to get her out.'

Arnie Ratledge was irritated. At times when deep reflection was called for, he'd don dark glasses, a flat cap and head for the Tesco cafe, within easy walking distance of his fiefdom.

Selecting an out-of-the-way table, he'd sit there quietly, sometimes with a newspaper, pen and notebook, wrestling with problems, real or imagined, and thankful for the anonymity. The limelight was welcome, but only at times that served his agenda.

Today, the quiet he sought was not being reciprocated by two grossly overweight girls who had parked themselves at the next table.

In between shooting unfriendly glances at them, he guessed their ages at anything from mid-teens to early 20s. Endless layers of fat made a more accurate assessment impossible.

He flirted with the idea of moving tables as their prattle continued: 'If you're up the duff, Amy,' Roxanne's mum continued, 'I wouldn't worry a shite. They give you so much help these days, it's a fucking doddle. Best thing I ever did, having our Roxy.'

Of Roxanne there was no sight, and Ratledge idly wondered who she'd been parked with. Somebody, somewhere would have been left holding the baby while mum chinwagged over coffee with all-ears Amy.

Yes, in every society, the young, the old and the sick would always need protection, but it all ended up being so crazily, impossibly expensive.

And would the likes of Amy, mum or even baby Roxanne, ever pick up the tab for future generations of the elderly – those care-home residents destined to succeed the current crop?

Chances were that Amy and co would not live long enough to help – unless there was a serious, nation-wide assault on obesity.

His thoughts provided some distraction for Ratledge as he pondered the greater question of whether Scully would even pick up the phone in two days' time.

He had no grand idea to put to Scully, even if he could get him to Lancashire. The master plan – 'hope,' really – was to string him along with inflated crumbs, picking delicately at the open wound of his mother's care-home death. Then, when his old comrade was fired up, mine his inevitable tirade, hoping for some golden nugget of an idea that he could jump-claim as his own.

In the best traditions of the worst politicians, it was how Ratledge operated.

Mum's voice jolted Ratledge back to reality as she reeled off to Amy, and any Tesco customer within earshot, all the material benefits of motherhood.

'Me being a cheeky cow,' she announced proudly, 'I asked 'em for the play centre I was entitled to for our Roxanne.

'You should've seen the bleedin' look on the health visitor's face. "You're not entitled to any play centre, Miss Shorrock," she says, coming over all snotty like.

'Well I told her, didn't I, that I'd heard it with my own ears at that pre-native thing I went to before Roxy was born. Some foreign woman had said that after every baby you get a play centre.'

Ratledge now found it impossible to concentrate on anything as mum ploughed on. In between fits of laughter, he caught a few further snatches. It was enough.

'It's that bleedin' thing they pull out of your fanny after the baby's born. It looks like a pound of fresh liver and they call it a fuckin' play centre. I'm not joking, Amy.' Even the placid Amy dissolved into giggles.

Ratledge gulped down the rest of his coffee, gathered up his pen, paper and notebook and marvelled at an education system so in tatters that the great unwashed could give birth, yet not have a clue what a placenta was.

Assuming they survived the obesity epidemic, was this a generation that could be relied on to service care homes, an industry already said to have a very patchy record?

His own contemptuous snort gave the answer as he trudged back to the Town Hall for what he hoped would be a productive meeting with his Finance Officer.

The coffee had not been an entire waste of time. Ammunition could be picked up anywhere and Ratledge knew how to store it.

***

Stanley Vincent, having finally convinced himself that Ratledge was not planning mass murder, had been thorough. His professionalism was all he and his wife – a childless couple – had left.

He would serve the despised Ratledge to the best of his ability, as long as there was a glimmer of hope that his own reputation could be rescued from the ashes. This time, however, he would protect his own back. Ruthlessly.

To Ratledge's delight, Vincent had been very busy. All thoughts of the Tesco Two evaporated as he eased back in his chair to digest the details. The basics were as he suspected.

Across the country most fees ranged between £555 and £855 a week for residential care homes (between £28,860 and £44,460 a year), but as he already knew, some were higher.

In his own patch the average was nearly £43,000 and there were around 12,000 residents who were being taken care of.

The higher than average figure surprised him, but there it was in black and white. It was another number, however, that made him sit bolt upright.

Figures on the Dept of Works and Pensions own website showed that average life expectancy after entering a care home was just 19 months.

After three times asking for – and getting – cast-iron assurances from Vincent that the figures were correct, his Finance Officer dropped a further bombshell.

About half of dementia sufferers admitted to care and nursing homes died within a year. Drily, as if reporting on the latest currency exchange rates, Vincent added that malnutrition and pressure sores helped them on their way.

Ratledge let out what he thought was a low, soft whistle, but sounded more like a 'raspberry.'

As with so many skills, the art of pursing lips together while expelling air was beyond him.

'This is dynamite. No wonder the politicians, pre-election, were saying that none of the old codgers should have to fund their own care for more than two years. Most of them are bloody dead by then.' Vincent remained deadpan.

'Getting sent to a care home must be like a death sentence. No need for those one-way tickets to Switzerland, eh?'

Vincent stressed that the figure was an average and some hung on for much longer. A lot depended on the quality of the care.

Ratledge's mind raced ahead. 'If you want it crudely, Stanley, I would say it's all so blindingly obvious. It's the ones who are well looked after ... who hang on the longest ... they cost us the most. They drain our coffers instead of filling the coffins.'

Two parallel thoughts merged in Ratledge's mind. He felt confident that such shocking figures would speak to Scully in a way nothing else could.

He also knew that presented cleverly at the opportune moment, significant political capital could be mined.

However, routine condemnations would not be enough. Answers ... answers ... were needed.

The more radical, the more headline-grabbing, the better. Scully's importance was growing by the hour.

***

'Just tell him to fuck off, Ludo, it's as simple as that. Better still, don't take the call.'

Lucy was out of patience. Vacillation was not her bag, and she loathed it in her man.

For her, everything foundered on the great mystery of why Scully still evidently believed Ratledge could ever achieve anything for anyone.

A two-time loser whose only achievement had been self-enrichment, Scully still seemed to be drawn to Ratledge, like a moth to a flame.

Time and time again she pressed the question, only to be sidetracked into alleys of political guilt, social obligation and personal grief where Scully's demons slumbered lightly.

Lucy was aware of the wretched family poverty, which stood out even in the dirt-poor streets surrounding Manchester's Strangeways Prison.

Scully often went begging with his mother to two charities: The trump card who tugged at the hearts of the men and women on the charity panels. It was one way of supplementing the three pounds or less his boozed-up father gave his mother each week to feed the family of five.

The strain of trying to put food on the table under impossible conditions took a terrible toll on his mother. Scully watched, little fists clenched, powerless, as she'd sob uncontrollably, veins bulging in her neck.

Lucy Milner, who in adult life grew into a small-time antiques dealer, making scant use of her classical Oxbridge education, occupied a different planet.

While she rode ponies on her father's smallholding in North Yorkshire, a taste still with her, Scully's childhood entertainment cost nothing.

His favourite was to spread false rumours that someone had died. Many unknowing 'widows' were stopped in the street by sympathetic neighbours, condolences duly conveyed.

'It's that lunatic Ludo,' the 'bereaved' spluttered, descending on his mother, demanding she silence her 'nutter' of a son.

Local police could only scratch their heads, having nothing in their legal armoury to cope with little boys prematurely 'burying' half the neighbourhood.

It was his mother's care-home treatment, decades later – reducing her to a living skeleton within months – that proved to be a life-changer for Scully, seeding an irrational hatred for all such homes.

At visiting time, Scully had the urge to push his mother's wheelchair through the ugly doors of the care home and keep going.

But what paperwork was in place? What would be the health, legal and financial implications, the Lilliputian threads that slyly tied her there?

He had not been told by his despised older brother who had made the arrangements – and he had not asked. He was guilty of the sin of omission, not saving his dementia-afflicted mother from a lonely and miserable death in a place where even her false teeth were left on a side cabinet, gathering crud.

Sometimes, behind drawn screens, he could hear her cry out in pain as blank-faced care assistants, perhaps the same people who helped administer her cocktail of injected drugs, moved her bed-ridden, seized-up body as it progressively set in its near-foetal position.

Lucy knew from bitter experience that mention of Scully's mother was difficult. Over the years she had tried to move him on, urging self-forgiveness. What his mother had suffered was not unique. The problem lay within the loosely regulated care-home system, she'd argue.

Her approach lessened some of Scully's self-blame, focussing instead on the homes themselves. Each time a story broke about some mistreatment of the old, both were as one, roundly condemning the 'inhumanity' of the system.

Lucy, above all, should understand his antipathy to care homes, Scully reasoned, as he tried afresh to bring her on board.

'What on earth makes you – and a man you can't even stand – think you have the answer to the elderly rotting in care homes?' Lucy asked, making no attempt to hide her disbelief.

'I'm sorry, Ludo, I don't want to sound cruel, but apart

from shooting the lot or discovering some eternal youth potion, you're wasting your time – and mine.

'Billions of pounds, euros, dollars, whatever, will continue financing this misery – it's the only game in town – and there's not a thing that you, Ratledge or Jesus Christ himself can do about it. Just forget it and let's get on with our own lives while we still can.'

An unpleasant half smile formed and it made Scully uncomfortable. 'You should think about yourself a little more, Ludo. I mean it'll not be that many years before you'll probably be a care-home candidate, peeing your pants, dribbling away in front of daytime telly, lost in memories of good times long gone. You should make the most of what you've got now.'

Scully disbelieved his ears. 'So you'd put *me* in a care home?'

'Of course. I mean I'd still be relatively young and you wouldn't want me to waste some of my best years caring for a dried up old stick, would you?'

Scully had serious difficulty stringing words together. 'You calculating … you … you unbelievable bastard … you …'

'Like I say, Ludo, make the most of what you have now.'

Lucy let Scully's red-in-the-face spluttering chug along for a few more seconds before smiling fully. But this time warmly.

'Do you know, for a man who's supposed to be clued up, you can be such an idiot, Ludo. Of course I wouldn't put you in a care home. I'd never leave you to their tender mercies, no matter what.

'The only person caring for you will be me. I really do love you, although sometimes you push me right to the edge.'

Scully's face was a mix of relief and still lingering doubt as Lucy delivered her central message:

'All I want, at this very moment, in this land of smiles and soft sea breezes, is to make you see how precious our time together is. It's criminal to waste it on a premier-league loser like Ratledge. I mean what credibility, what sway has he got these days? Zilch! Live, Ludo, live in the moment.'

With great effort, Scully regained his composure and stared at Lucy, eyes heavy with memory. It was true, women and the young viewed life through different prisms. And he'd be taking on both mindsets if he flew to see Ratledge. Could he really risk losing the girl he cherished?

He was back to those wheelchair-pushing moments at his mum's care home decades ago. Only this time would he go through the doors?

3

Worlds Apart

Mean to the last, Ratledge had held out against paying for Scully to fly First or even Business Class. For Lucy, that had been close to the last straw as she waved him off on his Koh Samui-Bangkok connecting flight. From there it would be Economy all the way to Manchester.

Scully had taken Ratledge's phone call, in the teeth of Lucy's bitter opposition. He'd tried to explain that if he didn't hear Ratledge out, he'd be wondering for the rest of his life whether he'd walked away from a genuine opportunity to do something, however modest, about care-home suffering.

Lucy had not been persuaded and compared him to a starry-eyed, teenage idealist, no smarter than the gullible Flower Power generation who'd been 'nourished on pie-in-the-sky from gurus who took their money and ran – to the nearest luxury-car showroom.'

She'd called him a fool, and the word still rankled, challenging the bait Ratledge had dangled in the second phone call.

Talk of 'shocking' care home death rates – without revealing too much fine detail – had, however, proved to be Ratledge's clincher for Scully.

Maybe, just maybe, this could be his one chance to avenge his mother, and thousands of others who had fallen victim to abusive and criminally neglectful hands.

Alternatively, he was indeed a fool, waving goodbye to a disgruntled and beautiful young partner on a paradise island, for however many days. Hadn't Lucy said repeatedly their time together was precious. He squandered it at his peril.

Easing himself into his seat aboard the Manchester flight, Scully's heart sank at the sight of his fellow passenger – 18 stone, he guessed – already sprawled in the wing-side seat.

He would be up against this man mountain for the next 12 or so hours. He'd read somewhere that the very fat were to be assigned extra large seats on aircraft – and surcharged accordingly. It certainly hadn't happened here. Maybe they had to be above a certain weight – 20, 25 stone? Madness!

It did not help that Alf, who couldn't wait to introduce himself, had resilient BO that battled its way through a sickly-sweet combination of deodorant and aftershave to assail any nearby nose.

A nervous passenger who tried to deal with his problem through talk, within a few minutes Scully learned that he was some sort of call centre manager from Lincolnshire, and had been in Thailand to meet possible brides.

His assessment of women in general was unenlightened and not to Scully's taste. He wanted no part of the conversation, particularly not this day of all days. Cabin crew were instructed to occupy their seats for take off, and Alf's sweat glands moved up a gear, along with his misogyny:

'They're users, all of'em fuckin' users.' As the plane trundled down the runway, lift off chimed with more obscenities.

'You're out of sight for a few weeks and before you know it they've found some shoulder to cry on – and that soon turns into a cock to suck on. I'm telling you, none of 'em can be trusted.'

Scully thought he'd wait till the plane was in level flight and then ask to be moved, but for the moment Alf's terror of flying ensured a silent, bone-dry mouth and Scully felt free to mull over the past 48 hours.

Scully had been approached by an anxious Visit, wanting to chat urgently. The resort owner had got his wires crossed and thought his much-prized guest was leaving for good, angered by the previous week's noise.

Visit was reassured it was not the case and he would, indeed, be coming back. Anyway, they still had Lucy as hostage, he'd joked. Visit still looked uneasy. Over a glass of quality Cognac that stretched to a few more, and well into the early hours, the owner had opened up to him a little.

He didn't want to 'dilute' the quality of the guests staying at Nam Horm, any more than he wanted to dilute the fine XO they were drinking. But he had to live in the real world and take whatever customers were available. Money was tight.

He'd embarrassed Scully quite unintentionally by confiding that if he could pick and choose his customers, he would just limit himself to a few older guests, like Scully, who were little trouble and just wanted to spend their later years enjoying warm weather, good food, a little alcohol, splendid beaches and pleasant company – the final observation accompanied by a knowing smile.

'Frankly, Mr Ludo,' he said, '20 or 30 guests like you each year and the resort – poof! – does not have problems.'

Scully empathised with Visit's dilemma and, as they both got steadily more drunk, bafflement at a world seemingly unable to get its act together became their common foe. Too many square pegs seeking too many round holes, Mr Visit, Mr Ludo and Monsieur Cognac agreed.

Scully smiled at the thought, but was interrupted by the mound alongside stirring back to life. Alf returned to the subject of women. Or tried to. This time Scully cut him short.

'Look, I'm sorry you've had bad experiences with women,' he said, 'but you can't generalise and put half the human race in the same boat.'

'You wouldn't say that if you'd been through what I've been through,' Alf whined. Scully, still intent on moving seats, looked for a stewardess, but was suddenly overtaken by a superior thought.

Twenty years earlier he'd gained his Private Pilots

Licence, simply because – like Everest for mountaineers – it was a challenge, and he didn't want to die regretting that he hadn't tried most things.

The biggest aircraft he'd ever flown was a four-seat Cessna 172, but he was proud of his licence which, disappointingly, looked like a building society paying-in book. He reached into his inside pocket and pulled the licence out.

'You're a bit nervous about flying, aren't you, Alf?' Scully asked in a friendly tone.

'Well, aren't we all,' Alf shot back, annoyed that anyone had sussed his fear.

'I'm not criticising you,' Scully re-assured. 'I just wanted to show you this – it's my pilot's licence. I don't fly anything big, like this plane, but the principles are the same and I always think all pilots have a moral duty to set passengers' minds at rest.'

'Wow, I'm sitting next to a bloody pilot,' Alf began and lost no time in posing his entirely predictable question:

'So, if something happened to the pilots up front, would you be able to fly this?' His eyes were popping in anticipation.

'Well, theoretically, yes, but it would all depend on how good ground instruction was, where we were and how relaxed and mentally stable I felt.'

Scully's answer was deadpan, delivered with the straightest of faces. 'The big problem handling a plane like this would be the weather.'

Alf's mouth grew even drier. 'Like rain and that?'

'Not really. Wind, turbulence, air pockets, things like that. You know, when the plane drops a bit and your stomach feels funny. That's when you have to be careful.'

'How d'ya mean?' Alf asked, dreading the answer.

'Well, I'm supposed to be re-assuring you and I'm not so sure I should be telling you this, but you're a big lad so what the hell.'

Scully then explained in infinite detail how wings have

their stress limitations and how excessive speeds and other strains can rip them off.

He also pointed out, helpfully, that the wing tip movements Alf could observe from his porthole were signs of that stress, but as long as they kept within a few inches all would be well.

Alf bothered Scully no more, and over much of the remaining flight sat with his eyes glued to the port-side wing of the aircraft, emitting the odd whimper when undue flexibility seemed evident.

Scully could not have wished for a more compliant travelling companion.

In between meals, he was able to doze much of the way, only waking fully as the plane made its final descent into a rain-swept Manchester.

***

Ratledge was much as Scully expected. Time had added, rather than taken, its pound of flesh; in fact, many pounds, Scully calculated. Sagging jowls underpinned the still boyish face, and Scully was mildly unnerved to note the eyes had changed little.

The same innocent powder blue, more watery perhaps, and now framed by eyelids that had thickened with the years, exaggerating the crevices.

Disturbingly, the eyes had lost none of their ability to open wide in an instant, affecting an innocent air, surprise, a sense of victimhood – whatever the demands of a given situation.

Many times they had come to Ratledge's rescue when lesser mortals might have been shredded. Yes, still a man adept at worming his way out of most things, Scully registered dispiritedly. He's not changed.

The added weight was not so apparent on Ratledge's torso, but Scully was privy to the reason. Not work-outs, as

Ratledge would have the world believe, but specially tailored corsets underneath the expensively-cut suits.

Still taking everyone for a ride, Scully noted as he sank into the luxury leather of the civic limousine, winding its way from the airport.

The destination was Wigburn's Central Hotel. The 'best hotel' Ratledge had promised, and so it was. The best in Wigburn, which only boasted four buildings that could reasonably be described as hotels.

The two men exchanged opening pleasantries on the 40-minute journey. Scully had not expected his old boss to turn up at the airport and was unprepared.

'Well, comrade, the years have certainly been kind to you,' Ratledge gushed as the chauffeur nursed his passengers through the Lancashire countryside.

'I would appreciate it if we could drop the "comrade" bit, Arnie,' Scully requested in a tone of tired irritation. 'Those days are dead.' Ratledge fell silent.

'I've had a bust up with my partner and flown half way round the world because of you. Just let's stick to business and cut the usual crap.' A polite cough from the driver caused Ratledge to slide shut the partitioning window.

'No need for unpleasantness, Ludo,' Ratledge said, instantly switching his eyes to full 'hurt' mode. 'If we're going to work on this thing together, we need to show each other a little respect.'

'Oh, I've no problem with showing respect, Arnie. It's just that I'd like some in return. I'm too old to be patronised or taken for a mug any more. I don't take kindly to it. And that's why – for your sake and mine – I hope that what you've told me is accurate.'

'Of course it's accurate, Ludo. Would I lie to you?' Scully paused.

'I would hate to think, Arnie, that you've got me here under any false pretences. I'm looking forward to hearing all these big ideas.'

Ratledge, swallowing hard, a finger tugging at his suddenly over-tight collar, swore further assurances.

That night was not a comfortable one for Ratledge. Tomorrow he would be under Scully's scrutiny. Presenting the care-home problem would be a doddle, and, if past performance was any guide, somehow, some way, Scully himself would come up with an answer – without even realising it. It would be tricky, very tricky, but Arnold Ratledge could handle it. It's what leaders did – pinch the ideas of others. As his dad used to say, 'That's how they grab OBEs – Other Buggers' Efforts.'

Not entirely reassured, Ratledge finally drifted into a fitful sleep.

4

Angel Lies

Ratledge's office was much as expected. Scully thought his old boss had been relatively subdued in the ride from the airport, but he'd put it down to their one sharp exchange. He assumed, rightly, that Ratledge would slip back into more familiar cocky mode when surrounded by the trappings of power.

The meeting had been fixed for 9am prompt; Scully arrived seven minutes past, offering no apology, just inwardly enjoying Ratledge's known aversion to late-comers.

All the figures were laid out in neat rows, each number representing a death, or the cost of continuing care. The Mayor's secretary and Stanley Vincent attended. The council's terminal financial situation was also present.

Scully had the knack – found in journalists and lawyers – of absorbing vast quantities of information quickly, discarding the dross, arrowing in on the significant. His notes were rigorously focused.

For the first hour he hardly spoke, except to ask the odd question extrapolated from the documents. When he did speak at length, there was no mincing of words.

'As I understand it,' he began, fixing his eyes on no one in particular, 'this council is knackered financially because some idiot' – Ratledge squirmed – 'or idiots' – Vincent joined the squirm – 'put huge amounts of public money into Icelandic banks that failed.'

'Can we avoid the offensive language,' Ratledge requested. Scully ignored him.

'And it looks like the government will have to step in,

using taxpayers' money to save the people of Wigburn from you lot. Have I got it right so far?'

Heads nodded reluctantly, as if attached by rusty hinges. 'And you think you can turn this whole mess around and save your political skins – sorry, skin – by doing something about care-home costs for the elderly?'

'I wouldn't put it quite like that,' Ratledge hissed, straining for self-control.

'Well, you tell me, Arnie, how would you put it?' Ratledge cleared his throat.

'Come on, Ludo, you can't think it right that a huge chunk of public money is enriching private care-home owners, in some cases a grand a week or even more. And for what? The figures you've got in front of you don't include the most shocking statistic of all – the thing I hinted at on the phone.'

'And what's that, Arnie?' Scully pressed.

'OK, I warned you the death rates were scandalous, but can I first ask you a personal question, Ludo?' His ex-employee nodded.

'How long did your mother spend in a care home before she died?' Scully spat out, '16 months.'

'Well, Ludo, you might be interested to know that the average life expectancy after entering a care home is just 19 months. And for half of those suffering from dementia, they're dead within a year of entering a care or nursing home.'

Scully's composure cracked a little, enough for Ratledge to sense his moment was arriving.

'Think about it. These, these …' he feigned searching for a word that was waiting on his lips '… these parasites, some raking in tens of thousands of pounds a week for keeping a few dozen old people in squalor.

'That's right, squalor. Soaked in their own urine, some smeared in their own faeces, fed crap food, plonked in front of daytime telly, even the heating probably turned down.

And for many, the reward for suffering this living hell is an early death.'

Ratledge's office, not known as a place of quiet reflection, enjoyed total silence for six seconds as images took root.

The word 'heating' triggered thoughts that now ran amok in Scully's head. He was already missing the warmth of Lucy, the heat of Thailand and its blisteringly spiced food. The contrast with UK life could not be more vivid.

An average Thai factory worker earned £40 a week, and for that people could live a poor-ish but reasonably happy life in families that generally stuck together through the generations.

What would Thais think of a society that had gone mad, paying £1,000 a week to keep old people in conditions that – in some cases – shortened what little time they had left. He thought of his mother and an incendiary mix of anger and disgust compelled him to speak straight from the heart.

"Yesterday I flew in from a country where £40 a week is the average for an industrial worker. It's incredible that some of our old people can't get decent care for 25 times that amount.

'What is wrong with this bloody country? In Thailand the elderly are truly respected, and you know something, the Thais would look after our old people a damn sight better than we do – and for a fraction of the money.'

At that very moment, Ratledge, a life-long atheist, came the closest he had ever done, to muttering a silent prayer of thanks to any god within hearing distance.

Scully's words had ignited a blinding flash of pure opportunism. He'd expected … hoped … Scully would come up with something, but this was of a different order entirely; the stairway to heaven or, more accurately, the golden path to political rehabilitation on the national stage.

Exhilaration and relief surged through Ratledge as, for the second time that morning, he made enormous efforts to keep himself in check, asking Scully:

'Do you believe in telepathy, Ludo?'

Scully shook his head.

'Well, I really can't believe what I've just heard. You've stolen my thunder, young man.'

Scully looked perplexed.

'Why do you think I brought you over here, Ludo?' Without waiting for an answer, Ratledge continued:

'That's right, to explore the possibility of our old people finding happiness overseas, in a place where the elderly are wanted, loved even, and where they don't charge too bloody much. To be perfectly honest I wasn't thinking of Thailand, more sort of China,' he lied.

'I figured they export so much to us, why can't we export our elderly to them. But Ludo,' he cooed, 'Thailand sounds an even better bet.'

Scully scrutinised Ratledge's face for any hint of anything untoward. Not so much as an out-of-place wrinkle could be found around the guiltless blue eyes.

Meanwhile, up in the heavens, where the angels are said to dwell and where one dies whenever a lie is told, an entire division succumbed to Ratledge's monumental porky.

***

The meeting now took on a fresh energy, with Ratledge, untypically, allowing his Finance Officer to occupy a brief place in the sun.

'I asked Stanley here to draw up a situation document on the state-of-play in the entire country,' he puffed, 'and he's done more than that, projecting where we're all likely to be a few years from now. He's done an excellent job.

'If you think care for the old is bad at the moment, it's all gonna get a whole lot worse. I'll try to summarise the position, and if I get it wrong I'm sure you'll pull me up, Stanley.' Vincent moved not a muscle.

'A commission set up by the Health Secretary has been looking into the whole business of financing care for the elderly.

'And they really have been examining the lot. I'll quote you the commission's brief: "How best to meet the costs of care and support as a partnership between individuals and the state."

'All three of the main parties have pledged to end the need for pensioners to flog their homes to pay for the cost of care, but you know what politicians are like.'

Scully and Vincent shot meaningful glances at each other. A muffled noise from Ratledge's minute-taking secretary was swiftly stifled, dressed up as a yawn.

'I wouldn't trust 'em an inch. There's still this idea of a death tax kicking around, levied on whatever's left after death; new schemes that could force everyone to save for their old age – whatever happened to the idea of care from the cradle to the grave, eh, Ludo – and then there's that business about handing over a lump sum of thousands in advance for your care.

'Bit of a gamble, that. Live a long time, you're in pocket. Pop your clogs soon after and they've screwed you yet again.

'None of 'em have any idea, really. It's all a lottery that falls on the individual, and if they or their family can't stump up the cash, then it's down to you and me – the taxpayer. Whether it's national or local government, it all comes out of our pockets in the end.'

Pleased with himself, Ratledge paused for breath and took a sip of water, sensing it was time for back-up. 'Am I right, Stan?'

Vincent despised the barrow-boy rhetoric, but technically there was nothing he could object to.

He inclined his head once, in what Scully registered as the most grudging support he had ever witnessed. He was warming to Vincent.

'Look, let's not pull any punches here,' Ratledge continued. 'The situation's bad in the short term, but over the next 20 years another 1.7 million will need care and spending could soar to £26bn.

'We're talking about you and me, folks, our generation. Unless you're already at death's door or virtually destitute, the state will not fund you. It's as simple as that.

'One in five of us will be over 65 in 15 years, that's around 13 million people. The situation will be impossible unless there's a bloody miracle. Let me give you an example of what's happening now.

'At Trafford they've already ended free swimming for the old. Their council can't find the money. Yet swimming is one of the best ways of keeping fit.'

Ratledge sensed a swift involvement of Scully would pay further dividends.

'I bet you find that's the case in Thailand, eh Ludo, not to mention all that other stuff they do, that Tae Kwon something or other.'

'It's Tai Chi,' Ludo corrected.

'Well I knew it was Tae something,' Ratledge smiled, irritated that he'd encountered his first correction.

Now well into his stride, Ratledge reeled off more figures, including a reminder of the 'scandalous £23,250 – if you've got assets above that, the state won't pay a bean towards your care home costs in old age,' he stressed. 'It'll come out of your own pocket.

'And what do you think other councils – local authorities like us – are trying to do? Most of 'em, bugger all.

'So maybe we'll end up going the way of the Russians – drinking ourselves to death with cheap supermarket booze before we ever get old.

'You'll be interested in this, Ludo: Only 50 per cent of today's 18-year-old Russians can expect to reach retirement age. And that's because they're shovelling so much plonk down their throats.

'Maybe there are some people in Britain who wouldn't mind us going down that road. It'd solve lots of problems for lots of people, including us here in Wigburn.'

Ratledge rose from his chair as if addressing an audience of thousands, switching to sombre mode as he glanced down at his official papers.

'And now we come to the heart of the matter, the position on our doorstep. Yes, Ludo, you're right, this council is financially knackered, and unless we come up with a solution, the state will step in and we'll be as popular as cancer.

'This is not just about me and the Finance Officer; it's about the proud history of Wigburn and all that it stands for.' Scully sighed deeply.

'In the short term we can buy ourselves a few months by juggling the bills. Far more important is to come up with some idea – think of it as a pilot scheme – that shows little Wigburn can navigate its own way out of hard times.

'And if that idea is revolutionary enough, it could also point the way for other councils to dig themselves out of a hole; maybe even help tackle the country's national debt.

'I honestly believe Wigburn can lead by example and the answer might well lie not in China, but in your Thailand, Ludo. We need to get to work.'

***

Within four days Ratledge had put together a task force charged with exploring the possibility of moving, en-bloc, the residents of an entire care home to the Far East, most probably Thailand.

Willingness and fitness to migrate; family agreements; detailed funding arrangements; asset management; health care; legal ramifications; burial considerations; all was to be looked into, employing some of Wigburn's finest.

Scully's task was to head the Thai end of things, from

finding suitable premises to liaising with the myriad departments that made up the complex bureaucratic structure of the country.

Scully hesitated before committing himself, only too aware of the cultural minefield he would be entering. A simple wrong word could prove disastrous, transforming run-of-the-mill tasks into the stuff of nightmares.

More than that, did he really want to rekindle a working relationship with Ratledge. The money his old boss had offered him – some of it out of his own funds – was unusually generous, which told Scully that Ratledge genuinely believed he was on to something special. Nevertheless, he would still have to consult Lucy before making his final decision.

A selection of Wigburn care homes for the pilot scheme had been pored over in double quick time, a shortlist drawn up, and all agreed that tentative soundings should be taken at the Heaven's Haven Care Home.

Sixty per cent of its 31 residents were funded directly by Wigburn Council, others by private means. For Ratledge the home was a classical example, in microcosm, of the problem plaguing Britain.

It was at the most expensive end of the charge band, raking in from taxpayers and families deemed able to afford it, the thick end of nearly £43,000 for each resident – more than £1.3m annually.

Success with Heaven's Haven, repeated at other care homes, could slash Wigburn's deficit by tens of millions, maybe even put the borough in the black. There was also another reason for selecting Haven.

An old union colleague who had taught Ratledge many of the populist tricks of his trade was in residence there; and in life it never did any harm to have a man on the inside when planning something.

Ratledge had met up with Joe Dean just two months earlier. Dean had gone straight to the top and bitterly complained to Ratledge about Haven's assistant chief carer, 'Mother' Theresa Gill, who he'd labelled a religious crackpot.

According to Dean, long-term resident Ken Oates had suffered a damaging fall at the home and needed an urgent operation.

It was, however, fraught with danger, the most serious of which was the risk of total blindness for the rest of life. 'Mother' Gill had got wind of this and tried comforting Oates, who was very fearful.

'Don't you understand,' Oates told Gill, 'reading is one of the few pleasures I have left in life. For me, to go blind forever, would be like an immediate death sentence.'

'But it wouldn't be forever,' Gill had assured him.

'You're not hearing me,' Oates said. 'That's what I've been told.'

'And you're not hearing me, Joe,' Gill persisted in her calm, soothing voice, eyes glazed over in private rapture.

Oates looked totally blank.

'If things were to go wrong, Ken, you would only be blind until the day you died. After that you'd forever be in the bosom of the Lord, and you can't really believe the Almighty would want you wandering around heaven in a state of disability, bumping into things.'

Oates had immediately pressed his alarm buzzer and asked other staff to 'get this lunatic out of my sight while I've still got eyes to see with.'

Ratledge had not been able to do anything about the situation, but the incident had registered with him. Dean had nodded sagely when Ratledge noted that a name like Heaven's Haven was bound to attract religious fruitcakes.

5

Coming Together

Since flying back to the UK, Scully had spoken to Lucy just once; to tell her of his safe arrival and to give her his hotel number. Mobiles, although he was forced to use them, were not his style.

Holding something 'substantial and meaty' in his hand was his preferred means of communication. That's what I prefer, Lucy had joked all those years ago, and so a tradition of much-enjoyed telephone sex was born.

The levels of passion they could reach simply by painting word pictures when physically apart had amazed and thrilled them both.

For days Scully had thrown himself into a preliminary study of what was possible Thai-wise for the Ratledge plan, pumping the embassy for information without giving any hint of the reasons for the trawl; surfing the Net for the fullest background on the country's economy, culture, health and longevity record, climate and diet details.

Every night or morning he had expected a call from Lucy, knowing that geography had never acted as a barrier to their verbal intimacy before. It never came. On the fourth day, Scully broke his silence and rang Lucy, although in the past they had always taken it in turn.

He'd chosen his time carefully, 5pm UK, midnight Thailand, the hour when his partner was normally at her sexiest. He was not disappointed.

The voice down the phone was surprisingly wide awake, and after a few, not entirely convincing apologies for her non-communication, they were soon into their stride, graphically describing what they would do to, and for, each other if not apart.

Lucy's passion reached a peak of sorts in what seemed like indecent haste, but Scully dismissed the thought, smiling to himself that indecency was what it was all about.

The seamless path to mutual arousal was interrupted only briefly as Lucy switched her phone to loudspeaker so that her hands were free to make use of whatever 'toy' took her fancy.

Scully thought he could hear her wetness as they pleasured themselves in utter abandonment amid much laboured breathing and muffled cries. Lucy repeatedly gasped for her clitoral hood to be pulled back and the tonguing she craved delivered forthwith.

A tiny voice noted in the back of Scully's inflamed mind that none of Lucy's demands had been aimed at him directly and for a moment he wondered whether someone else was in her room.

But as more peaks were scaled, Scully flattered himself with the belief that just a few days' separation had made his young partner hungrier than ever for him.

Spent, exhausted and with Lucy's phone still on the loudspeaker setting, they showered each other with endearments, making up for lost time.

Lucy was evidently in no mood for sleep and Scully used the opportunity to fully brief her on what Ratledge planned. In that languid state that can at times make a woman receptive to almost anything, she was all ears as he unfolded the plan.

Scully revealed the large fee Ratledge had dangled before him, half persuading Lucy that this was serious stuff after all.

It also persuaded another set of ears in Lucy's bed: Wanlaya Vatayanon, the jaw-droppingly pretty, diminutive daughter of Nam Horm's owner.

Scully's fellow passenger Alf, the obese bundle of

misogyny, flight fear and special smells, had been perfectly correct. Within 48 hours of Scully's departure, Lucy had indeed found a shoulder to cry on, or more accurately the shoulder had found her.

But it had not metamorphosed into a penis to dine on; instead, mutual cunnilingus was now the house speciality; served often. And with relish.

It was open to question which of the two women was the more demanding, but the important point for Lucy was that a void had been filled in every sense.

Scully's phone call could not have been better timed, and Lucy smiled inwardly at the innocence of 'sweet Ludo' who could not know it was Wanlaya's tongue she had in mind as they reached the heights of telephone passion that night.

Wanlaya had enjoyed the charade, but it was what Scully had said post-sex that now exercised a business brain every bit as nimble as her tongue. It was, in fact, business that had brought them together on the second night after Scully's departure.

Wanlaya's family had noticed Lucy's red-rimmed eyes at meal times and still suspected that the resort's problems must have had at least something to do with Scully's sudden flight to Britain.

When Wanlaya knocked on Lucy's door she was on a genuine mission of discovery, still fearing that the resort's best customers might be slipping from its grasp.

Re-assured, yet again, that the trip was purely business, the real voyage of discovery began as the two women, loosened by mildly iced Mekong whisky, began paying each other heavy compliments.

It was Wanlaya who had made the first move, slipping her arm around Lucy's shoulders and gently kissing away her tears as she revealed how much she was missing Scully, and so soon; they hadn't parted on the best of terms, she confided.

As they sat on the bed, which doubled up as a sofa, Wanlaya's lips opened for her tongue to take on the task of removing the still trickling tears, licking them from eyes and cheeks.

Moments later, she seamlessly journeyed down Lucy's face until their mouths met. Wanlaya thrilled to the thought that there was not the slightest resistance from this nymph, who could easily have emerged from some classical canvas.

Lucy mentally returned the unspoken compliment, overjoyed that a ravishing young Asian beauty, with the figure to die for, might actually desire her.

All fear and hesitation melted as both mouths opened, tongues probing.

Seconds later both women drew back, panting and gazing into each other's eyes. 'I wanted you the first time you walked into our resort,' Wanlaya confessed, 'but I didn't think you liked women.'

Reddening slightly, Lucy revealed that she'd never been quite sure about how she felt towards her own sex, only ever experiencing schoolgirl fumbles.

'Riding horses gave me my kicks,' she laughed shyly, before quickly adding. 'But seeing you, Wanlaya, brought back memories of those fumbles. You could easily pass for a schoolgirl – only far prettier than those I ever went to school with.' It was Wanlaya's turn to change colour.

'The truth, Wanlaya – and I never told Ludo – is that I fantasised about you quite a lot. I just can't believe it's coming true.'

Both women had wasted no more words, enjoying each other at every opportunity each night, with Scully's phone call providing the extra dimension. Wanlaya's face now turned serious.

Snuggling close in the tender, yet fragile, bloom of early trust, Wanlaya spoke tentatively: 'Lucy, there is something you should know.'

For an icy moment Lucy thought the Thai girl might be host to some exotic STD and now it was post-coital, confession time. Harbouring such cliched notions unsettled Lucy who now felt a twinge of guilt.

'What is it, Wanlaya? You can talk to me about anything you like,' she urged, slightly inching away from the stickiness that glued both bodies together. For a moment the Thai girl hesitated.

'You must promise not to say anything to my father,' she implored, 'no one is supposed to talk about it outside the family.'

Lucy felt her concern growing and sat upright on the bed, noting with alarm the gathering tears in the perfect almond eyes she gazed down at.

'It's this business, the resort, it has big problems, very big problems, and I'm worried my whole family could lose everything.' Lucy sighed, doing her best to cover up the relief in her voice.

'Dear, dear Wanlaya,' she soothed, falling back on the bed and into her lover's arms, pressing the full length of her body against the tiny frame.

'I thought it was something really important you had to tell me; that you were seriously sick or something.'

'In some ways that would make me happier, Lucy. Then the whole family would not have to suffer. If one person gets sick and dies, the rest of the family can still live, carry on, but it's the resort that's sick; and if that dies, there will be no end to the suffering for all of us.'

For a moment Lucy lay quiet, disorientated by the mix of self-sacrifice and intense family loyalty that exemplified the Thai way. She tried to conjure up a vision of such behaviour in the West. She could not. The East was a different mindset, not just a compass point.

Finally, she broke her silence: 'Why are you telling me this now, Wanlaya?' Lucy felt the question was well grounded. A relationship a few days old was hardly the solid foundation on which to reveal family secrets.

'Forgive me, Lucy, I was not spying on you,' the Thai girl ventured, sheepishly, 'but you left your phone on the loudspeaker setting when you talked to Mr Ludo and I heard what he said about looking for a place for old English people to live in Thailand. Do you think that Mr Ludo might consider Nam Horm?'

Lucy was stunned at Wanlaya's swift change of direction. Eyes that minutes earlier had been misted with tears were now wide awake in child-like hope. Again, Lucy groped for the right words.

'This is a holiday resort, Wanlaya. People who are old need special carers, doctors, English speakers, legal things sorted out. It's not as though they're coming for a few weeks' holiday.

'They would be coming to your country to spend their remaining years, hopefully well cared for and happy. And …' Lucy's voice trailed off.

'And what?'

'Oh, nothing.'

'Come on, Lucy, tell me what you were going to say.'

'Well, they then die and someone has to make all the sad arrangements, sending their bodies home, or disposing of them here, in your country.'

Wanlaya looked, by turns, thoughtful and puzzled.

'You westerners make a big fuss about bodies, but it's only a shell for the spirit that soon finds a new home.'

Lucy sighed. 'It's not some philosophical or religious thing I'm talking about, Wanlaya, I'm thinking of the practicalities of death.'

'How do you mean? Why should this be any problem?' the Thai persisted.

Lucy, careful not to cause offence, turned her head sideways as she allowed her eyeballs a skywards roll. For a woman of education, Wanlaya, at times, could seem maddeningly obtuse.

'Well, think about it. When the old people come to the end of their stay they won't be acting like normal holidaymakers. And for a very good reason. They'll be dead. There would be lots of things to do, not just sort out the body.

'Doctors, police, any relatives, the British Embassy, maybe even a post mortem – an autopsy like the Americans say – could be involved. It's not a simple business and can be very chaotic, involving lots of complications.'

For reasons beyond Lucy's understanding, Wanlaya still looked blank. One final attempt at context was attempted.

'Let me put it this way, Wanlaya. The old people will not be going to reception the night before they die, asking for their final bill to be made up and announcing that they'll be vacating their room by noon the following day. When you're nearing the end, death is a very random business. It's not all neat and tidy.

'The Grim Reaper, as we call death, doesn't knock on the door or phone up and say, "Sorry to be a nuisance, Lucy, but could you let reception know that you'll be checking out tomorrow, for good. It's your final day on earth."'

The ludicrous nature of the conversation, lubricated by topped up glasses of fruit-based local hooch, suddenly struck both women, sending them into laughter spasms as each vision of dead souls queuing at reception outdid the other in anarchy.

Exhausted and satiated by the night's events, they fell back into each other's arms, sleep finally drawing a curtain on all activity. But not before Lucy had given Wanlaya a solemn undertaking that she would at least mention the idea of the resort to Scully.

Wanlaya had heard the figure of around £1,000 a week – 50,000 Thai Baht, a small fortune – that the English paid to look after one old person. She imagined the resort being filled with a plentiful supply of such people, and did the math.

Gentle smiles on both slumbering faces, but for different reasons, completed a picture of bliss under the star-studded tropical sky.

***

Scully's first reaction was one of anger as he quizzed Lucy harshly two days later.

There was no suggestion of any repeat phone sex between them as he rigorously questioned how anyone could know about Ratledge's care-home plan and the possible involvement of Thailand.

Scully emphasised it was a closely guarded secret with potentially important political ramifications. Lucy had concocted a cock-and-bull story about hearing garden furniture being disturbed outside their quarters while they were on the phone.

'Remember, Ludo, I'd had to set the phone to loudspeaker to keep my hands free,' she teased. 'Maybe some voyeur outside heard our conversation – and the care-home talk.'

'Yes, but how would the resort's owners get to know?' he persisted.

'I don't know, Ludo, they're not saying. Maybe it was one of them who heard, or someone mentioned it. The point is they now know, so what do I say to them?'

Reluctantly, Ludo bought into Lucy's explanation. He had little choice. Initially he had dismissed outright the idea of the resort being turned into a care home, for many of the same reasons Lucy had given Wanlaya.

But a flood of news items over recent days was now giving him a fresh perspective on what was and wasn't possible in a world turned upside down by increasingly bizarre political agendas.

The manifesto of the Monster Raving Loony Party

would look respectably dull, he mused, compared with the screaming headlines he was digesting:

Councils had been exposed for spending taxpayers' money on prostitutes, lap dancing clubs and exotic holidays for the disabled.

One Norwich man who'd been 'disabled' by mental ill health following a devastating divorce was given a free holiday in Tunisia with a 'friend.'

Even his Internet dating had been paid for, driving lessons thrown in, art materials supplied – all courtesy of the taxpayer.

What had particularly attracted Scully's attention, though, was that the break in Tunisia still worked out significantly cheaper than a week in taxpayer-funded institutional care.

Scully sensed that nothing was unthinkable any longer, the tectonic plates of what was socially acceptable were shifting.

It was a view strongly re-enforced by the news that a local authority had agreed plans for a 21-year-old with learning disabilities to have sex with an Amsterdam prostitute.

The money had been provided under the Personal Care Budget (PCB) scheme that gave lump sums to the disabled or their families, leaving them to decide how it's spent.

Predictably, organisations like the Taxpayers Alliance had gone mad, while the disability network, Radar, welcomed the move, its chief executive arguing that the desire for sexual relations 'was a matter of human rights.'

Scully's brain was racing. Infirmity came with old age, and what was that if not a disability. Why not go the whole hog and make the final years of Britain's old folk a real joy with sun, sea, sand and – yes, whatever else came their way, for those still up to it; men and women.

PCBs for the elderly already existed, although there had only been a 25 per cent take-up because managing a budget was not easy. But even if there were no PCBs and money was still handled in traditional council ways, that didn't mean it had to be spent in the same old manner.

Could some of this new thinking really be brought together in Thailand? Scully wondered.

Why, if tentative estimates were right and serious money could be saved by re-locating to the Far East, even the dry-as-dust Taxpayers Alliance might come on board.

Confidence growing that Ratledge might well be on to something, Scully felt a frisson of excitement and let his mind drift back to Lucy's words.

The mythical 'informant' had mentioned the £1,000-a-week cost of caring for the 'English elderly' to the resort's owners, Lucy had told Scully.

The entire Vatayanon family had then lost no time in letting Lucy know that, based on preliminary investigations – sounding out all the relevant authorities and making in-house cost calculations, including specialist staff hire – there was no reason why the resort could not do the job for about a quarter of the price.

Of course some resort alterations would have to be made, and cast-iron contracts entered into, ensuring a steady flow of residents, but 'please tell to Mr Ludo that all, as you say, is do-able,' Visit Vatayanon's parting words to Lucy had been.

She had dutifully relayed the resort's figures to Scully who could not stop weighing 'a quarter of the price … a quarter of the price …'

The information could not have been more timely. Official UK Government statistics had just predicted that 10m people currently alive in Britain would live beyond 100, a figure the pensions minister had described as 'staggering.' The financial implications were incalculable.

Scully now felt that something potentially huge could be bubbling up – and was about to share it with Ratledge, Finance Officer Vincent and an increasingly bemused Eileen Faulkner, who over the past week had found her secretary's job taking her in some very odd directions.

A minor twitch in the right corner of her mouth had appeared, and a sudden need for sleeping pills had swiftly embedded itself as habit. With events beginning to move at a dizzying pace, her modest spinster cottage became more sanctuary than home.

***

'How well do you know these people, Ludo?' Ratledge quizzed, eyes narrowing into watery slits so tight they threatened to imprison the moisture. Business brooked no levity.

Scully filled in the details, adding that in all his years at the Nam Horm, he had never found the owners to be dishonourable or disagreeable. In fact, the very opposite.

Mention of the 'quarter' cost, under £250 a week, had seriously whetted Ratledge's appetite, but he wanted to know more, much more.

'You never can tell with foreigners, Ludo,' Ratledge pressed. 'They're not like you and me, you know. They can be all smiles one minute and cut your throat the next.'

Ratledge's office grew quiet. Vincent pressed all 10 digits together, tip to tip, in the manner of prayer. Eileen Faulkner instinctively fingered her single row of cultured pearls, as if caressing a rosary.

'Well, Arnie, let me put it this way,' Scully responded, keeping his voice even and measured.

'There are people in Thailand I would trust far more than some of the shysters in this benighted land. And the resort's family come into that category.'

Scully fixed his stare on Ratledge who met his gaze eyeball to eyeball.

'You seem to be pushing the idea of this resort, Ludo, when we've not even checked out Thailand's established care homes yet.'

Scully jumped in: 'I'm pushing nothing. I'm in two minds about the resort myself. I am simply giving you information.'

'OK, so what about their established care homes?' Ratledge pressed'.

'I've got people checking that out as we speak, but I think you'll find there aren't that many to check. For starters, not many Thais can afford them. Besides, it's not really the Thai way of doing things, you see, Arnie. They are really funny people that way.'

'How do you mean?'

'Well, the thing is, they respect, honour and revere their old people. And when they're not busy with false smiles and sawing their way through throats, they actually like to take care of them – at the family home, not in some soulless, clinical Colditz stinking of stale piss and cheap disinfectant.'

Ludo's sarcasm breathed fresh life into Faulkner's left hand, as her pearl-fingering intensified. Scully watched absent-mindedly as each pearl was now threaded – systematically, neurotically, left to right, right to left. The early stages of some mental health problem, he guessed.

Ratledge could barely keep a lid on his anger, knowing that Scully, 'this Manchester guttersnipe,' had shamed him in front of junior colleagues. The taste of olive stones welled up in his mouth.

'If you can leave the snide stuff aside for a minute,' he almost spat the words at Scully, 'what exactly are you saying here? That it's worth talking to these resort owners in detail? You wouldn't be on a commission would you by any chance?'

Ratledge regretted the crude attempt to get back at Scully as soon as the words had left his mouth.

Scully stood up. 'So you think I could be on the take, eh, Arnie? Right. You either make a full apology to me now, in front of your colleagues, followed by a written apology, or I leave this office never to return. And you can shove the whole project up your backside.'

The pearls clattered to the ground, the thin string giving way to a level of pressure it was never manufactured for.

Arnie Ratledge felt hopelessly cornered, the olive-stone taste now thicker then ever. He was hanging by a thread. The demanded words were uttered through a bone-dry mouth:

'I am sorry, Ludo, I never meant to impugn your integrity in any way. It was a very bad joke and it was stupid of me to make it. I say hand on heart you are the most honest man I have ever met and I fully apologise to you without the slightest reservation.

'Eileen, when this meeting is over, please draft a letter to that effect to Mr Scully which I shall sign.'

Frantically scrabbling for the precious pearls with one hand, Eileen Faulkner scribbled her instructions with the other. The mouth twitch increased both its arc and rate. Ratledge's approach to Scully was now on an entirely different footing; for the present.

Playground words of wisdom occupied Ratledge's mind: 'He who fights and runs away, lives to fight another day; he who fights and stands his ground, gets his blinking clock knocked round.'

He had no intention of entertaining Scully at the expense of his 'clock.' His time would come. He would fight him another day, on different ground.

Clearing his throat and mustering whatever shreds of dignity he could salvage, Ratledge spoke quietly to the man he both loathed and secretly, very secretly, had a grudging regard for:

'Now that we have that very unfortunate misunderstanding out the way, I suppose you are the man best placed to judge this resort's offer, Ludo.'

His fleeting nemesis said nothing, enjoying the awkward silences that seem to have lowered the physical temperature of the office, making the warmth of Thailand and Lucy seem more remote than ever. Ratledge picked his words with extreme care.

'It's just that to me, sitting here, it seems incredible that some holiday camp on the other side of the world would have a clue about what to do with dozens of Lancashire old folk – some hardly able to walk, others probably incontinent, going gaga, whatever – when they've never done the job before. I mean they've never run a home for their own old folk, never mind a bunch of foreigners.'

Scully, tired with Ratledge and half swayed by the tempting prospect of sinking back into Lucy's arms, even for a short spell, easily fashioned the case for a quick trip back to Thailand to explore the resort's offer in detail.

'I don't think what they've managed before is that important,' he said. 'What matters is the quality and expertise of the staff they employ, or even sub-contract, to do the job.

'Take Heaven's Haven, right here on our doorstep. The rates are astronomical, but apart from criminal checks, what detailed probes have been carried out on the staff who work there; on whether they are the right people, psychologically and professionally, to look after our elderly?

'You yourself, Arnie, told me about that man who fears blindness, and the religious nut who's supposed to be taking care of him.' Vincent and Faulkner exchanged puzzled glances.

'There are people running these homes who rake in millions, yet they employ staff – some on a pittance, the more senior ones on more – who shouldn't be left in charge of a budgie.

'You used the words "holiday camp," Arnie, and I'll tell you who the real holiday campers are: the perma-tanned care-home owners, living it up on an ocean of cash and human misery.'

Ratledge allowed his eyebrows a slight elevation. He was back. The angry young man. Yesterday's communist was resurfacing for a final wave of crimson. He let him have his moment.

'So, yes, these people run a holiday resort at the moment, but if they can get the right staff and turn it into a resort-cum-care home at the rates they've promised, why not explore the possibility at least?

'Or is the good life – or what's left of it for Wigburn's elderly – only to be spent by a sun-kissed elite who themselves never experience the joys of day-time TV in a grey, Lancashire concrete block?'

Scully's late sprinkling of class warfare almost prompted polite applause from his audience of three. But while arm and hand muscles did not spring into action, Ratledge's words were all the reward Scully wanted.

'Do you think it might be worth flying back to Thailand immediately and talking to this family in detail, Ludo?'

'I think it might be worth a shot, but what I also want to do is carry out my own independent checks in the Koh Samui area and make doubly sure that what they're telling us actually stacks up on the ground.

'I've got some excellent contacts on the island, among both the Thais and the ex-pat community.'

Ratledge expressed concern that Scully's inquiries might lead to others cottoning on to 'his' idea.

'Relax, Arnie . I'm not bad at developing cover stories. No one will guess what I'm about – as long as the resort family keeps quiet. The longer things hang in the air, though, the greater the risk that someone will blab and the whole idea gets stolen.'

That final observation ensured Scully a return Thai Air flight two days later – Heathrow-Bangkok-Koh Samui – with no overweight fellow passenger to disturb his tranquility. First Class travel did not allow it. Ratledge's purse strings had loosened a little more for 'comrade' Scully.

As the 747 crossed the inhospitable North Sea, Ratledge crossed the equally uninviting threshold of Heaven's Haven, trying desperately to ignore what his sense of smell was telling him.

***

The warm blast of air as Scully descended the aircraft steps on to the Koh Samui tarmac had never felt so welcome. The picture-perfect airport, fringed by the Gulf of Thailand and a riot of tropical vegetation, was the perfect antidote to the grey of Lancashire, and immediately sent his spirit soaring.

The jewel in the setting was Lucy, clad all in white to offset her deepened tan and waiting impatiently behind the flimsy arrivals barrier that tantalisingly separated them.

Lucy had guessed correctly that their intense passion for each other, after a separation that had stretched to 10 days, would not survive a 40-minute ride to the resort and had wisely chosen a self-drive hire car.

They had hardly cleared the airport boundary before Lucy pulled the Suzuki into a private-looking copse. Such was their mutual heat that neither worried too much about being seen, tearing at each other's clothes with animal urgency.

This was wham, bam, thank you mam – and man – without any pretensions to anything else. Scully's erection was of a hardness that delighted them both, but led to an almighty tussle to release it from the confines of his jeans.

'Cheap sodding zips,' he cussed. Lucy acted, ripping the zip from its moorings. Within minutes, bodily fluids were traded in embarrassing amounts. Lucy's loud insistence on being taught a real lesson for being an 'exceptionally naughty girl' was met in full, with some extra homework thrown in.

The sweat-soaked couple paused for breath. 'So what have you been doing that's made you into such a naughty girl,' Scully asked, playing along, but seeking that extra bit of re-assurance all men search for after a lengthy separation.

Lucy never got to answer as the sound of voices brought all entwinements to a halt. Two herdsmen were trying to move a water buffalo to fresh pastures and the Suzuki was blocking their path.

Scully smiled at the herdsmen and, with as much dignity as he could retrieve, slipped behind the wheel and drove off, his briefs risking entanglement in the brake and accelerator pedals.

At a decent distance, both dressed, agreeing their unfinished business could be taken care of back at the resort. As the sun slowly slipped below the horizon, its rays burnishing specks of cloud in pink and gold, the couple smiled contentedly at each other.

Scully didn't know quite what, but there seemed something behind Lucy's eyes that was richer, warmer, more sensuous. Probably just the contrast with Lancashire playing tricks with his head, he thought.

As they pulled into the resort, Scully felt honoured at the mini reception committee waiting by the entrance: Wanlaya, her sister and their parents all flashed the broadest of smiles.

It felt good to be 'home.' Bags were swiftly unloaded and no, Scully had not forgotten a special present that Lucy had asked him to bring.

***

Without question, Ratledge had drawn the short straw when he and Scully parted for their respective destinations. The blast of warm air that hit Wigburn's leading politician as he entered Heaven's Haven had not been tinged with the frangipani and jasmine fragrancies of Koh Samui.

Instead, more gritty odours greeted him as he pushed open the care home's faded pink swing doors: human waste smells (solid and liquid) dominated, closely followed by bodily gases, sweat, cheap cooking oil and harsh cleaning fluids, all melded together in a heavy fug.

Ratledge mused that in a different setting, and perhaps with a little tweaking – more carbolic here, a little less oil there – the whole concoction could pass off as some black market, cut-price poison gas, available to impoverished Third World armies.

How people lived and worked in such an environment was beyond him, and by all accounts Heaven's Haven was not the worst.

Shouts of 'get out you mad bastard, leave me alone,' interrupted his silent promise to himself that whatever life threw at him, he would never end up in such a place.

The shouts got louder, even drowning out the crucial answer to Noel Edmonds' 'Deal or no Deal' question, blasting from the common-room TV.

'Nurse, nurse, he's doing it again,' a man in dirty white pyjamas and a purple dressing gown bellowed from a wheelchair. Above him towered another man, dressed only in similarly-coloured pyjamas.

Ratledge, who guessed both men were in their 80s, stood transfixed at the cause of the commotion. For reasons unknown, the man standing had a piece of sticky tape attached to his own upper lip, fixing the other end to his nose.

The man – a failed stand-up comedian called Phil Malden, Ratledge later learned – was pacing the room, addressing wheelchair man. 'Come on, Sam, play the game. Who am I and what's my problem?'

'Your problem, Phil, is that your charades are crap. Now just piss off and leave me alone, I want to watch Deal.'

Malden was having none of it. 'Come on, if you saw someone in the street looking like this, what would you think?'

'That he's a lunatic who needs locking up. NURSE!!!'

'No, Sam, you'd think 'hair lip,' and that's the answer. My name for today is Herr Lip.'

Those still able, had bolted for the door of the common room as soon as Malden appeared, sticky tape in hand. Those less mobile, or deep in liquid-cosh land, now stirred as Sam's cry for help grew louder.

It was a regular routine. Each day, 'Mad Malden' as he was known, adopted a different identity which others had to guess.

Ratledge approached Malden, intent on pacifying the situation, when a carer poked her head around the door.

'And who are you?' she asked sharply, immediately getting Ratledge's back up.

'Arnold Ratledge, Mayor of Wigburn Council. I'm supposed to have an appointment with your Chief Executive Officer at noon.'

'Well his office is on the second floor, you shouldn't be in here,' the carer snapped.

'Well maybe if you were doing your job and not leaving an old man shouting for help, I wouldn't be,' Ratledge shot back, his face reddening.

'Anyway what's your name?'

'I'm under no obligation to tell you that,' the carer said.

Resident eyes were on the two of them, minor wars forgotten for the moment, as Ratledge strode for the door, tried to bang it shut, but was thwarted by his sleeve's entanglement with a hook.

Not bothering with any lift, he found the stairwell and took the steps two at a time as he searched out the office of Stephen Boyle.

He had entered Heaven's Haven with the intention of going through the list of residents with Boyle, assessing those who might be ideal material for his ground-breaking project, subject to their individual agreement.

Media-savvy as always, Ratledge realised that for maximum impact he needed to 'export' old folk already in a UK care home so that instant cost comparisons could be made.

He was wary of contractual obligations with Heaven's

Haven, having been fully briefed by the council's legal department, and had, unusually for him, been prepared to deal reasonably with the owners.

'Creative co-operation' was going to be his weapon of choice. And only when absolutely necessary would limited compensation be offered. These amounts could, however, be quietly topped up under 'special arrangements,' with no questions asked about the origins of the extra cash.

Experiences in the common room had, however, unsettled Ratledge and marginally hardened his approach.

Mustering a fake smile, he entered Boyle's office and wondered why the stench of the building had almost vanished.

Maybe the upper floor had a different ventilation system. Or could it be that he was just getting used to the stink. Perhaps carers and residents no longer noticed after a certain time.

Ratledge sat alongside HH's owner, who doubled up as the CEO, as name by name they ploughed through the list of the residents below.

He took an instant dislike to Boyle, noting how the man sitting alongside him – pointed features sitting atop a slight, crouched body that moved in a darting, jerky manner – would have been a much more fitting recipient of his own surname, with its rodent allusions.

In fact there was nothing man-like about Boyle at all. Even his masculine smell of freshly-cut wood was explained by a pencil he'd just sharpened, notebook at the ready.

Ratledge declined the offer of coffee and brought out his own notebook. Because the matter was still of the utmost 'commercial sensitivity,' both men had agreed no secretaries would attend.

***

Refreshed in all senses after a night of unbridled passion

with Lucy, Scully seriously reflected on why he had ever left the delicious company of his partner.

Who in their right mind slams the door on a tropical paradise for the life-sapping greyness of Lancashire, even for 10 days. I do, that's who, he muttered as he gazed longingly at the sleeping beauty beside him on the king-sized bed.

Gently and quietly, so not to disturb her, he massaged his aching jaws and patted his overworked tongue, both of which had been in great demand during the hours of darkness.

He'd often wondered why Thai beds were so huge, and now his imagination offered endless debauched answers. Oceans of space had certainly smoothed the frequent transition from 'regular' to oral sex, which was just as well. Lucy had wanted his head between her thighs so much that at one stage Scully seriously feared suffocation.

The resort's owners had invited the couple to a special 'welcome-home,' breakfast that morning and time was moving on. With reluctance, Scully kissed Lucy awake and after a bout of sensuous showering that threatened to make them late, they joined the Vatayanons.

Within minutes, before the opening course of exotic fruit had a chance to be digested, Visit handed Scully a single piece of paper.

With a mixture of amazement and admiration, he read through closely-typed plans of how Nam Horm could be turned into a care home for the British elderly within months. Nothing had been left to chance as the fine detail burned into Scully's brain.

Under a bloc arrangement, partially funded by insurance companies, health organisations would ensure medical care around the clock.

Teams of personal carers, virtually one for every two 'guests'– Scully liked the use of the word – would be available 24/7, staying on the premises, in their own quarters, in shifts.

The carers, who would generally be young ladies in their

teens or 20s, supervised by an older team leader, would be available from an employment agency that Visit had already listed.

All legal requirements for permanent residence in Thailand would be taken care of by a respectable law firm with headquarters in Bangkok. And even the tricky business of death had been thought through.

There would be the option to fly the body back home – built into the costings (assuming no complications) – and if disposal in Thailand was preferred, there were a number of choices, one of which was not yet available, but could be in the near future.

Scully was agog as he read on. In the US and Belgium a new method of disposal called resomation had been developed and it could come to Thailand. It essentially involved dissolving the corpse in a special solution.

Said to be less polluting than cremation – the preferred option in Thailand – what was left of the dear departed could still be returned to next of kin in an urn-like container.

Scully looked up from the document and stopped eating his second course of noodles with lightly fried squid and chilli sauce. He wondered whether he could be in the company of a fantasist.

'So Thailand could soon be in the business of dissolving bodies. Is that right?' Visit's eyes twinkled.

'Oh yes, Mr Ludo. The Belgians and six American states are trying to get permission to do that. If they succeed, I think we could soon have this system in Thailand.

'We are always very pleased to get the latest technology in our country. We Thais will still go for cremation, I'm sure, but maybe you farangs would prefer this … errr … solution.'

Scully paused for breath, gazed into the middle distance and understood why countries of the Far East were in the forefront of human advance. The main interest was in getting the job done, efficiently and economically, utilising advanced science.

As if reading his thoughts, Visit continued: 'If we get the dissolving system, I think it would cost less than cremation or burial.

'I spoke to an American friend who knows this idea. He says he is certain it is cheaper. That would save money for your friend's council and my resort, Mr Ludo.'

'Wow, that sounds really promising, Mr Visit.'

No one spoke for a few seconds and Scully felt obliged to say something knowledgeable about death and innovation in Britain.

'Mind you, Mr Visit, I suppose we can all be creative in our own way when it comes to death.'

'How do you mean, Mr Ludo?'

'Well a widow I once knew had the ashes of her husband ground very fine and put in an egg timer.'

'An egg timer?'

'Yes, you know, those glass things that normally have sand in them. They run for about four minutes. Perfect eggs every time.'

'So why swap the sand for her husband's ashes, Mr Ludo? That is not very respectful to his memory.'

'She told me he'd never done a real day's work in his whole life and "now that he's dead the lazy good-for-nothing will at last be doing something useful."'

A stony silence came from the Thais as eyes were lowered. Lucy fought desperately to suppress a major giggle fit. Scully feared he'd crossed some cultural red line and immediately re-buried his head in Visit's document, digesting the details:

Pocket money for the 'guests;' clothing and an on-site shop for life's remaining pleasures; yoga and tai chi lessons for those who could manage it; special diets; supervised swimming in the main pool or on an ultra-safe, shallow section of the beach; embassy liaison for any serious emergency back home; video-phone links to friends and relatives across the world; films, games, music; visiting specialists, from barbers to manicurists; everything was covered on the two sides of the one-page report.

Even the addresses and contact details of all the individuals and organisations involved had been listed so that 'Mr Ludo' could check it all out if he wished.

Scully passed the document to Lucy and fixed his eyes on Visit's now blank face.

'You know, nothing is certain about all this?' Visit nodded his understanding. 'It all depends on what happens in England.' Visit again nodded.

'Why have you gone to all this trouble – so much detail – when nothing might come of it?'

Visit now delivered his broadest of smiles. 'In my country, nothing is too much trouble for our old people. That should be the same for your old people.'

Scully sat back, humbled. Visit's next words stirred very different emotions:

'Besides, Mr Ludo, this is a very good idea. Much money, we think, is being wasted in your country and other lands in the West. If your council does not make a deal with us, we will talk to others. Maybe in other countries as well.'

The old familiar enemies of fear and resentment welled up in the pit of Scully's stomach. He couldn't blame Visit for hedging his bets, but he would do whatever necessary to make sure that this baby of his – and Ratledge's, as he mistakenly believed – would be sourced to its correct parentage.

Scully immediately went up a gear, laying it on with a trowel: 'It is an honour, Mr Visit, to know that your respect for old people extends to the elderly of my country.

'We might be the ones who develop the new technology – and not always that any more – but when it comes to life's real values, and what could be more precious than an old and wise head, we have a great deal still to learn from the people of Thailand.'

The entire Vatayanon family nodded their appreciation of the kind words.

'I can assure you that I will do everything in my power to get your proposal accepted by Wigburn as quickly as possible.

'If necessary, I would even be prepared to fly back to England tomorrow' ... the sound of Lucy choking on her cup of jasmine tea punctuated his speech ... 'to make sure that Wigburn and Nam Horm strike this historic deal. That's how determined I am.'

'Like hell, you will,' Lucy thought. But then she caught Wanlaya's seductive, smiling eyes and the threatened pain of another sudden wrench from her beloved began to soften.

Lucy's splutter with the tea succeeded in reining Scully back a little. 'Of course, Mr Visit, Wigburn will expect me to check out some of these sub-contracting agencies you have lined up, so that will obviously take some time.

'But please don't misunderstand me. I fully trust what you've set out here, but, as I'm sure you'll appreciate, it's normal business practise to see things for oneself,' he explained defensively.

'Of course, Mr Ludo,' Visit smiled. 'I understand perfectly.' As the sun rose higher, Ludo began to feel stickier than usual in his slightly over-tight western shirt.

'Obviously, my offer to return tomorrow was a little exaggerated,' he smiled.

'Of course, Mr Ludo.'

6

Beautiful Schemers

'You made a bit of a tit of yourself at breakfast,' Lucy chastised, as their re-hired Suzuki bounced down a half-paved road on the outskirts of Samui's chaotic capital, Nathon. 'Flying back tomorrow … egg-timer ashes … I don't know, Ludo, what are you like.'

Scully tried to focus on the road, dodging the weaving motorbikes that seemed to follow traffic rules all their own. They reminded him of flocks of starlings taking wing; diving, weaving, soaring in a tight, black cloud; never an observed collision.

'You try a business meeting when you're jet-lagged and you've hardly had a wink of sleep all night,' he snapped.

'Aaah, so you would have preferred a good night's kip to servicing your beloved,' Lucy teased.

'Don't wind me up. Just keep your eyes open for the agency. It should be somewhere along here on the right.' A few hundred metres on, the Kantor Koh Staff Agency finally came into sight.

A two-storey building of some elegance, the overall effect was marred by an ill-conceived attempt to blend traditional Thai with minimalist European add-ons; an afterthought that ought never to have been given skull room. KKSA was listed on Visit's all-embracing document as the preferred care-worker provider.

A swift scan of the highly-polished company name plate revealed that it also supplied staff of many different callings: Office temps, waiters and waitresses, cleaners, cooks, bar staff, masseurs and masseuses, tour guides, interpreters, dance instructors ('Thai traditional and western'), and health advisers who doubled up as teachers of yoga and tai chi.

What caught Scully's eye in particular, and Lucy's, was that a KKSA offshoot, Hearts Apart, acted as an international dating agency. Lucy couldn't resist a final dig:

'There you are, Ludo, tailor-made for any randy old Wigburners who want to cop off – unlike some people I know who prefer to nod off.'

'Enough, Lucy. Go and see what damage you can do with the credit cards. There seem to be plenty of shops around.'

Lucy, who had zero interest in sussing out a 'boring old employment agency,' didn't need asking twice, agreeing to meet back at the car in an hour.

Scully entered the building and immediately congratulated himself on having the good fortune to be alone. Whatever credit card damage Lucy inflicted, it could not possibly blight the eye candy he now feasted on. It was as though he'd stumbled into the middle of a major beauty contest.

Scully stepped back outside to ensure that he'd not taken the wrong entrance, but no it was the right place. It was the people who seemed all wrong.

No care-worn carers, no crushed cleaners in sight. Just stunning young women, and men, and some who seemed to occupy the in-between territory that the Thais termed lady-boys.

Even KKSA's own administration staff, sitting demurely behind a huge reception desk, or taking notes in little cubicles, could have stepped straight out of the pages of some health and beauty magazine.

He could not tell who was offering what service exactly, and stood gawping in what seemed to be the central reception area.

'May I help you, sir?' a girl asked. Clad in a figure-hugging Chinese *cheongsam* slashed to the thigh, her even-white teeth, set in finely-sculpted features, dazzled Scully into momentary silence.

Finally he trotted out his cover story about an elderly, semi-infirm father who liked to spend winters in Koh Samui, but needed a carer to look after him 24/7.

Kamphan Champa radiated charm, sympathy and concern in equal measure as she asked him to follow her through a door at the far end of the reception area.

This Scully was happy to do, eyes riveted on buttocks shaped by the Chinese dress into the firmness of two hard-boiled eggs. He now understood how this simple item of clothing had enticed so many western men into self-destruction over the centuries.

Seating herself behind a small teak desk, Kamphan offered Scully something cold to drink as she rummaged in the drawers. A green folder was eventually produced, out of which a form was extracted for Scully to complete, giving his 'father's' personal details. He kept the answers as general as possible, feigning forgetfulness with some of the more awkward questions.

The ice-cold coconut juice was delicious, but did little to cool his burning curiosity.

'I thought I'd come to the wrong place for a minute,' he smiled. 'Why was that, sir?' Ms Kamphan asked, eyes wide awake in a mix of innocence and gentle humour.

'Well … there were so many people milling around … and … and …' she waited patiently for him to finish his sentence … 'and, please don't take this the wrong way, they were all so, well, so good looking.'

Kamphan laughed and for a moment Scully feared, for the second time that day, he was making a fool of himself in front of Thais.

'Sir,' she asked, 'who told you about our agency?'

'Oh, a man I met in a bar in Bangkok,' he lied.

'Well, sir, he should also have told you that our speciality is in supplying the best-looking staff we can find for our clients.' Scully looked puzzled. Kamphan explained:

'There were many stories about us in the newspapers two years ago, claiming that we were discriminating against less beautiful people, but we won the argument and in fact the publicity was very helpful.

'Our staff are now in demand all over Koh Samui and in other parts of Thailand. And we have plans to open offices abroad – if we can win the legal challenges about discrimination.'

Scully was even more perplexed. 'May I ask you a very direct question?'

'Of course.'

'Why should it matter whether a cook, a cleaner, a carer, or an interpreter for that matter is beautiful or handsome? I can understand you trying to get good looking people on the books of your Hearts Apart dating agency, but why should it matter for the staff you supply? Surely the only important thing is that they do their jobs well.'

Kamphan shifted in her chair and gently passed her tongue between her lips, moistening them slightly before speaking.

'Sir, may I ask you a question?' Scully nodded.

'Do you enjoy looking at a beautiful flower, a painting, a beautiful sunset, a sea that's emerald green and inviting; white, unspoilt beaches framed by coconut palms; beautiful homes adorned with exquisitely carved furniture; food, particularly vegetables and fruit, that my people spend hours carving into shapes of such great beauty that you feel guilty about eating it; even bars of soap fashioned into intricate, delicate flowers – items of so much beauty that people hesitate to wash with them?'

Scully, deeply impressed with the girl's passionate advocacy, delivered in flawless English, nodded tamely.

'Thailand is not only the land of smiles,' Kamphan continued, 'it is a land that values beauty in all its forms, including the human.

'Yes, people also have beauty within, and the staff we supply must have that, too – and, of course, the necessary work skills – but having a person of beauty around increases human happiness, a subject I believe your Prime Minister once expressed an interest in.

'People, if their heart is good and they are not of the jealous type, like to work with, share homes with, be taught by and be cared for by the beautiful of this earth. It lifts the spirits – and this applies to everyone, regardless of age.'

With that final flourish and her eyes now firmly fixed on Scully, Kamphan opened the green folder. Scully tried with some effort to continue his form filling as picture after picture of oriental, and some European, beauties leapt at him from the pages.

Brief biographical details and work history accompanied each picture, but Scully found it difficult to tear his eyes from the photos. Why on earth, he wondered, had Nam Horm listed this as their preferred agency.

In the company of such ravishing carers, he couldn't see the residents of Heaven's Haven surviving a week. He feared that the mere sight of the women would send pulses racing to destruction. Maybe it was all to do with some Thai belief in dying happy.

With a sense of unease, his mind skipped back to Visit's unsettling interest in the resomation method of body disposal. Scully began to wonder what he was really getting into. Kamphan's voice intruded on his thoughts.

'Are there any of these girls you'd like me to make contact with?' she asked, running her eye down Scully's barely legible handwriting. 'Yes, the bloody lot,' he fantasised.

'Errr, I need to think about all this and discuss it with my father. Have you perhaps some brochures with … samples I could take away?'

'You mean of the carers?'

'Yes please.'

A sheaf of glossy brochures, booklets, pamphlets and newspaper cuttings was presented to Scully.

***

As ever, Lucy was late returning to the car, and what she found was not the man she'd left 75 minutes earlier.

'Sorry,' she said automatically, both hands gripping bags of 'must haves' that were most likely to end their lives in cupboards and wardrobes before the year was out.

Scully muttered his forgiveness, head buried in the KKSA literature. Lucy glimpsed some of the pictures.

'Where else did you go?' she queried instantly as he continued devouring the contents.

'Nowhere, I've been with one of the KKSA girls who's been telling me what the organisation is all about.' Lucy took a more detailed look at the pictures.

'These are not care workers, Ludo.

'Of course they are. All this stuff is from KKSA. It's their literature.'

'Ludo, I've seen umpteen girls like this outside high-class massage parlours. Be honest, that's where you've been and I've caught you drooling. You slipped out for a quickie. Just don't lie to me. No wonder your eyes are all shot.'

Scully snapped, 'Look for yourself, what does that say in big, bold letters, or has the sun burned your brain away – "Kantor Koh Staff Agency" – they are the girls they have on their books as carers. Even their cleaners, their cooks, they're all lookers, like this lot.'

'You're joking!'

'No, I'm not. They have this insane policy – or I don't know any more, is it insane – that every person on their books must be a cracker. There were stories about it a couple of years back. Anyway, it's all explained in this bumph. Read!'

Scully thrust the papers on Lucy's lap. 'So you think I

went for a quick jump. The only jump here is from you – jumping to conclusions.'

Lucy saw the word 'carer' below one of the pictures. She read further and her mood gradually softened from anger to disbelief.

'But why, why would anyone with such stunning beauty want to work as a carer or cleaner, for God's sake. It doesn't make sense. I'm sure most of these girls – or boys – could get jobs as models, or well-rewarded "escorts."

'And why would Nam Horm want such stunners to take care of people at death's door? It's all completely crazy.'

Scully treated Lucy to a potted version of the beauty philosophy he'd been subjected to. Her response was succinct, conjuring up her equestrian past:

'Horse shit.'

Tempers cooled, both agreed their next port of call should be back at Nam Horm for some serious questioning.

***

Ratledge had not had an easy time with Boyle. Predictably, money had been the sticking point. Heaven's Haven owner had raked in millions over the years, with much more on the horizon.

Running an all-male residential home had been an astute move by Boyle. Men died earlier than women and rates would always be adjusted upwards for new residents filling the inevitable vacancies.

The cost to the council of breaking agreements with the home would be high, and no 'special arrangements' could disguise the fact.

More importantly for Ratledge, large severance penalties would not just be a monetary blow. They would eat into the financial benefits of any relocation to Thailand, clouding the crucial political message that he was pioneering a ground-breaking, cost-cutting scheme for others to follow.

Instead of being seen as the trail-blazing saviour of taxpayers' cash, he would be labelled an imbecile without equal, squandering savings from 'his own,' potentially great, idea.

Other local authorities would inevitably step into the breach, 'exporting' the elderly in a more professional, clear, cash-saving manner … and the media would mock Ratledge for shooting himself in the foot yet again; only this time severing an artery back to the political mainstream.

They would give him no second chance, to develop 'his' brainchild, ensuring he fell at the first hurdle as others, more competent, swept passed.

Always the media calls the tune in this bloody country, he sighed, self-pityingly. Can't trust any of 'em. That's what his mentor Joe Dean had said, and he was right. The only half-decent hacks were old ex-Left-wingers like Scully, and he certainly wasn't sure about him any more.

A mild depression settled on Ratledge as he sat alone in his office and reached for a file on other care homes that might be open to a deal or could soon be facing closure.

He was on the second page when thoughts of Joe Dean resurfaced.

Joe – his man on the inside, his personal Fifth Column at Heaven's Haven – he would be sympathetic, understand what his old protege was facing.

Maybe Joe knew something that could drive the price down, the odd skeleton in the cupboard … or one about to rattle its way in. Haven still had to be the answer.

Ratledge poured himself a whisky, topped it up with spring water, sat back in his chair and loosened his collar. His mind shifted to murkier territory.

If anything untoward were to happen at Haven, the residents would have to be taken care of elsewhere. And if Haven were at fault, any broken contracts would be their responsibility – and penalty-free as far as the council was concerned.

He was warming to the dark track of his thoughts as the whisky kicked in. And if something quite scandalous closed Haven, that could easily be spun as extra brownie points for rescuing the old folk. He was now in overdrive and sat upright, deeply impressed with his own genius.

Not only do I transport these people to paradise in a pilot project that saves public money – blazing a trail for others – I also rescue them from some headline-grabbing event; premises found to be not fit for purpose, perhaps even structurally unsafe; or staff suspected of ill treatment … abuse; financial irregularities in the handling of residents' cash. So many possibilities. Brilliant, he almost said out loud. Who needs a Scully?

An inner voice cut through the whisky and self-congratulation: 'You do. Who's got it in for care homes? Who's the best man for punting out damaging stories about Heaven's Haven? The man with the right media connections?'

'Scully,' Ratledge answered himself audibly. What's the bloody man up to anyway? Nearly a week since he flew back and I've not heard a peep. Probably not got out of bed yet. He always was a bugger for his oats.

***

Oats had been the last thing on Scully's mind as he sat down with Visit Vatayanon in a corner of the public dining area, viewing him with a less than trusting eye.

The resort's owner sensed the change and seemed genuinely sad at the lack of the usual light-hearted banter. 'I can see you are not very happy, Mr Ludo, I hope I can help you.'

Scully launched straight in, unwisely dispensing with the opening pleasantries that were an expected part of social interaction in the Far East.

'I've visited the KKSA and I need to know what kind of

organisation it really is.' Visit looked startled.

'I don't understand, Mr Ludo. You know what organisation it is. It's an employment agency for all different kinds of staff. You have the list I gave you. You have just told me you've been there. You must know.'

'What I saw, Mr Visit, were some of the best looking people I've ever seen in my life, offering themselves as cleaners, carers. It just doesn't happen. It doesn't make any sense. Please be honest with me. What are they really up to?

'Is it some sort of front for trafficking? I'm a journalist, Mr Visit, please don't take me for an idiot.'

Scully realised too late that he'd overstepped the mark. Visit rose from his chair, accidentally knocking over a single orchid in a glass vase.

Scully knew well that he had broken the cardinal rule about not showing anger in public, especially to a person of note. Inevitably it would be followed by someone's loss of face, which could have devastating consequences. Visit came the nearest he'd ever seen any Thai come to unchecked fury.

'Mr Ludo,' he said, face reddening by the second, 'I do not think of you as an idiot. I have great respect for you and your wife. But you have shown no respect to me by the way you have just spoken. You have asked me to be honest with you, which means that you think I have not been honest in what I have told you about KKSA.

'That is a very bad insult to me and I am sorry but I can speak with you no longer unless you withdraw your words and apologise.'

Scully, stunned by the ferocity – for a Thai – of Visit's response, searched for the right words, aware that any etiquette failure now would probably end their relationship.

Desperately he paraphrased the first thing that came into his head; a waiter's fulsome apology for a dirty fork, lifted from an ancient Monty Python sketch

Bowing almost double, he began, 'I am humbly, most

grievously sorry for the terrible hurt I have caused you by this grave offence, Mr Visit.

'Please be so kind and good enough to accept my sincerest and most deeply-felt apologies. Nothing, and I say this with hand on heart, nothing of this nature will ever happen again.'

Scully had no idea what the Thai for 'you give great grovel,' was, but the satisfied look on Visit's face as he resumed his seat seemed to have done the trick.

The resort owner then launched into the self-same spiel about beauty that Scully had heard on the premises of KKSA. Scully began to fear for his own sanity and wondered whether he was losing the plot.

Could it be possible, really possible, that there were important people in Thailand who believed that beauty was the major factor in spreading happiness.

Try as he might, it just didn't ring true in his jaundiced take on people and the things they got up to. He was now edging towards Lucy's hard-boiled 'horse shit' assessment, when another thought elbowed its way into his brain.

What if KKSA was indeed a front for traffickers? The whole notion of operating in broad daylight, under the cover of some fake mission to bring beauty to the world, was nothing short of genius.

KKSA's Kamphan Champa had said quite openly that plans were already afoot to open offices in other parts of the globe. What a story, and not just a national tale, but one with international reach!

The journalist in him had never died, he told himself, just hibernated in the soft world of public relations where he now frittered away his talents, polishing the images of tossers and the tosh they sold.

Like those nodding dogs in the backs of Cortinas all those millions of years ago when the world was a more fathomable place, Scully's head had been rhythmically jerking up and down to the resort owner's now-honeyed words.

He felt bored with the beauty message and wanted to listen no more, but wondered how to extricate himself politely. A sudden urge to mix with ugly people made him long for a poster of Marty Feldman or Charles Laughton's Hunchback of Notre Dame.

'I think I now understand why beauty is of such importance to you and your people,' he lied to the owner.

'May I say it is a beautiful idea that you have, and tomorrow I will contact my people in the UK and explain all this.

'Thank you so much for opening my eyes. It is so sad how farangs like me can be so suspicious and only see the ugly side of life. But please understand, I was a journalist for so long and we learn to think that way. It curdles our brains.'

As with Ratledge, another flock of angels disembowelled themselves at Scully's words.

For Visit, though, it was the icing on the cake. A fulsome apology, plus a conversion to the Thai way of thinking was more than he could ever have hoped for at a single bite.

The 'conversion' was perhaps a little too readily offered, though, he noted.

***

Lucy seemed mildly surprised, almost disinterested, that Scully had come around to her 'horse shit' take on KKSA. He had braced himself for the expected stream of 'told you so' admonishments, but none came.

At Scully's suggestion, Lucy had been on a fishing mission of her own, chatting cosily to Wanlaya at a quiet end of the long bar.

It had not escaped Scully that Lucy seemed to be getting on with the owner's daughter particularly well of late, and he'd suggested she raise the KKSA business with her casually, but his expectations were low.

Lucy had, however, delivered and Scully was intrigued to

learn she had been given the identical beauty spiel that he'd now heard – twice.

Maddeningly for Scully, though, Lucy now seemed to be moving in the opposite direction to him, no longer dismissing the possibility that there could be something genuine in KKSA's way of looking at things.

'It's all very Thai, isn't it, Ludo,' she sighed in a voice that was uncommonly soft and distant.

Her eyes again had a warmth and mistiness that slightly unnerved him and he wondered whether the whole business with the care homes was turning her a little odd too.

Scully toyed with the idea of forgetting the Nam Horm resort altogether:

'Maybe we should check out other possibilities on the island; maybe other islands or even the Thai mainland,' he suggested as Lucy poured a couple of beers.

The sound of pouring stopped abruptly and Lucy stiffened. Her demeanour took a 180 degree turn and Scully was suddenly listening to a highly focussed, analytical lady, lasering in on the situation.

In this mood, she could probably give any of the world's sharpest CEOs a run for their money, he reflected, as she got into her stride.

'You're in a no-lose situation, Ludo, think about it,' she ordered, more than suggested.

'If you're right and this KKSA outfit is in the trafficking business, you're probably onto one of the biggest stories of your life. Surely you can see that. Imagine exposing all this eastern beauty appreciation stuff as a cover for international prostitution.'

Scully recoiled fractionally at Lucy's outright relish for a hatchet job on a culture he largely admired. Lucy paid him scant attention as more angles unfolded:

'How could so many girls and boys be threatened, persuaded, conned, drugged, blackmailed, whatever, into such a life?' she questioned.

'And what of the punters, those who use the agency's services? Individuals. Companies. Are they in on it, along for the ride or being taken for a ride?

'And how on earth would this resort benefit by having some of Britain's old and sick taken care of by beauties who should be spending their time in discos and clubs, trying to catch the eye of talent scouts, model agencies, film producers and the like?

'And are there fixers, middlemen getting their cut?

Drinks finally served, she paused briefly to take a sip, before sketching a picture of the flip side.

'And if it is all genuine, then fine. Either way, Ratledge is shelling out for you to look into the care prospects for old Brits. Do that – AND find out what's really going on at KKSA, in case it all goes pear-shaped.

'In effect, he's financing your investigative journalism as well.' Lucy smiled extra sweetly. 'You're on a winner either way here, Ludo. I should drag it out a bit.'

Such ruthlessness in such a sweet, sweet angel, Ludo mused. Truly, truly, women had depths that men could only grope towards – in every sense.

'Is your agency OK back home?' Lucy suddenly added as an afterthought. Scully nodded. 'Well then,' she observed mischievously, 'there's nothing holding us back. Let's enjoy the ride.'

With that she pulled open the bottom draw of her bedside table and fished around for a newly-bought tight black swimsuit that would never see water.

It was to be an occasional alternative to the jodhpurs and school uniforms and appealed as a fabric that would lend itself to some serious spanking; an ideal starter to the main course that now had to be performed to some very exacting standards:

Vaginal G spot fiddled about with; oral in play, tongue

hard at it; labia nicely massaged; clitoris lavished with attention; anus fingered a bit; nipples sucked; orgasms aplenty. Job's a good 'un.

Sometimes, though, Scully felt more gynaecologist than lover and understood why women complained of headaches: Too much bloody technique to remember. It all needed organising properly.

Scully drew on his pilot training, recalling that a good mnemonic could be an invaluable memory aid – like BUMPF, used by aviators the world over for vital pre-landing checks:

B: Brakes
U: Undercarriage
M: Mixture
P: Pitch
F: Fuel

Scully dug deep, seeking a pattern in Lucy's preferred order of business that would lend itself to a mnemonic. His mind erupted with the highly inventive VOLCANO

V: Vagina
O: Oral
L: Labia
C: Clitoris
A: Anus
N: Nipples
O: Orgasms (hopefully)

His interim report to Ratledge was due in the morning. He feared he would not be at his best.

***

'Can you not stop yawning,' Ratledge again requested as

Scully presented his filleted report over a remarkably echo-free line.

Unusually, his former boss had been as good as his word and invested in all the state-of-the-art communication tools Scully had needed.

'It's this heat, Arnie,' Scully half-fibbed, 'it gets really sticky at night.'

'Yeah, I'll bet it does.'

'No, really, it's no joke trying to kip when its nearly 34c outside.'

'Come on, don't tell me they don't run to air-conditioning.'

'Of course they do, but it's not the same thing and it's bloody noisy.'

'Yeah, Ludo, whatever.'

A double-dip yawn and a hefty pause increased Ratledge's irritation. 'These calls are not cheap, Ludo. Can we just get on with it.'

'As I've said, Arnie, all the details and my comments are being e-mailed across. Everything seems to check out fine, the firms involved all seem kosher, the figures add up, it's just … just …'

'Another fucking yawn's on the way,' Ratledge sensed …

'It's just that the employment agency supplying the carers, well they operate a, a, ahhhhaaa...' The yawn stretched into a six-second humdinger.

'Go and have a bloody kip, Ludo, and ring me back when you're in better shape. This is ludicrous.'

Scully ignored him, determined to finish his sentence. 'They operate a policy of having beautiful people on their books – carers, cleaners, tour guides, whatever.'

Ratledge thought he'd mis-heard and rushed to get his question in before the next yawn hit. 'You did say "beautiful people?" Scully nodded, forgetting he was on the phone.

'HELLO! "BEAUTIFUL," RIGHT?'

'That's right, Arnie. It's some sort of Thai obsession; they do it with soap and carrots and all sorts. It's supposed to make you happy.'

Ratledge removed the phone from his ear and looked at it stupidly. He hesitated before returning it to its correct position, fearing what might spill out next.

'OK, Ludo, what've you been on? You're gonna get yourself locked up and this whole project's down the pan.'

With a huge effort that came close to dislocating his jaw, Scully stifled a mega yawn and explained KKSA philosophy as best he could. Ratledge cut to the chase.

'So they think beautiful things and beautiful people make other folk happy? So what? Do you think any of the poor buggers stuck in Haven are gonna complain about being looked after by some gorgeous bint?

'They'll think all their birthdays – and some of 'em must have had over 90 – have come at once.'

'They're real crackers, though, Arnie, and I'm worried that the excitement of seeing such beauts might, you know, bring on heart attacks, strokes, that sort of thing.'

'I repeat, so what? How would you like to go out, Ludo? That way, or gazing into the eyes of some religion-crazed Lancashire Nurse Ratchett?'

'OK, Arnie, if you don't think there's a problem...'

'Problem? Problem? There's no contest, Ludo. No contest. If you want to hear about real problems, I'll tell you what's happening at Haven. The place is run by nutters and lazy good-for-nothings. It's just a cash-cow, squeezing the taxpayer by exploiting the old.

'I now understand something of what your poor mother must have gone through,' Ratledge added hastily, not wanting to waste an opportunity of getting Scully even more on side.

'That bad, eh?' Scully yawned more than asked.

'Yeah, I'll tell you about it later, but Ludo I can't take any more of these yawning gaps from you. It's annoying the hell out of me. Get a nap and then ring me back, if it's not too late your time. Meanwhile, you can send me those e-mails.'

"Yawning gaps," cynical old sod, Scully thought as he half sleep-walked to his computer. A few minutes later he flopped on the bed, relieved that Lucy was nowhere to be seen. Probably teamed up with her new best mate, Wanlaya, he dozily speculated before heavy eyelids closed on a nightmare world of grotesquely outsize genitalia.

***

A two-legged mammoth vagina was chasing him down an alleyway, engorged lips snapping at his prominent nose. He struggled desperately for breath, arms flailing, until the voice of Lucy jerked him back to reality.

'Ludo, Ludo, wake up!' She shook his shoulder roughly. 'You've just hit me on the neck.'

Bathed in sweat, Ludo prised open his terror-filled eyes to the red mark below her left ear.

'You've been having a nightmare, screaming all sorts of obscenities, half the resort must have heard. And look what you've done.' The redness was rapidly developing into a weal.

Still half asleep, Ludo mumbled his apologies, though still not quite sure what had happened, and glanced at the time.

'Christ, I've got to ring Arnie back,' he said, rummaging for the phone. 'Anyway, where have you been?'

'Oh, getting stuff out of Wanlaya,' she answered truthfully. 'What I want to know is why you've been screaming. Is Ratledge giving you a hard time?'

'No, not at all. It was just some monsters chasing me; you know, kids' stuff.'

'You're a bit old for that sort of thing, but I suppose we can't control dreams. How did you go on with Ratledge?'

'No problem. He thought I was making a fuss over nothing.'

'Just as I thought,' said Lucy, who rarely resisted registering a triumph, no matter how tenuous or minor.

Scully let the comment pass. He accepted it was part of a long-term healing process for an ego bruised by erstwhile 'friends' who had sneered openly when they first learned Lucy had thrown in her lot with an older man.

The manner of her meeting Scully had not helped either. They had both been evicted from an upholsterers in circumstances that made the local paper.

Lucy was choosing some mid-brown hide for a chair that had to match older furniture. The conscientious salesman, urging caution, demonstrated how, when the leather was stretched on a frame, it took on a lighter colour.

Scully, next in line for the salesman, was unable to resist a loud comment: 'If Michael Jackson had known that, he could have saved himself a bloody fortune.'

Scully was evicted amid allegations of racism. Lucy, who had never clapped eyes on Scully before, was shown the door for laughing hysterically.

They often joked that it was stretched skin that brought them together and now bound them tightly in all sorts of imaginative ways.

Scully smiled at the memory and stirred himself into giving Lucy's ego a further healing hand.

'Yes, you were right, love. Ratledge thought the Wigburn old folk would take to pretty girls like a duck to water, and not believe their luck.

'He mentioned some further problems at that Heaven's Haven place, though. It sounds like a real nightmare and he wants to talk some more about it. What exactly did you get out of Wanlaya?'

'Oh, pretty much what I got last time, but she went into much greater detail. She showed me a world of beauty that I never even knew existed, Ludo. She really is some girl, and goes to great lengths to make her point. She knows so much, I felt like a relic from the Dark Ages.'

Scully couldn't remember a time when Lucy had ever waxed so lyrically about another woman. Nor could he know that he had hit on the right word. When she met up with Wanlaya, the Thai girl had just returned from a full Brazilian waxing, removing all body hair.

The mere sight of her most precious few square centimetres, intimately exposed as never before, had been the trigger for Lucy to reach unimagined heights.

'If there was anything significant she revealed, just tell me later,' Ludo requested. 'I must ring Arnie now.'

'Will do,' Lucy shouted from the bathroom, smiling.

***

'Anything look out of place to you, Stanley?' Ratledge queried as both men flicked through the e-mailed fruits of Scully's Thai-side research.

Vincent had glanced at most of the material quite quickly, nodding his approval, but seemed to spend an inordinate amount of time poring over the lavishly illustrated KKSA literature that had been scanned across. There was a reluctance to replace it on Ratledge's desk.

'I'm no expert on Thai rules and regulations and how their companies operate, but at first glance I would say this all seems to be pretty standard stuff,' Vincent said, trying hard to add timbre and gravitas to his voice as his eye fixed on a particularly well-proportioned cleavage.

'Certainly the costs are well within the original estimates, it's just ... well ... just this ... err ... material,' he said in a low voice uttered by men of a certain age when buying top-shelf magazines in the seedier newsagents.

'Not you as well, Stanley,' Ratledge sighed. Vincent was forthright. 'Well, I must be honest here. These women look like prostitutes. I think we would be failing the elderly of Wigburn if we didn't check this ...' Vincent stopped mid-sentence.

'Hang on, hang on, Arnie. Prostitutes. Has this got anything to do with taxing prostitutes by any chance – that old chastity belt nonsense? Because if so, you can count me out of this whole business.'

'No, of course not, Stanley, nothing further from my mind. Not that I accept it was nonsense. I mean, whoever comes up with a foolproof way of taxing prostitution...'

A light came on in Ratledge's eyes, a light that said completely different things to the two men. To Ratledge, it spelled 'idea.' To Vincent, 'dread.'

'... just think what it could do for the economies of countries where the sex trade is rife,' Ratledge added before shutting down the subject.

Vincent stood up and spread the KKSA material on Ratledge's desk, feeling relieved that he had not kept silent about his fears.

Ratledge cleared his throat noisily, but the decibel count was matched by the ringing phone.

'I've Mr Scully on the phone from Thailand,' Eileen Faulkner announced. 'He couldn't get through on the other lines and has had to come through the switchboard.'

'OK, Eileen, and could you bring me in the Heaven's Haven file.' Ratledge felt relieved that he could escape all the beauty explaining with Vincent, immediately volunteering Scully for the job.

'Just tell Stanley why the KKSA women are such crackers, Ludo. He thinks they could be on the game.'

Scully did as we was told, unaware that a minor drama was simultaneously unfolding in Ratledge's office. Faulkner handed Ratledge the Haven files and stepped back in shock at the site of KKSA's prime offerings sprawled on her boss's desk.

Over recent weeks Ratledge had grown increasingly concerned at his secretary's behaviour, which seemed disconnected and erratic. He felt sure he'd smelled alcohol on her breath some mornings. Many times he'd asked Vincent for a second opinion, but got no straight answer. Only Faulkner herself knew the reality.

Returning to her desk, in a state of mild shock, Faulkner rummaged in a bottom drawer and from under a pile of papers extracted a flask of vodka.

Faulkner had been a quick learner in the substance-dependency department, effortlessly navigating a seamless switch from pills to booze. She now took a cossack-size swig, her third of the day.

The rapid 'hits' had helped her bury, or at least give some perspective to, the swiftly evolving events at Wigburn Council.

As the vodka dutifully kicked in, she let her imagination soar. 'Could they be thinking about using Thai prostitutes? Are things really that desperate here? Does it mean I could be implicated? The police; the newspapers.'

The alcohol continued on its all-powerful path, zig-zagging at will. Whimsy now took its turn, softening the hard edge of her skewed reality:

'But then again, prostitution is the world's oldest profession and was a respectable calling in ancient times. Aaaah, let people enjoy themselves, be happy, be merry and if it brings in the money who cares. Money … maybe he's back with the chastity belt thing.'

Tolerance morphed into licence as the vodka now seeped into fresh byways.

'Sometimes I wouldn't even mind giving it a shot myself … a few years younger … who knows.'

A second reach into the bottom drawer was interrupted by Vincent leaving Ratledge's office. The pitying look on his face as he gently shook his head sobered Faulkner, but only slightly. An aggressive coarseness now took over.

'What's bothering that dried up old stick? Imagine any poor girl getting a punter like that. Be like taking a corpse to bed. He's already half dead, always moaning about his prostate. That's it, that's what he needs: A prostate-tute, not a prostitute.'

Mirth derailed any further thoughts as Eileen Faulkner rested her head on the desk for 40 winks ... wishing it could be 40 wanks at the hands of some young stud.

***

Scully's words had reassured Vincent that Wigburn's oldest and finest were not going to be at the mercy of 'holesalers' as Ratledge had once crudely described them.

Both Ratledge & Scully knew the importance of keeping Stanley Vincent on board. Those who handle the cash normally know where all the bodies are buried – and only idiots alienate them.

How to deal with Haven was, however, business of a very different order. Ratledge and Scully discussed penalty clauses, possible contract loopholes and the structure of the company that owned Haven.

Ratledge again breathed fresh life into the ghost of Scully's mother as he described in imaginatively fleshed-out detail the greed, cynicism and mental suffering that was 'said' to go on behind the closed doors of the home.

'Said' by who exactly was neither revealed nor questioned as lurid embellishments papered over all ticklish gaps in Ratledge's disturbing narrative.

He claimed that some years back a bargain-basement comedian – the entertainment budget had been cut to the bone – caused uproar at Haven.

The comedian's opening line had been to ask how many of the residents had Alzheimers. A few hands went up. 'Well, I'm safe telling you lot the old jokes then.'

Furious Alzheimer victims almost lynched the comedian. Scully queried his name.

'None of them can remember,' Ratledge said, deadpan.

Scully's dislike for a care home 7,000 miles away – one he had never actually visited – grew into disgust as Ratledge's revelations did their intended job.

The single trigger word that kept running through Scully's brain was 'abuse' as visions of his mother re-appeared. What Ratledge had described needing exposing.

'Sadly, Arnie, all this reminds me of those old tales of care home abuse that used to do the rounds, and still do.' Ratledge kept silent.

'At one penny-pinching home they even employed an epileptic barber. He'd fall asleep standing up – right in the middle of cutting someone's hair. Long-term residents got used to it, but it killed a new bloke.'

Ratledge's interest grew. 'How, Ludo?'

'Well, nobody told him what to expect and he was being shaved with a cut-throat razor. Suddenly the barber nods off for a couple of minutes, razor resting over the poor bugger's jugular. The shock killed him and the barber was sacked.'

Ratledge, seeing no mileage, moved Scully on. 'And what else?'

'It was terrible what they uncovered at some homes. Dirt, bed sores, food poisoning, bullying, mental and physical abuse by staff, vermin on the premises. A few got closed down eventually, but not many.

'There were even some cases of sex abuse by staff. Horrified the nation those cases did. Authorities shut the homes within days, pending investigations. They didn't have a clue what was going on – right under their bloody noses. As soon as it got into the papers that they were being investigated – whoosh, that was it.'

Ratledge smiled the quiet satisfaction of the cat that had caught the pesky mouse and been rewarded with a bowlful of the finest clotted.

He might be a pain at times, but press the right buttons and 'my boy, my Ludo' still came up with the answers every time. Without ever realising it.

'You know, Ludo, you're making me think. Maybe what I've found out is just the tip of the iceberg. I wonder what really goes on when no prying eyes are around. Some of Haven's residents certainly give me the impression they're too scared to talk.'

'Well, if you do unearth something really big, you know where to come for national exposure. I'll do anything to shine a light on these slime balls. But tread carefully, Arnie. Proof. Evidence. All vital.'

There was a long pause from Ratledge. 'You know, Ludo, it's been a pleasure talking to you … and without those bloody yawning gaps.' Both men laughed.

'You managed to get some shuteye then?'

'Yeah, but I had some funny dreams.'

'Well, we all get those, Ludo, it's just that I can never really remember mine and anyway they seem to get cut short.'

'It's probably because you think you're renting them, you tight-fisted bugger.'

The two men laughed some more and agreed to talk three days later, unless some urgent business intervened.

In the meantime, Ratledge had a little extra job for Ludo, nothing to do with care homes, but something he would be handsomely paid for.

'Ludo, could you pop into a brothel, massage parlour, whatever, for me?'

'What!'

'I want you to find out whether the sex industry – you know, the girls, the madams, the owners – pays any tax in Thailand.'

'Why on earth do you want to know that, Arnie?'

'It's just something to do with a little idea I've got kicking around. I'll explain it to you when you're back over here.'

'I've done dozens of brothels in the UK when chasing stories, Arnie. It's a nowt job. I just make my excuses and leave in the time-honoured fashion when I've got what I want.'

'Good man.'

'But I'll have to have a word with Lucy first.'

'Of course.'

Against expectations, some warmth was being rekindled between the odd couple in the face of the common care-home enemy.

Ratledge felt a double glow of satisfaction. And not without reason. His 'little idea' was nothing less than the mass resurrection of the chastity belt invention, only this time flooding the fleshpots of the Far East.

It all made perfect economic sense. The potential income for governments in the region should mean no shortage of Research & Development funding to get the little 'belters' absolutely spot on this time. China could do the manufacturing, and that would reduce transport costs.

No harm in having an extra sideline going. He'd have Scully talk to Thai government officials once he'd completed his initial 'research' with the 'holesalers.'

Nothing, however, must get in the way of the far more important care home project.

***

A nagging itch now pestered Scully's head. Had he adopted too much of a broad-brush approach to care homes? He had promised to do 'anything' to expose those care home 'slime balls.'

Was he repeating the folly of earlier years when he believed there was no such thing as a good capitalist, tarring all with the same brush?

He had been wrong, utterly wrong, accepting late in life that there were indeed good and bad capitalists. He was now one himself!

Similarly, there must be good and bad care homes. What

if Ratledge had been exaggerating the problems at Haven, distorting facts to suit his agenda, with more of the same to come; and egged on by Scully.

It was a moment of truth partially brushed aside by the return of his mother's emaciated face. The care industry owed him one – a huge one – his mother.

Why in this world was it only he, Ludo Scully, who had to play by scrupulous rules? But then again, what was life without rules and values. Scully's head felt mushy.

Ratledge tried buzzing his secretary with a request to contact Joe Dean urgently at Haven. It took a few seconds before Faulkner answered in a voice that sounded half awake. A yawn confirmed Ratledge's suspicions. What is it with everyone today? he wondered. They all seem knackered.

***

Joe Dean bounced into the Tesco coffee shop two days later for his meeting with Ratledge. Told to say nothing about their get-together, he was excited by the prospect of a bit of clandestine stuff.

Nothing of consequence had been said over the phone, but he knew that when his old protege went into secret mode, something of interest must be afoot. And whatever it was, it had to be better than rotting away in a care home he loathed.

'You want me to do what?' Ratledge moved quickly to lower his old mentor's tone.

'No way, Arnie, I can't do that. They'll think I'm a fruitcake or something and lock me up. What proof would I have. Anyway, what nurse in her right mind would want to sexually abuse me? I'm an old man for Christ's sake. I couldn't pull a muscle.'

Ratledge sighed. This was going to be tougher than he thought. 'I'm not asking you to do this on your own, Joe. To make the allegation sound right, there would have to be two, maybe three, of you. The no-smoke-without-fire mood would need fanning. Are there any others at Haven who would go along with the idea if you suggested it – just one at a pinch.'

Dean looked at Ratledge with a fresh eye.

'What's wrong with you, Arnie? Even I won't go along with it. What's the point of talking about others? Anyway, it's criminal, it's lying stuff.'

'Fair enough, Joe, if that's the way you feel. A pity, mind.'

Dean's eyes narrowed a little. 'It's just not right, Arnie.'

A few seconds went by. The eyes narrowed some more. 'Not that I'm interested; just curious. What would have been in it for us?'

Ratledge had saved his strongest card till last and prayed that he hadn't overplayed his hand.

'OK, Joe, here's the deal, which I'm telling you in strictest confidence. 'Wigburn's trying to pioneer a scheme in which care home residents are looked after in other countries.

'We think it's a scandal that some care firms in the UK are ripping off the taxpayer, draining the economy and people's assets – sometimes charging over a grand a week – for treating our old folk like dirt.

'We think the elderly deserve better. Care could be much improved and cheaper elsewhere.'

Dean was having none of it. 'So that's the game. You know we've been hearing rumours for weeks with all the comings and goings at the home and relatives being talked to. Let me see if I've got this right, Arnie.

'You want to ship us all off to some basket-case land – away from friends and family – where the labour's dirt cheap. You can then paint yourself as some sort of financial saviour. Is that it?' Ratledge felt it slipping away.

Rummaging in his briefcase, he pulled out the Thai material. 'No, Joe, no basket case land, but a place I'd jump at in your position: Thailand.' Dean's eyes swivelled as they fastened on the KKSA brochures.

'These, Joe, and I'm not joking, are a sample of the carers who would be looking after you, but that's only the start. Please hear me out.'

Dean's posture gradually became more relaxed as feelings long dormant began to stir.

Ratledge painted the best picture he could of a people 'obsessed, obsessed, I'm telling you Joe, with beauty,' drawing on Scully's descriptions and again embellishing as required.

'You see, Joe, this outfit that supplies the carers has taken this beauty business one stage further and thinks that everyone deserves to be surrounded by beauty, whether it's a vegetable …'

'What, you think we're all vegetables at Haven, well I can tell you …'

'No, will you just listen, Joe. The Thais get these carrots, artichokes, tomatoes …'

'A tomato's a fruit, not a vegetable.'

'Well, whatever it is, you nitpicking old bugger, they get these fruit and veg and, like, carve 'em into beautiful shapes so they look really good on the plate.'

'What's the point if they're gonna be eaten? Sounds like a crackpot job-creation scheme to me.'

Ratledge was beginning to wonder whether his involvement of Dean had been a mistake. You can take the man out of the trade union, but not the trade union out of the man.

He was an argumentative, grumpy old git and a character change was as likely as the earth reversing its axis spin.

'You're missing the whole point, Joe. They want everyone – even a pain-in-the-arse like you – to be immersed in beauty, from the moment they wake up …'

'I bet they can't carve bacon and egg …'

'Shut up, Joe … till the time they're tucked up in bed by some lovely lass, maybe after a relaxing massage.'

Ratledge drew out the word 'relaxing,' accompanying it with a sly smile.

'Aye, I've heard about these Thai massage places,' Dean again chipped in, as mixed memories began to edge out the more combative side of his character.

'There was a particular one in Blackpool that was always very popular with delegates at conference time.'

Ratledge let him ramble on, sensing that some of the hostility was beginning to evaporate.

'Didn't matter whether it was my own union, Labour Party or TUC, that massage place did some right business, virtually queuing round the block they were. I mean those conferences could be hell on the back, sitting for hours, listening to some right wankers. Not that I ever went for a massage myself.'

'Of course not, Joe.'

'No, seriously, Arnie, I mean if the papers had got hold of it, picture in *The Sun*, they would have made it look like a knocking shop. Missus, may she rest in peace, would have gone absolutely barmy. Edith was never one to tolerate that sort of "nonsense" as she called it, Arnie. Strict upbringing and all that.

'Don't get me wrong, she was a good wife in other ways, food on time, house kept clean, shirts well ironed, but when it came to a bit of the other, I reckon she missed her way. St Catherine's Convent should have been her calling.'

Ratledge suddenly felt a twinge of sadness for his old mentor. He was of an age when the goods weren't sampled before marriage, and after marriage it was too late, with the taint of scandal surrounding divorce. And if the goods were sampled pre-marriage, working class lads did the decent thing and wed the lass.

Now you could have your cake, eat as many slices as you wished, vomit it all out, move on to whole cake shops, and the word 'marriage' wouldn't even have to pass your lips.

A different world, and the past a foreign land, in many ways more foreign than Thailand seemed.

'You know, Arnie, looking at these pictures, many of the lasses are dead ringers for those at that Blackpool massage place ... errr ... I saw 'em in the adverts like.

'But I suppose they all look a bit similar out there. They're certainly bonny lasses, I'll give 'em that.' Ratledge seized his opportunity.

'Look, Joe, none of us knows how many years he has left. I don't want to be morbid, but I could go out of here and be knocked down by a bus.

'You could go to sleep tonight tucked in by that religious nut. Suddenly she gets it into her head that she's an angel of mercy sent by the Lord to smother you all to death so you can be in His bosom.'

Joe Dean felt fearful and vulnerable, familiar companions to the old. 'Stop it, Arnie, you're frightening me.'

'But some terrible things have happened at care homes, you know, Joe. Trust me, people can flip. Anyway, I've said my piece.

'Great food, warm weather, beautiful sand and sea, surrounded by carers who really respect and revere the elderly – and are only too ready to take care of their every need.' Ratledge paused.

'Alternatively, you can spend the rest of your days at Haven. The choice is yours. I need an answer very quickly. Haven would have been the ideal home to pioneer this project, but if it can't be done, I'll have to search for some other place.'

A long silence followed Ratledge's ultimatum. Finally, Dean spoke. 'What exactly would I have to do, Arnie? I'm not saying I will do it, but what exactly would be involved?'

Ratledge ordered another round of coffees and rang his office to say he'd be late back. His meeting was still running. He twice had to repeat the message to Faulkner and wondered what she'd found so hard to grasp.

***

Scully crept up behind Lucy and playfully squeezed her waist. He felt confident that Ratledge was mulling over their conversation and would probably discover more about Heaven's Haven. No need for either of them to be too pernickety, he'd finally decided. Nothing in life was flawless.

Scully was on his own voyage of discovery, finding out afresh what it was like to feel reasonably good about himself, enjoying some respite from his older demons. There would never be complete escape, but at the moment, respite would do.

Even the resurrection of reasonable relations with Ratledge felt pleasant, as though a decades' old rock had been lifted.

'What's put you in such a good mood then?' Lucy probed in between ticklish squeals of delight.

'There are some hiccups at the other end, but nothing to worry about,' he soothed, afraid that any gloomy news might accidentally find its way to the ears of the resort's family via a drink too many with Wanlaya.

'Anyway, what's this Wanlaya thing you were going to tell me about?' he said, nuzzling her ear. 'You two seem to spend a great deal of time together. I'm amazed that you can find so much to talk about.'

'Who said anything about talking? Lots of the time we just stroll along the beach, taking in the beauty of this place, listening to the sea, feeling the breeze. Sometimes we don't say a word for minutes on end.

'Other times we'll just lie down and gaze at the stars, wondering at the mystery of it all. When we do talk it can be very profound – and there is something you need to know.' Lucy turned to face Scully.

'We had a heart-to-heart about the staff on the KKSA

books and she admitted that all is not what it seems.'

Scully braced himself. Lucy saw the change and moved to re-assure him. 'It's not anything terribly bad, Ludo, but it does change the picture a bit.

'What does?'

'This whole thing has only been looked at from the punters' perspective. No-one has ever asked why some of the most beautiful, and, yes, sexy people I've ever seen should actually want to care, clean, cook, interpret, whatever, for others.'

'OK, Lucy, out with it. They're all dying of some terrible disease. Aids is it?' Lucy acted as though Scully had not spoken.

'It's simple really and I'll explain it as Wanlaya did. Life is a long business and beauty fades fast, and that's particularly true with most women.'

'Not with you,' Scully interrupted, ingratiatingly. This time Lucy gave him a weak smile, but still ignored his words.

'The girls on KKSA's books – I'll stay with them for the moment – are mostly from dirt-poor backgrounds, some from neighbouring Laos, where the poverty is among the worst in Indo-China.' Scully nodded.

'What they all have in common is the knowledge that within a few years their major asset will be gone. None of them wants to become a prostitute, but what they do want is the chance to meet people who, by their reckoning, are rich.

'In many cases that means Westerners, but it can be any nationality, rich Japanese, for example, but in general Westerners are preferred because, rightly or wrongly, they are seen as kinder.

'The age and looks of who they meet are utterly unimportant. All they want is the chance of that meeting – as a private cleaner, a carer, a cook – and for those more educated with their sights set higher, as interpreter, tour guide, you know the sort of thing.' Scully again nodded.

'That meeting gives them the one formal chance, the opportunity to impress, stun, enchant, and change their lives forever, maybe ending in marriage, even becoming a long-term mistress or, what for many can be the jackpot, being remembered in an old person's will.'

'But there are dating agencies for that sort of thing,' Scully protested. 'KKSA has an offshoot that bloody well runs one.'

'That's exactly the point I put to Wanlaya.'

'Well?' Scully's impatience irritated.

'Dating agencies, especially here in Thailand, attract a certain type. It's a bit like cold canvassing in a meat market. There's no spontaneity in how the people meet. In each other's minds they will always be thought of as some sort of inadequates for whom a relationship – and Wanlaya stressed any form of relationship – had to be artificially constructed.

'With the best will in the world that puts a break on feelings. People have dignity and want to feel they have come together naturally, organically, if you like. That's the genius of KKSA. It humanises what has too readily been dehumanised.

'If people feel that fate and mutual affection has brought them together, that generates real happiness and warm feelings, even if those feelings can only be expressed in the tender way bed-sore dressings are applied in the last few months of someone's life.

'Or, at the other end of the scale, re-kindling the embers of a long-dead sex life.'

Scully was impressed with Lucy's grasp of emotional detail as she sketched the broader reality.

'Wanlaya said that KKSA's own internal studies showed that non-dating-agency relationships were far more fruitful for the girls, money-wise. When someone's felt affection for you, looked after you, it normally generates some kindness in return.

'And, as I said, it can be some act of life-changing

generosity for the girls. That's why so many are queueing up to go on KKSA's books. And you know the real irony of all this?'

'Go on.'

'Many of the carers will end up using the money to look after their own families, especially their old folk. To many of them, the idea of shoving their own parents or grandparents into a care home, to be looked after by strangers, is anathema. It's the wheel turning full circle, Ludo.'

Scully sat stunned. 'Jesus! So they'll be sacrificing themselves at Nam Horm, looking after our old folk, to earn money to take care of their own old folk?'

'Yep, I suppose many of them will.'

'Wanlaya spilled all this to you?'

'Yes, she did, and much more.'

' What more?'

'Oh, just women's stuff, you wouldn't understand. It really does take a woman to really get to the heart of what this KKSA is all about.'

'Couldn't it be argued, though, that for some of the girls it's just a form of sophisticated prostitution?' Scully persisted.

'No more than some marriages or partnerships are,' Lucy noted. Scully sensibly retreated, switching the conversation to Ratledge's 'extra job.'

'Oh yeah, I almost forgot, Arnie wants me to check out a brothel or massage parlour and find out whether taxes are being paid. It's nowt to do with care homes, just some other idea he's got on the boil.'

'What idea?'

'He wouldn't say. It's all hush-hush, as ever with him. He said no one must know tax is involved and he'd explain it all to me back in the UK. You don't mind do you?'

'Not if it's work. Just take a condom with in case you get carried away.'

'No chance. I've done this sort of thing dozens of times

in Britain. You know, making my excuses and getting out.'

***

Two days later Scully walked into a massage parlour in a side street, running off Nathon's main coastal road.

Within five minutes, price agreed, he was down to business and his underpants.

'Aaaah, you do nice work but not much money eh?' he asked as oily hands steadily massaged their way nearer his groin. The girl answered readily, 'No, very little money, you leave me big tip, please.'

'Yes, I give good tip, but Government take big tax off you, yes?'

'Tax?' the girl queried, interrupting her oily journey.

'Yes. You, the manager, the big boss, all pay tax, yes?'

'Why you want know about tax?' the girl asked, frightened.

'It's OK,' Scully soothed, 'no reason, I'm just interested in how many baht the government take from you all.'

The massage continued with one hand while the girl pressed a concealed buzzer under the bed.

Within seconds, one of the largest Thais Scully had ever seen joined them.

In rapid-fire Thai, Mr Big exchanged words with the girl and turned on Scully.

'Why you talk tax? Here sex. Not tax. Sex. You spy for government? You go now. You fuck out of my place. Now.'

No further words were wasted as Scully, clad only in underpants, clutching whatever clothes he'd been able to grab, was bundled into the street.

A passing party of schoolgirls giggled uncontrollably. For Scully, the only upside was that he had not needed to invent any excuse to leave.

Clad in trousers, no shirt and a single sandal, he persuaded a reluctant taxi driver to take him back to Nam Horm at double the normal fare.

A puzzled Wanlaya saw Scully leave the taxi and head straight for his bungalow from where a phone call was made direct to Ratledge's home. It was 4am UK time.

'Never, ever give me any extra "little jobs" again, he thundered to a half-asleep Ratledge. 'I've just been thrown out of a massage parlour – in Thailand, for fuck's sake, Thailand! – because of you and your bleedin' tax.'

Ratledge tried in vain to calm him down.

'I couldn't give a shit about any of your other ideas, Arnie. I don't want to know. This is all about care homes for me. Nothing else.'

'OK, OK, Ludo. I get the message. Just care homes it will be from now on. Now, if you don't mind, I'd like to get back to kip.'

Scully slammed the phone down so hard it brought Lucy running from one of her interminable showers.

'What the hell happened to you?'

'I got chucked out of a fucking massage parlour, would you believe.'

'What!!! This is Thailand, Ludo, anything goes.'

'Except questions about tax. They went absolutely ape.'

Lucy gazed at her half-dressed man and couldn't resist laughing hysterically.

The amusement continued into the evening when she snatched a sticky hour alone with a curious Wanlaya who wondered why Scully had returned to the resort half naked.

Lucy could not resist telling her that he had been thrown out of a massage parlour, inventing a story that he was carrying out research for a friend back in Britain who was writing a book on sex habits in the Far East.

She told Wanlaya that Ludo did not disclose the precise reason for his ejection, sending the Thai girl's mind into overdrive.

Every perversion under the sun – from animals to anal nut-cracking – went on. What hidden, depraved mind did this mild-mannered Englishman really possess, she wondered.

Scouring her memory, she did recall one massage parlour rumpus involving an Austrian tourist, a girl and the trunk of a baby elephant.

But it had been the elephant that had trumpeted its excuses and left, crashing straight through the door.

Wanlaya was beginning to see Scully in a fresh, tingly light. She was not alone.

Ratledge had not been able to get back to sleep for some time, recognising that he'd pushed 'his boy' too far. Scully was right, concentrate on the biggie, the care homes. The other stuff could be shelved for now. No harm done.

Fancy, getting chucked out of a Thai massage parlour. Eeeeh, you do come up with 'em, lad. With that final thought, Ratledge drifted off to sleep, a rare smile on his face.

***

Joe Dean was slowly edging towards the Thai light, though still wracked by doubts wrapped in a morality born of another age.

Stand-up comedian Phil Malden was wracked by nothing more than an intense desire to live long enough to make the move.

Malden's enthusiasm had been infectious, telling Dean in expletive-peppered language that anyone who did not grab the chance to get out of Heaven's Haven – by fair means or foul – was 'fucking insane.'

The KKSA brochures that Dean flashed to Malden had weighed heavily.

Although generally disliked by many of the other residents, Malden's madcap approach to life had attracted Dean and an odd chemistry had developed between the two men who despite their advanced years and entrenched political differences, still hankered after some show of rebellion.

Each in his own way was an example of Lancashire cussedness, still fighting the Wars of the Roses against whatever foe could be substituted for a Yorkist enemy.

Every morning, usually between the hours of seven and eight, just before, during or after a breakfast of two boiled eggs, Malden would fart noisily, accompanied by exactly the same sentence: 'Eeeeh, we've not much money, but we see life.'

Fortunately the flatulence was usually odourless, but the utter predictability of the morning disturbance had an added corrosive effect on the already bottom-drawer Haven morale.

Some residents, working on the ' if you can't beat 'em' formula, ended up joining the morning chorus of 'Eeeeh, we've not much …' others sincerely wished that each morning would be Malden's last.

'I've seen this nutter in action,' Ratledge protested, when Dean half-heartedly revealed that Malden was more than willing to be his partner in crime.

'He tormented some old geezer in a wheelchair, talking about "Herr Lip."The man's as mad as a spoon. Drives people crazy with his farting, I've heard.'

'No he's not mad, Arnie. Just someone who's lost everything over the years; a failure at anything he's ever put his hand to, but he never kissed arse, no matter the cost. And he just keeps himself going by making his own entertainment, no matter how lousy.'

'"Entertainment?" Tormenting someone in a wheelchair?'

'Things are not always what they seem, Arnie,' said Dean

'The man in the wheelchair, Sam, is forever banging on about what a staunch trade unionist and socialist he was; a bit of a gob shite in my opinion, not the genuine article.

'Phil Malden thinks Thatcher was a great woman, a second Churchill who saved Britain from ruin by the unions. Well, you can imagine the fireworks. Others at the home just moan quietly and wish they'd both shut up.

'The Herr Lip bit was just one of his nutty charades, and he was taking a bit of extra piss because Sam's surname is Lipton and some call him Lippy. No, don't ask. The place is like an asylum sometimes.'

'How did you ever keep sane there, Joe?'

'Oh, that's nowt. If you want genuine nutters, Arnie, you should see Mick and Eric in action; we call 'em "The Readers."

'They each get out a book of similar length and read aloud from it as fast as they can. They sound like monks in full chant. The first one to finish is the winner. They don't take in a word of what they're reading, just shout to each other occasionally as they plough through the pages, "I'm on Page 47, where are you?" "Page 49."'

'Jesus, Joe, it's a wonder you're not raving.'

'Well Malden's convinced I am for even hesitating about the Thai move.'

'Can Malden be trusted, Joe? He sounds like someone who could shoot his mouth off at any time.'

'He's desperate to get out the place, Arnie. Some evenings when he's not fooling about, I've seen him near to tears, and he talks about just ending it all. He plays the fool, but he's no mug.'

'Did he have any reservations about making claims against the home?'

'Not in the slightest. His exact words were: "I'll do anything to get out of this shit-hole. Just name it."

'He helped convince me, although I'm still uneasy about it all. I'm your weakest link, Arnie, not Phil Malden. But OK, yes, against my better judgment, I'm on board.'

Ratledge opened his diary and prepared for the weeks ahead. The massage parlour affair now buried, Scully had assured him that the Thai end was all in order. The resort had completed most of the bureaucratic groundwork.

All that remained was for some minor building alterations to be made to the resort itself, improving overall access and mobility, and for specialised vehicles to be ordered once the green light had been given and contracts signed.

Ratledge pencilled in a frontal assault on Haven's reputation for the end of the following month, giving just over six weeks to crank up the rumour mill of damaging stories at the home, softening it up for a crippling, if not mortal, blow.

On no account was Scully to be made aware of the sex abuse deception or any other creative porkies. He must be convinced all was genuine. Scully would be drip fed tales of ill treatment, making full use of his media connections and story-placement expertise.

Truth, exaggeration, outright falsehoods were of no concern to Ratledge, only perception. If Scully fully accepted the ill-treatment tales, he would fire on all cylinders to get them out into the open.

In that sense, Scully was really no different from the herd, Ratledge mused. Just better connected. And articulate. In Lenin's words, the perfect 'useful idiot.'

Ratledge mentally fast-forwarded two to three months: If all went according to plan, Haven's old and tired, the sick, the weak and the deranged, should be jetting off into the sunset aboard a chartered flight of hope; a flight that could blaze a trail for developed economies groaning under the weight of care for the elderly.

And it would all be down to him, the much-mocked Arnie Ratledge, whose power of oratory and skilled manipulation of others, would always put him at the head of the pack. He almost brought a tear to his own eye.

PART TWO

7

Explosion

'WHAT SORT OF A COUNTRY IS THIS?' screamed *The Sun*; 'A STAIN ON US ALL,' thundered *The Times*; 'BRITAIN SHOULD HOLD ITS HEAD IN SHAME,' wept the *Express*.

Red top, quality, middlebrow – not a paper in Britain missed the bandwagon of public outrage, softened up brilliantly by 'leaks' to the *Wigburn Sentinel*.

For weeks, its steady drip of increasingly alarming stories coming out of Heaven's Haven had been a master class in manufactured outrage, channelled diligently to the nationals whose coverage oscillated between nothing and the odd paragraph to the occasional page lead.

Poor food, only supplemented by a diet of force-fed religion, mice, cockroaches, unwashed inmates left in their own filth for hours on end, staff bullying, all inhumane life was there.

Slowly, but undeniably, Heaven's Haven was making a hellish name for itself.

Ratledge had made full use of his contacts among Wigburn pond life who, for the price of a pint, would spread rumours their own mum was on the game.

The malicious gossip surfaced in council offices, pubs & clubs, in graffiti and on slickly-written anonymous stickers.

No local media worth its salt could ignore what was being alleged, and all Haven could do was issue milksop-strength denials, to which the standard public response was 'no smoke without fire.'

In truth, Heaven's Haven never had a prayer against a

campaign so professionally and energetically pursued.

The smouldering fire blazed into a raging national inferno, courtesy of Dean & Malden's double act. The claim that staff had hosed their genitals in ice-cold water as punishment for some minor misdemeanour almost led to Haven being trashed by an angry mob.

There was a miniscule kernel of truth in the claim. Staff, angered by rowdy behaviour, had on occasion 'accidentally' altered pre-set shower settings so that some residents got a brief but cold dowsing.

This fact eased Joe Dean's conscience a little, but it was a massive stretch to spin that into what was now being claimed.

Dean and Malden were deliberately vague on dates and staff identities, claiming faces were half covered by surgical masks. They were old men, not expected to remember details.

Senior staff, fearful of fresh harassment claims, got nowhere with their questioning of all residents.

Social Services and the police fared no better, with one detective assigned to the case requesting special sick leave after spending a full day grilling Mick and Eric, The Readers.

Scully felt uneasy about the whole story and thought it had emerged a little too conveniently. The steady drip of 'tales' out of Haven during the preceding weeks had, however, corroded his own judgment as old emotions were freshly stirred.

The icing on the cake for Ratledge was the media's discovery that Malden was a war hero, having been awarded the George Cross in WW2. He had repeatedly risked his life in Normandy, saving wounded soldiers stranded in a live minefield.

Scully's national contacts had been priceless in accidentally unearthing the war-hero angle.

Both Dean and Ratledge were amazed that Malden – who thought himself a total failure – had been a success when it really meant something in life. Malden absolutely refused to discuss Normandy with anyone, limiting himself to the single observation that he 'could have saved more.'

The thought of such a modest hero being subjected to humiliating physical and mental torture drove the country wild. Police were occasionally deployed around the perimeter of Haven, and at one stage Ratledge feared his whole scheme could be derailed by some uncontrollable act of violence.

But he also knew his finest hour had arrived.

A meticulously-planned press conference was called for noon on a Saturday, with the intention of generating maximum coverage in the Sundays when Joe Public is traditionally at his most suggestible.

Wigburn had never seen so many journalists and cameramen on its modest patch. For the first time in its history, the Town Hall's main council chamber was opened for a purely media event.

Ratledge would make a speech scripted, re-written, honed and polished many times over; then take questions. Scully was by his side, his third trip back from Thailand over recent weeks as his involvement deepened.

Ratledge cleared his throat a couple of times, sipped some mineral water, and made his bid for immortality.

The words were to be delivered impeccably, highs and lows inserted to perfection, pauses judged to within micro-seconds – all parcelled up in a body language that had its own sub-text.

Scully would not give his former boss so much as a glance during the 10-minute delivery. Instead his eyes would remain riveted to the piece of paper in his lap – the full text of the speech – anxiously checking against delivery.

Scully's concern was understandable. The final text was almost entirely his own, after some draining consultations with Ratledge. Puppet and puppet-master were, as in years gone by, once again in harness, and now there was no delicate blurring of the roles.

An outsider might still have found it difficult to discern which was which, but Ratledge knew who pulled the strings.

'It's said that when a new idea is born, sometimes events become its timely midwife,' Ratledge opened.

'For much of this country, Wigburn has become a byword over the past few weeks. Not a byword for anything we can be proud of, but a source of deep shame and dishonour, whipped up in a tsunami of claim and counter-claim.

'As elected mayor of this council, I will not run or hide from my share of the responsibility for what is said to have happened at Heaven's Haven.

'If the allegations are true – and I promise you, time and the wheels of justice will tell – then this town will have been stained and I will be part of that shame.

'For legal reasons I will not repeat the sickening claims against the home, but what I can say is that I am not prepared to put its old folk at risk one day longer.

'Think for a minute. Imagine having your parent, or grandparent, in a home that's under suspicion. Hand on heart, who here could sleep easy, wondering what might be happening to a loved one.'

Murmurs of approval from a packed public gallery, unusually thrown open to the press conference, eased Ratledge further into his stride.

'I can announce, therefore, that all of Haven's elderly will be removed from the home next month – and I can say categorically they will not be returning.

'If Heaven's Haven clears its name completely, not leaving any scintilla of doubt, of course it might accommodate other "resssidentsss" sometime in the future ...' the word was delivered in the manner of a hiss, practised with Scully the night before ... 'but the vast majority of Haven's current folk will be starting life anew on the other side of the world.'

Journalists glanced at each other, assuming a puzzled look. To Scully's consternation, Ratledge couldn't resist an aside – 'No, you didn't mis-hear; the other side of the world' – before returning to his scripted lines.

'It's a move that could put Wigburn on the nation's lips for very different reasons than at present, and could perhaps lead the way in solving one of the greatest financial and demographic problems facing the entire Western world: Our elderly and how to finance their care.'

Some journalists openly yawned their contempt. Ratledge was back in his old megalomaniac skin that he'd never really vacated.

Unfazed, Wigburn's Mayor poured out the financial facts and figures, asking rhetorically, 'And what do the old folk get for these colossal sums of money. Well, for some it means being kept at levels of squalor that we wouldn't tolerate for animals. In fact, if we were talking about pets, the country would have been up in arms years ago.

'Yes, we've all heard the odd tale about neglect in some care home or other, but since Haven hit the headlines, I've heard horror stories from across the country, repeated to me in great detail. My phone has not stopped ringing. And what I'm told fills me with shame.'

Ratledge's secretary winced, her bloodshot eyes executing an acute sideways glance. Apart from the incessantly phoning media, she had logged just five calls relating to care homes outside Wigburn.

'As a nation I fear we could be on the brink of unearthing something so foul and so widespread, that I shudder to think of the consequences.' Ratledge paused.

'I am not in a position to do anything nation-wide, but I can act in my own tiny patch. And that's why, next month, a few Haven residents will be moved to other Lancashire care homes, but the vast majority – with their full consent and the agreement of any responsible relatives – will be spending their remaining years – and I hope it's many years – in … Thailand.'

A TV camera swiftly panned to the Press reaction and caught one of the more senior print journalists falling off his chair. The clip was repeated endlessly over the following days.

Most of the public gallery was equally stunned:

'Did he say Leyland?'

'No, Thailand, bloody Thailand.'

'No, I think he said the Highlands.'

'No, Thailand, I'm telling you.

'Leyland, the Highlands, they're not the other side of the world. Why don't you bloody well listen to what the man says.'

Raising his voice above the tumult, Ratledge felt the adrenalin surge back into long-starved veins. This was his destiny, where he belonged, the leader doing what he was born to do.

'And now for the other important bit, the news that can give Western economies and the elderly cause for real hope: Havens's old folk will be looked after at a cost that is around one quarter of what we pay some care homes here.

'If followed through in the rest of the Wigburn area, this will not only help to straighten our finances out after the Iceland setback, it will ultimately enable us to reverse some cuts in public services – even perhaps reduce council tax. It lights a beacon for other councils across the country to follow.

'It could even reduce government subsidies to local authorities – and that could mean lower income tax. Even the Taxpayers Alliance would applaud that. And if the whole idea really catches fire, overall Government debt, that crushing burden on all our shoulders, could be significantly reduced – not just here, but across the Western world.

'Out of the trauma of Heaven's Haven, little, insignificant, unknown Wigburn might well be playing a pioneering role in helping the economies of the developed world back to financial health and solving one of the most challenging social problems of our time:

'Responsible, genuine care of the elderly – without breaking the public purse, or the backs of the rest of us.'

A much needed sip of water gave the buzz from the Press bench and gallery a chance to gather volume. It also provided an opportunity for a planted shout from the gallery. Ratledge had prepared well:

'How do we know our old folk won't be treated worse out there, and anyway, if it's that cheap, it must be cheap labour.' Ratledge smiled:

'I was just coming to that. Anyone who's ever had dealings with me knows that I would never exploit workers anywhere in the world.

'I can assure you that all the staff directly involved in looking after our old folk will be paid at least double – maybe more – the average Thai factory wage.' Ratledge did not put a figure to the wage.

'Yes, pay is lower in Thailand and much of the Far East, but then so is the cost of living. You know, it amazes me how we're all happy to buy cheap goods from the Far East – and they're cheap because labour costs are lower – and there's hardly a peep.

'They flood our markets to rake in the pounds, dollars and Euros, so what's the difference if we flood them with our old people, clutching pounds, dollars and Euros ... assuming the Euro's still around, that is?

'We live in a world where goods and capital largely travel freely. So why not our vulnerable elderly, who pose absolutely no threat to those foreign labour markets. In fact, they would generate jobs.

'But it's not just about money. It's the whole Thai attitude to the old that I have found deeply impressive.

'The fact is – and I'm also revealing this publicly for the first time – the Far East has been on my radar for some time as a possible long-term answer to care for the elderly. It's the events at Haven that have brought matters to a head earlier than I intended.

'My old colleague here, Ludo Scully,' he pointed to the top of a bent grey head still poring over paper, 'has in fact been in the Far East over recent months, carrying out vital research on behalf of the council and negotiating with potential carers.

'What he's unearthed is nothing short of inspirational. Their respect for the elderly is at a level we can only dream about these days; or for those of a certain age – a long distant memory.

'Imagine a society in which care for the old folk gets pride of place, no matter what. A society in which old people don't sit shivering in their homes, either from cold – or fear of the next terrifying visit from some neighbourhood yob.

'A society in which the last act is not to be shoved into greed-driven care homes and left to the tender mercies of the cynical, the uncaring and – yes – the brutal.

'The Thais love – yes, love – old people and they think their final years should be spent in the bosom of their own dedicated families, or if that's not possible, looked after by caring human beings who will surround them with kindness, affection and beauty.'

Scully worried that the treacle was being applied a mite too thickly. Ratledge's delivery of the next four sentences banished all fears.

'Is it too much to ask – and I address this question to everyone here and to the country at large – that our elderly are treated in similar fashion.

'Through eyes that have faded with time, they are looking to us and our children to see them through their final challenge.

'Don't let the generation that fought Hitler, or those who lived as kids through the privations of war's aftermath, say to themselves that this was Britain's most shameful hour.

'Wigburn's finest, and millions like them, deserve their place in the sun.'

Applause from the gallery trickled through to the Press benches, evolving into a standing ovation throughout the entire chamber that only left a sprinkling of journalists seated.

These tended to be the older hacks, which left the younger ones puzzled. But then few of the younger ones had prior experience of Ratledge.

They had heard of Hitler, but as far as contemporary British history went, they were clueless – the fruits of a half-baked education system shredded by political tribalism.

Ratledge and Scully shot each other a swift glance. To have 80 per cent of the Press joining a standing ovation for Ratledge was unthinkable, beyond dreams. Script now abandoned, they sat back, expecting the odd tough question. None came.

Instead their inquisitors were largely a mix of the sympathetic and the embarrassingly ill informed. Among the older, awkward squad, there seemed to run a thread of tired resignation, thoughts drifting to their own near-retirements.

Ratledge's economic figures had aroused some mild curiosity, once the shock of Thailand had worn off, but as any jaded journalist knew, numbers could always be twisted to suit any case.

The failure to grasp fully the significance of Ratledge's speech would, for some journalists, bring the date of their own retirement forward, but not in a way they would have wished.

Press interest for now, though, was largely focussed on what vetting there would be for the Thai carers and whether any particular home had already been chosen.

Ratledge, occasionally guided by Scully, negotiated the vetting subject competently, alternating between honesty, exaggeration and obfuscation as the situation demanded.

He revealed that a specially adapted resort in Koh Samui would be the most likely venue for the project, but some minor details had yet to be ironed out.

How exactly the very elderly, the infirm and the mildly demented would be transported to the other side of the world was a question he left Scully to answer, having introduced him as the project's special adviser – and a qualified pilot.

Scully had reddened, reflecting that only Ratledge could brazenly link a pilot who'd never flown anything bigger than a single-engined, four-seat propeller aircraft with the very different world of special-needs-adapted jets crossing the globe.

Merely getting Haven's residents on and off the plane would be a demanding task in itself, and the insurance costs threatened to be prohibitive.

But, as Ratledge knew, Scully had not been idle and had already been in touch with an old Russian pilot friend from his communist days who now ran Air Troika, a charter line.

Its safety record was not of the highest, but Sergey Chuikov had assured him that 'how you say, comrade Scully, it's all a piece of cake.'

Scully avoided details, only disclosing that 'negotiations with an airline charter company are already underway and I've been assured that a specially modified aircraft can do the job in safety and comfort.'

Questions swung back to financial savings as Ratledge resumed his ringmaster role, and assurances were sought that adequate monitoring of the Haven situation would be maintained in the run-up to the big move.

Ratledge gave promises on all points, adopting a well-practised fatherly tone, although he himself had never sired anything, preferring the second option in the perennial dilemma that confronts egomaniacs:

Do I allow the world to experience my seed, which may

or may not live up to the high expectations I have set; or do I leave that reputation unsullied, in the certain knowledge that I was unique, a one-off that could never be repeated.

The following day's headlines, elevating Ratledge to near hero status, confirmed his belief that he had made the right choice during his many brief affairs and his one, equally brief, marriage.

***

Scully, as he prepared to fly back to Thailand, was now a busy man, battling on two fronts. His concentration on the care home project had meant less time for his PR company and he had paid the price in the loss of a major client.

This made him more dependent on Ratledge, a development that Wigburn's Mayor both desired and had quietly worked towards. A clear demarcation line between master and servant – no matter how talented the servant – was always important.

Lance Crowther, an employee with Scully's Luscu PR company for just over a year, had inexplicably sent a catastrophic e-mail to a cosmetic surgery client.

The copy was prose of the highest order, dealing with the sensitive issue of the human profile. Crowther, digging deep, described the nose, chin and lip sculpting at Sebastian Clinics as in a class of its own.

'Truly speaking, the finely calibrated labours of Sebastian Clinics could mount a serious challenge to that most famous profile of all – Cleopatra's,' he wrote.

Unfortunately, Cleopatra had been substituted by Punch in the sent e-mail. The text had been circulated among the clinic's sniggering staff, and ultimately landed on the desk of Sebastian Simon who immediately terminated all work with Luscu PR.

Crowther had given Scully a series of unconvincing explanations, claiming it was just a joke that had gone too far and that he hadn't really intended to press the 'send' button but something he couldn't really explain had come over him.

In what Scully described as the most ludicrous attempt at a defence he had ever encountered, Crowther said that humour sometimes takes over if he works with his left elbow on the desk, his hand pressing on that side of the neck.

Conversely, if he worked with his right elbow on the desk, his copy seemed to be more serious. He thought it was all to do with the blood flow to the brain.

'I suggest you put both hands on both sides of your neck and squeeze very tightly,' Scully advised before sacking him on the spot.

To his colleagues, Crowther didn't seem at all fazed as he waltzed out the office, but then they couldn't have known of the £20,000 in a brown-paper envelope that had been delivered to his flat, as promised.

Like Scully, Ratledge had not been idle either.

***

'Mr Ludo, I can say with certainty that the special beds will be in place by the agreed date, as will everything else, including the ramps,' Visit Vatayanon assured.

'Can you guarantee that all of our new residents will arrive on time? For us it is imperative that Nam Horm has continuity of income.'

Scully gave the necessary assurances and explained some 'minor' transport hiccups to the resort's concerned owner.

'As you'll appreciate, Mr Visit, these are frail people who will be travelling half way across the world, and they can't simply be shipped across by any old plane.'

'I understand that, Mr Ludo. In Thailand we are well aware that the elderly need special consideration. I sincerely hope the rest of the world might also understand that one day.'

Scully picked up on the prickliness and proceeded with

care: 'I have this old friend, a Russian guy called Sergey Chuikov, who owns Air Troika, an air charter company. He assured me that one of his charter fleet is already being prepared.'

'Have you got that in writing?'

'Yes, but he's not a man who would lie to me. We go back over 20 years. Flying, politics and vodka we had in common …' Scully trailed off, lost in long-dead years.

'Anyway, Sergey said the problem had been finding a plane that could make the trip from Britain to Samui with minimum refuelling stops. Obviously there can't be any change of plane en-route, but the length of the Samui runway has been a pain.

'The biggest jets can't land here, and smaller jets have to refuel often. The more refuelling stops, the greater the discomfort for the passengers, Mr Visit, something I'm sure you are perfectly well aware of,' Scully tacked on hastily.

'So selecting the ideal aircraft – one that could also be physically adapted to the needs of old people on a long flight – was a bit of a challenge.' Scully looked pleased with himself, and slipped into lighter mood.

'You know, Mr Visit, Sergey predicted that fuel costs will one day force the aviation industry to have a fresh look at the whole business of carrying passengers.'

Visit, ears ever alerted to modest investment opportunities, looked interested.

'Sergey sees himself as a bit of a prophet and, you know, on many things he's been right. He made millions, and I'm not talking baht, when the old Soviet Union collapsed, getting in and out of markets always at the right time, and setting up specialist consultancies no one else had thought about.'

Visit's interest was deepening by the minute.

'Well, he thinks that in a few years, in-flight food, toilets – all that sort of thing – will be seen as unnecessary, done away with. That'll make space for more passengers.'

Visit's interest turned to incredulity: 'No passenger would ever fly without food and a toilet. Was your Sergey drunk when he said this?'

'No, no, Mr Visit, he's serious. He predicts that passengers of the future will simply be given a pill or injected with a drug that puts them to sleep for the entire journey.

'They'll be stacked like boxes, know nothing about it, and wake up nice and refreshed at their destination

'In fact, he said it would have saved a hell of a lot of trouble – not to mention money – if the residents arriving here could have been given some sort of jab. But of course the authorities would never have allowed it.

'Always ahead of his time is Sergey … always ahead …'

Visit looked horrified. 'And this is the man you're trusting to bring your old people here?'

'Absolutely,' Scully assured, and wondered whether he should have kept his mouth shut.

'There's nothing to worry about, Mr Visit, that's just the way the Russians think. They're a practical people, yes, a very practical people. For them, what matters is what works.

'Their Ladas never looked the best, but they always got the job done; a bit like their T34 tanks, eh, as Hitler soon found out …'

***

'I'm getting the feeling that Visit thinks I'm a bit odd.'

'Why's that?' Lucy asked, distractedly, as she sought Scully's help in pulling off her riding boots.

'Well, I was discussing air transport with him and when I'd finished he just sat there, eyes glazed over, muttering something about making special offerings to his ancestors. He didn't look at all well.'

'I expect it's all the pressure, he's under, Ludo. It's a big step for the resort, and if it all goes wrong, they could lose the lot.

'Wanlaya was telling me they've had to take out an extra bank loan, but not to mention it to anyone, including you. Her father would go bananas.'

'Yeah, well, they're not the only ones taking a big risk. I've just lost Sebastian's.'

'The cosmetic clinic?'

'Yep. Crowther sent them a lunatic e-mail that really pissed them off. They closed the account immediately.'

'What did he say?'

'It doesn't matter now, it's too late.'

Scully lapsed into silence as he helped his partner wriggle out of jodhpurs that seemed to be tighter than ever.

'There's something I don't understand here, Lucy. The sort of stuff that Wanlaya's telling you about loans and things is commercially sensitive information. I mean if it got to Arnie's ears he'd already be thinking of ways to drive costs down. It's the kiss of death if he thinks he's got someone over a barrel.'

Lucy looked frightened. 'You're not going to say anything?'

'Of course not, but I'm really mystified by Wanlaya. Why does she open up to you so easily?'

'We've already touched on this, Ludo. It's this deep friendship we have. Magical, spiritual … it's … it's … like we even know what each other's thinking before we say it. I … oh … oh …'

Lucy's response was immediate as the jodhpurs finally gave up the fight and Scully's tongue started its tantalisingly slow journey southwards.

'Aaaah, aaaah,' sharp, shallow breaths and the familiar scent of a woman in heat heightened all Scully's senses, but Lucy seemed determined to keep Wanlaya in play.

'She's like nothing I've ever come … aaaah … come across in my … ohhh ... life.'

Scully felt sure that talk of Wanlaya was adding to Lucy's

arousal, but let the thought pass in the heat of his own ardour, hands and tongue burrowing into sodden briefs.

'Oh, my love, you've shaved,' Scully gasped delightedly. 'What a good girl you are, preparing a nice smooth surprise for naughty uncle.'

Stubbornly, Wanlaya resurfaced. 'Aaaah … not shaved … Ludo … a Brazilian … thank Wanlaya.'

Scully's intense train of erotic thought was brought to a screeching halt on its well-warped tracks.

'What the hell has Wanlaya got to do with you having no pubic hair, Lucy? What's going on here? Are you two lovers or something?'

Lucy's fury at having her conjugals interrupted was instant and unrestrained.

'Ludo, you're an idiot. Don't you know what a Brazilian is?'

Scully knew full well the craze for removing all body hair with a Brazilian waxing, but was determined to exact a price for the 'idiot' slur. She wants 'idiot,' she'll get idiot.

'Someone who lives in fucking Brazil.'

Lucy spluttered, 'You, you ignorant …' Scully cut her off.

'Of course I know that a Brazilian's a waxing. What I don't know is what it's got to do with her.'

'Because women talk about bodily hair, under the arms, on the legs, on the face – and in the place where men most like to be. I just asked Wanlaya if she knew where I could get a Brazilian and she told me.

'I meant it as a special treat for you and you've just fucked up, like you fuck everything up.'

Scully, still reeling from the loss of Sebastian's, felt an odd disconnect that he hadn't experienced for decades; that history was revisiting in a familiar form and control of his own life was again beginning to ebb away.

Apologies to Lucy rang out hollow and inept as he mechanically went through his coupling duties; connected, yet not. The intense heat of the moment had dissipated and they failed to scale the longed-for heights.

The worm of sexual dissatisfaction was making inroads, undermining both their souls. Scully wished for a quiet corner to crawl into.

8

Motionless Flight

'Do you realise their combined age is nearly 2,500? That's 500 years before Christ.'

The observation by *The Sun*'s Ned Lubbock caused an extra buzz at Manchester Airport's packed observation area.

The media had arrived early, jostling for the best view as Haven's 27 prepared to be loaded onto the Air Troika Tupolev. Some would mount the aircraft steps unaided; others, only with assistance; a few would have to be wheeled up special ramps; and two stretchered aboard.

Mick and Eric, The Readers, seemed intent on delaying embarkation, halting at every opportunity as they tried to outdo each other in rude hand and arm gestures to anyone in sight.

'It's probably just their way of saying goodbye to Britain,' Scully lamely suggested to the Press corps as he prepared to take his own leave.

Back in Britain for the fourth time in as many months, Ratledge, Sergey Chuikov and Visit Vatayanon had all thought it a good idea that Scully, as link man for all three, should accompany the 27 out to Thailand. Scully had agreed reluctantly.

The idea of being 35,000 feet up in a sealed tube with over two dozen flatulent old folk did not appeal. He just hoped that Chuikov would not be cutting corners as some airlines did, re-cycling cabin air to save on fuel costs, rather than pumping in fresh.

His love of aviation and curiosity about the Tupolev 154 had finally tipped the scales in favour of making the trip.

Lucy had not been seriously opposed to the idea, leaving Scully bemused.

Some of the warmth – even heat – had crept back into their relationship and he'd expected objections, but apart from some mild bleatings, there were no strong protests.

'Right, boys and girls, Arnie and the council Press Office will be looking after you from now on,' Scully announced to the media.

'When we get to Samui, I'll be holding a short Press briefing at the airport, and as soon as the residents are settled in, there'll be another briefing at Nam Horm. It's all there in the handout.

'Liaison between the council and the resort will be on going and I'm sure there'll be plenty of "first impression" quotes for you to pick up on. And of course there'll be daily updates for the foreseeable future.

'Just remember that all times listed are GMT and we're seven hours ahead. So don't try ringing Nam Horm in the middle of the night. Our residents need their beauty sleep, and so do I.'

Chuckles all round left Scully buoyant as he made his way through check-in and immigration. The feeling evaporated the moment he set foot in the plane.

Cries for assistance from at least half a dozen voices dented hopes of a tranquil journey. Just two Russian carers-cum-stewardesses had evidently been deployed for the trip and they were already being run ragged.

Scully had been promised full communication facilities while aboard, plus access to the pilots. His request to speak to the captain was refused.

'Sorry, they are busy,' said Olga, the more senior of the two stewardesses. 'You must please be seated. You may speak with them when we are airborne.'

Attempts to ring Sergey Chuikov direct were also blocked. 'Mobile phone must be switched off now. You will have communication only when we say is permitted.'

'But are you the only two stewardesses on board?' he asked the younger Natasha, who was struggling with someone threatening to wet himself unless he could access the toilet immediately.

'Yes,' she smiled, while reaching for a bed bottle from the lower shelf of her trolley.

Complaints from all sides rang out thick and fast.

'Nurse, nurse, I should've had me pills an hour ago …'

'I've had nowt to eat for hours …'

'I've dropped me glasses, I can't see a bleedin' thing …'

Scully digested the reality of the new Russia. Chuikov had seemingly made a full-blooded transition from communist to cost-cutting capitalist without pausing for breath.

'The bugger's slashed staff to the bone,' he muttered to himself, and feared the worst from the cabin air as the aged Tupolev finally lumbered into the skies over Manchester.

Like all the passengers, Scully was heavily encouraged to eat a large apple compote, a traditional welcome-aboard treat from Air Troika, he was told. Rejection would be taken as only one step below an insult to Mother Russia. He ate.

***

Relief from the groans and moans of old age was largely located in the cockpit, which Scully was finally admitted to an hour into the flight.

He found Igor and Lavrenti to be a cheery pair with the usual touch of unflappability common to most aviators. Questions about the number of stewardesses were met by a shrug of the shoulders.

'Not our biznis,' Igor smiled, the inevitable gold tooth flashing. Air-recycling queries were met with similar stonewalling, buried in airliner technical jargon well beyond Scully's scope. His nose and possible post-flight infections might supply the only answers he was ever likely to get.

Scully stayed in the cockpit for as long as possible, ignoring broad hints that the Russians had work to do. He engaged them in basic aviation banter, swapping stories with the more talkative Lavrenti as pilots the world over do.

Finally, after receiving assurances that communication with Chuikov would be guaranteed within the next hour, he reluctantly vacated the cockpit to be met with a scene of bedlam.

Chief among the innovative adaptations for the flight had been the removal of every alternate passenger row so that the modified seats in front could be lowered to a fully horizontal position.

The idea was crude, but what each passenger had, in effect, was a passable bed. It wasn't pretty, but it worked. Now, alongside at least eight of the beds, pools of vomit decorated the aisle.

Reaching for sickbags had not been possible. They were horizontal to the deck, nestling in the back of the seat in front. No one had had the foresight to see the problem coming. Bags were accessed too late as wave after wave of retching echoed along the fuselage, each encouraging the next.

Natasha, sweat beading, was dashing from pool to slippery pool, wiping the mess with a rag and squeezing the contents into a bucket of water.

Olga, meantime, darted from seat/bed to seat/bed, taking extra care not to slip as demands still rang out, although now from voices distinctly weakened.

'Please, nurse, I need something to drink, I'm parched …'

'I need my heart pills …'

'I've got cramp in me left leg …'

Another full-blooded retching brought a fresh fountain of vomit onto the deck, splashing Natasha's shoes and stockings as she bent over an earlier deposit.

Scully felt a wave of sympathy for the two women, gritted

his teeth and offered to help. He didn't need to ask twice.

Without a word, Natasha brought a rag and bucket from the galley and pointed to the aisle. The stench was dreadful, forcing Scully to breathe through his mouth as he tried to isolate his nasal passages. Twice he came close to joining the vomiters' ranks.

A simple phone call from Ratledge and here he was, over four months later: business in trouble; thrown out of a massage parlour; and now wiping up a sea of vomit, 35,000 feet in the air, instead of making passionate love to his sexy partner on an island paradise.

'I really, really must be fucking mad,' he said aloud, thinking the engines would drown out his words.

Natasha heard, turned to face him and smiled through the stench. 'Thank you so much for helping us. You are good man.'

Scully felt bad about his whinging and wanted to put the girl at ease. 'That's OK, Natasha. It would be far worse if we had bad weather. You know, turbulence.' He made a rocking movement with his hand to ensure she understood.

'Oh, yes, yes, turbulence,' she laughed. 'The captain says we will not get that for another two hours. Bad weather over Balkans.'

Slowly, but blessedly, the moans, groans and retching subsided, giving way to some light snoring as the day's events began to take their toll on the 2,500-year-old cargo.

Scully and the stewardesses cleaned themselves up as best they could. Having leant a helping hand, Scully felt he was now owed one and intensified his request to be put in touch with Chuikov.

Natasha visited the cockpit twice to press his case, the second time returning flushed with anger but apparently successful.

'You will be able to speak with Mr Chuikov in five minutes,' she assured.

'Are you OK?' Scully asked.

'Russian men can be, how you say, a little bit stubborn.'

'I know,' said Scully.

'But Russian women even more stubborn. Uncle Sergey will be talking to you. You have my word.'

'He's your uncle?'

'Yes.'

He's even exploiting his own family, Scully mused. Can kids up chimneys be far behind?

***

'Ludo, Ludo, how are you? Natasha tells me you've become one of the crew. I must remember to put you on the payroll.'

For the first time in their long association, Sergey's jocular voice was not a welcome sound in Scully's ears.

'Sergey, please listen to me,' said Scully, ignoring the pleasantries.

'We have a difficult situation here. You can't expect just two stewardesses to look after 27 old people on such a long flight. Without proper care, some of them might die.'

'Ludo, what's happened to you comrade? Why are you taking life so seriously? Everything's in hand, all will be fine.'

'But Sergey, you don't understand,' persisted Scully.

'Passengers have been sick all over the place, the women are struggling to cope, bad weather's ahead. It's pure hell up here.'

'Trust me, Ludo. Any problems will be solved in the good old Russian way. Remember those days, when we believed there was nothing we couldn't do? Olga and Natasha are good women. They'll know what to do. I know them both very well.'

'Is Olga also a niece?' Scully probed. Sergey laughed.

'No, no, no comrade, she's my latest wife.'

A shell-shocked Scully almost let the phone slip from his grasp.

'Just don't worry so much, Ludo. Sorry, but I'm already late for a meeting. Dosvidanya, comrade.'

Cabin-air circulation had not even got an airing.

As forecast, weather over the Balkans lived down to expectations, creating a storm of foul air inside the aircraft – in direct correlation to the bad air without.

Each sudden loss of altitude was greeted by a fresh wave of flatulence, some contributions distinctly audible in the plodding plane.

Scully tried to wipe from his mind what must be passing through everyone's lungs, only to be forcibly reminded by some fresh assault on his nose. The retching returned with a new vigour, but seemed less productive.

Scully assumed that the stomachs of the more queasy had already given up all they had. Any further evacuation of solids would make their appearance at the other end, he reasoned, viewing the prospect with dread.

A few bedpans, alarmingly few, were already stacked near the emergency exit. A poetic touch. The turbulence intensified, occasionally joined by spectacular flashes of lightning in the darkening sky.

Screams and shouts now outnumbered retches and flatulence as Scully guessed that one air pocket must have cost the Tupolev 1,000 ft in lost altitude in about five seconds.

If that doesn't have them baying for the bedpans, nothing will, he thought, but the deluge never came; just one bedpan request.

Natasha passed by. Scully motioned towards the idle bedpans. 'I didn't expect to see them still looking so shiny and clean,' he smiled.

Dark-haired, petite and pretty, ticking all the Scully boxes, Natasha smiled back. 'Yes, I think nearly all will still be that way when we get to Samui.'

Scully shook his head. 'I think you'll find it's a different story after they've had their meals.'

Natasha chuckled. 'Aaaah, you English are very pessimist' – 'pessimistic,' Scully corrected – 'maybe you don't understand.'

'Understand what?'

'That we are a practical people.'

'I know that very well, Natasha. But apart from … errr … please forgive my words … apart from putting corks in people's bottoms, you can't stop them from, you know, relieving themselves.'

'Corks in bottoms,' Natasha repeated, dissolving into laughter.

'No, no, never, we are a civilised people. We always look for simple ways to solve problems. Something that works, no fuss.'

Scully was beginning to feel uneasy at the conversation's direction. Natasha now leaned forward over his seat, which had remained in the upright position. Her small breasts came within an inch of brushing his arm as she whispered in his ear.

'If I tell you a secret, will you please not to tell it to anyone?' Scully nodded.

'The compote.'

'What about the compote?' he asked, alarmed.

'Made to an old Russian recipe for when our people shit too much. I'm sorry I only know the bad word for this.'

'What's in it,' Scully asked through an increasingly dry mouth. 'Nothing bad, just apple juice and … errr … .errr … .yes, I remember the word now, cornstarch, the thing you English use to thicken your gravy.

'Lots of cornstarch makes the apple juice thick, like compote, and also makes shit thick inside people. I think we will get very little, or no, shit from these passengers.'

Scully looked up at sweet, smiling Natasha and didn't know whether to laugh or cry. It dawned on him that he too had eaten the compote and would probably be joining the ranks of the constipated for the flight's duration.

He momentarily reflected on how his creeping sense of diminishing life-control now extended to his own bowel movements, without him having had the slightest say in the matter.

'Remember, not a word to anyone,' Natasha winked, 'or whoosh.' A flat hand passed across her throat to emphasise the request. Scully assumed the threat was a joke, but was uncertain.

A battle raged in his head: A bit of cornstarch to control bodily functions a little. So what. Billions of bodies were in hock to far worse substances every day and no one gave a shite.

The word brought a slight smile to his face. Maybe the Russians were right; he should lighten up a bit. The trip would be over in a few hours and everything forgotten.

But darker thoughts wanted their say and now muscled in on his conscience. Serious constipation could be a killer. Presley had died on the bog in 1977 after days of constipation. The strain of trying to pass what was said to be a monstrously large stool had given him a heart attack.

The flunkies at his Gracelands Mansion had found him sprawled on the bathroom floor, pyjamas around his feet.

Presley was only in his 40s. Most of the 27 were in their 80s and 90s. What chance would they have, straining against cornstarch-induced constipation?

Alarmed, Scully now searched out Natasha. No way could he have the deaths of care home residents on his conscience.

'Tut, tut, tut, Mr Scully,' Natasha admonished, conjuring up a look of hurt pride. 'Do you think we are murderers. Do you think we do not know of this problem?

'You talk about the Presley singer dying because he could not make the shit. Someone far more important, our respected queen, Catherine the Great, died because she tries to make difficult shit. It gives her big stroke in the head.'

Scully looked stupefied.

'Before we land at Samui, everyone will be served a special meal that will help them make a shit on the ground. Then everything will be well. But your passengers must be taken to their new homes quickly.'

Scully spluttered out a few 'buts,' unable to marshal a coherent thought.

***

A refuelling stop in Mumbai had gone relatively smoothly, with most passengers now seemingly beyond the point of caring. Time was idled away snoozing, complaining, snacking, peeing, drinking or trying to talk to each other above the general hubbub.

Vomiting was now rare and turbulence rarer as they headed for the east coast of India and the final few hours of what had turned into a survival exercise – mental and physical.

This was almost as true for Scully as the 27, but the Russians seemed supremely unperturbed. Their stoicism and equanimity remained intact, treating each challenge that presented itself as all in a day's work.

A solid meal of blintzes, dumplings – a stew of uncertain provenance, Scully guessed bear – veg and a light salad was rounded off with a fruit-based yoghurt.

For drinks, the stewardesses served tea with a slice of lemon, fruit juice, and, for those deemed able to handle it, ice-cold vodka.

Scully was surprised to see both Olga and Natasha helping themselves to the vodka, but noted that they were at least taking it with juice.

He was flattered by an unexpected invitation to join them and, in a rare quiet period, soon found himself on the end of a flurry of questions about his life. The personal stuff came first: Widower in a current relationship; grown-up son living in Canada.

The women knew he was some sort of liaison man for a Thai care-home project, but could not understand why he'd joined the flight.

'The people I work with wanted it,' he explained, 'but I was also curious about the TU 154.'

'Aaaah, you like planes, Ludo,' they noted with satisfaction, slipping into first name use.

'Yes, I'm a pilot myself,' he said, trying to quell any hint of pride in his voice.

'But it's only light aircraft. A four-seat Cessna is the biggest plane I've ever flown.'

'Size isn't everything,' Olga chuckled.

'Anyway, is not difficult to go from light planes to the big ones, once you've learned to fly,' Natasha chimed in. 'It's all same principles.'

'Is that what uncle Sergey's told you?'

'No, we find out ourselves.'

Scully looked blank as Olga poured him another vodka but declined any more for herself or Natasha.

'How … how do you mean?'

'We learnt it at flying school. There are five pilots on this plane, Ludo. Natasha and I also fly.'

'Fly what?'

'Fly this.'

'This plane?'

The women nodded.

'Then what the hell are you doing working as stewardesses?'

'The agreement was the boys,' Olga nodded in the direction of the cockpit, 'fly the outward journey while we do the hard work, looking after your old people.

'On the return journey, we do the flying, while the boys, huh! the only nursing they do will be for big hangovers, not old people. Is not fair play. We fly back in the morning, the boys can party all night. We have not to drink for 12 hours before flying. Not fair.'

Dumbfounded, Scully put a question, the answer to which he already suspected.

'Are Lavrenti and Igor also family?'

'Of course. Lavrenti is Natasha's brother and Igor is my cousin. Sergey employ family because it cost less, but he still has one communist principle.'

'Tell me what it is, Olga. I need to hear it.'

'He makes sure that men and women get same pay. He is, how you say, an equal-opportunity exploiter.'

Both women fell about laughing before a cry for help from the passenger aisles ended the mini-party.

Scully returned to his own seat trying to put his thoughts in some order. How had it all come to this? So many wasted communist years – Russia's and his own. Parallel trajectories.

The old Soviet-era joke that had first opened his eyes to the fraudulent reality of it all returned like a warm-hearted friend's deathbed cautioning:

'Remember, capitalism's the exploitation of man by man; and communism's the reverse.' Scully tacked on his own take: But under capitalism you at least have liberty, the rule of law and the freedom to elect whatever set of sharp-suited speechifyers takes your fancy.

Scully dwelt on all this and concluded that Churchill had got it about right when he described capitalism as a lousy system, but still 'a 1,000 times better' than all the others.

***

As the sun rose in the east and Igor prepared to announce that seat belts 'and any other fastenings' should be secured for the Samui landing, he was marginally pipped at the post by Malden's 'we've not much money but we see life...'

No-one knew or cared whether his dawn ritual had been accompanied by the usual flatulence, but boiled eggs had certainly been provided as requested. Figs and prunes played a covert role in almost every other dish that made up the large breakfast served to all.

An air of listlessness seemed to have overtaken the bulk of the passengers as well-worn digestive systems struggled to complete what should have been a natural cycle.

It was Joe Dean who first caught sight of Samui and its surrounding islands, nestling in the greenest waters he had ever seen. He made a valiant effort to rally the troops.

'Try to get a peek out of the portholes, lads. This looks like a bit of all right. Certainly beats bloody Wigburn.'

The more able-bodied helped the weakest to glimpse what was almost certain to be their last resting place. Those whose eyes lacked the strength to absorb detail, were treated to word pictures painted by the more fortunate.

Slowly and unexpectedly, faint traces of smiles began to crease aged lips. Scully pictured children grown old being taken on one final, spectacular outing.

The trials of the flight began to melt away as he felt a surge of joy at the sight of eager faces pressed against perspex.

He battled to hold back a tear as the Tupolev made its final approach to land, a distinct line of white vehicles clearly visible in the distance, waiting to whisk the 27 to Nam Horm.

Reporters and cameramen were already at the airport, recording every minute of the historic scene as the plane taxied off the runway to meet the assembled ambulances and special buses.

Scully was able to squeeze in a hurried briefing, with well-practised reassurances that the flight had gone without a hitch, although there had been a 'little turbulence' en-route.

Arrangements had been made for a super-fast clearance through immigration and customs, with officials coming out to the aircraft.

The Thais were as good as their word and just 30 minutes after touchdown the convoy was threading its way along the narrow coastal road.

Whenever the situation allowed, the 27 gawped endlessly,

and not just at the outside scenery. The carers accompanying them were all from KKSA. The faint smiles that had surfaced on the plane grew more prominent as eyes met.

When the old men learned that these girls were to be based at the resort and would be part of the team looking after them for the rest of their lives, the smiles cracked into broad grins.

Malden put it into words. 'It's hot as hell out there, but I think I've died and gone to the other place.'

The girls who heard and understood him smiled so lovingly that he seriously asked one of them to pinch his arm. She playfully obliged, assuring him that he was neither dead nor in a dream.

'This is for real, Mr Phillip. We will look after you with all our hearts.'

'That'll do me, lass.'

***

The Nam Horm reception was worthy of a minor state visit. Some media, all four Vatayanons, their less immediate family, friends, eight more carers, two local dignitaries, reception staff, curious onlookers … and Lucy.

Scully had expected to see her at the airport, but knew that her workload had been heavy. Over recent weeks she had played a more active role in the care home operation, acting as a conduit for important messages to and from Britain, ironing out linguistic and cultural difficulties, and only facing serious problems when dealing with Ratledge's secretary, Eileen Faulkner.

She'd discovered that the earlier in the day, English time, a call was made via Faulkner, the better. After lunch, there was confusion, unanswered calls or semi-coherence. It was an issue she would be raising with Scully, but for now she was just happy that a potentially fraught chapter had gone smoothly.

Her man had made headway, and she embraced him lovingly as the bevy of carers escorted, wheeled and stretchered their charges to individual quarters.

In each room an orchid had been placed on a generous-sized bed, and a welcoming bowl of soft fruits sat atop the bedside tables.

Satellite TV, radio, recording and music facilities had all been upgraded, and videophone links newly installed. The air-conditioning hummed gently, churning together the heady scents of frangipani, jasmine, burnt coconut husks and ripening fruits.

All was complemented by the strong sunlight that streamed through the open French windows, mosquito-net shutters at the ready for any evening intrusions.

A writing desk, two chairs, an armchair, a modest fridge/freezer, a cooking ring, electric kettle, cutlery and crockery, a dressing table, cavernous wardrobes and an exquisitely tiled bathroom with shower and – unusually for Thailand – a full-size bath completed the picture.

Two emergency cords, one above the bed, one over the bath, signalled that Nam Horm intended to cover every conceivable situation.

Outside the French windows, an impressive 50-metre, four-lane swimming pool, previously enjoyed by holidaymakers, would now be for the exclusive use of Heaven's Haven former residents, and any other hard-currency, care home 'refugees' Nam Horm might absorb in the future.

Residual holidaymakers would now be restricted to the smaller pool nearer the sea. The adjoining, magnificent stretch of beach remained accessible to all.

Although tired, Scully had volunteered to show Joe Dean to his room, taking a little pressure off the carers who were still finding their feet.

Lucy tagged along, as did Wanlaya, the pair now

seemingly joined at the hip. Even when Lucy hugged Scully at the resort's gates, Wanlaya was only centimetres away, forcing an idiotic-sounding 'excuse us' out of Scully.

Dean examined the room in some detail, saying not a word. Finally, Ratledge's old mentor sat down on the bed, and looked up at all three directly. His tone was wistful, almost sad.

'I don't know how much Arnie's told you about me. Anyway, I'm not one for flowery words, but I want to say something from the heart:

'This lot is absolutely beautiful. Breathtaking I'd call it. What I want to know is why didn't somebody come up with this idea years ago?'

Ludo and Lucy could offer no answers. Wanlaya simply smiled. The trio headed for Dean's door, but the old man motioned Scully back.

'Can I have a word with you in private, Ludo,' he asked, a little embarrassed. The women took the hint and headed for reception.

'What is it, Joe?'

Well it's not just me, but quite a few of us have got this, like, medical problem. To put it bluntly, hardly any of us have been able to have a crap since we left Britain.

'Even those of us who've always been regular as clockwork, and that includes me, have produced nowt.' Scully felt a hot flush.

'It's probably just the excitement of the flight, Joe. You know what it's like when people get moved around, everything goes a bit haywire.'

'Yeah, I suppose you're right, but I would have thought flying has the opposite effect. That's probably why a few bedpans were lined up. I mean some of the lads were shit scared, especially when it got really bumpy.'

Scully did his best to re-assure. 'I'm sure that now you're all "home" you'll soon be passing more motions than a TUC conference.'

Dean enjoyed the joke. 'All that lot ever passed was hot air, a bit like us at the moment,' but then his face darkened.

'It's just that I feel really bloated. There seems plenty there to come, but it just won't budge. It's like a knot in the gut. And I've heard that it's dangerous to push too hard when you get old. It could bloody kill you.'

Scully promised to have a word with the relevant medical staff and headed to reception, a knot of a very different kind forming in his own stomach.

***

Nam Horm buzzed as the new residents were settled in gradually, with care and consideration; everyone briefed on the vital importance of first impressions.

Individual carers, their dazzling beauty inevitably contrasting with their wizened charges, showed infinite patience in getting acquainted with those whose well-being and happiness they would largely be responsible for.

Sanuk, the quintessential Thai sense of fun, was already in play.

At reception, as formalities were gone through, thick Lancashire accents struggled to master Thai names, said to be the longest on the planet.

Endless giggles from the girls, respectful but infectious, greeted heroic efforts to say their names.

Bemused holidaymakers watched in wonder at the good-natured banter between the old and the beautiful.

Some assumed that a party of western millionaires had arrived for a debauched time with hot ladies from Bangkok, and that was the real reason the larger pool had suddenly been put out of bounds.

Through the seeming mayhem and endless chatter, Visit Vatayanon dealt with every minor hiccup effortlessly, issuing a stream of instructions without ever raising his voice.

Both Scully and Lucy were impressed with the entire Thai end of the operation and judged it time to put Ratledge's mind at rest.

Persistent, inexplicable problems with mobile connections again forced Scully to use the council landline. After what seemed like an eternity, Faulkner finally put him through to her boss.

'You're going to have to do something about that secretary of yours, Arnie, she's in a different world.'

'Never mind that now, Ludo, how'd it all go?'

'Everything seems fine this end, although the flight was a bit interesting,' said Scully, choosing words carefully.

'The main thing is they've all arrived alive and well, right?' pressed Ratledge. There was silence from Ludo's end.

'Well, haven't they?'

'They're certainly all alive, Arnie. The same 27 that were counted in were counted out. How well they are, I can't say.'

'What do you mean?'

'Well, there've been no emergencies, but with old people how can anyone ever be sure? Some might go on for another 10 or even 20 years, others might pop their clogs tomorrow.

'How about your end?'

'Gone like a dream, Ludo. More and more councils are thinking about doing the same. The whole issue is going to be raised in Parliament as a possible, pain-free way of helping to dig the country out the mire.

'Even the media coverage has continued to be largely positive, but there are the usual jealous bastards who would love the whole thing to flop.

'That shit Charlie Wallis even wrote a column predicting the flight alone would kill some of the 27. He'd love to see me fall flat on my face, Ludo. It's eating him up that I'm flavour of the month at the moment. You know, if one or two of the Haven lot dropped dead, Wallis would be over the moon.'

‘Yep, there are certainly some bad ‘uns in this world, Arnie.’

‘Whatever you do, Ludo, make sure they’re well looked after, especially over the next few weeks. Nothing must go wrong; this whole thing’s about to get massive.’

‘I’ll do my best, Arnie, but, as I said, at their age no one can guarantee anything.’

‘Ludo!’ a distinctly Russian voice interrupted Scully who turned to see Natasha with Olga.

‘Got to go, Arnie, more things to sort out. I’ll call you in the morning.’

***

‘What are you two doing here,’ Scully blurted, forgetting basic etiquette.

‘Oh, we thought you think it is nice to see us,’ Natasha said, disappointed.

‘Yes, yes, of course, it’s just that it’s … a surprise.’

‘We look up Nam Horm address on plane’s manifest, hire car and here we are. You helped us and we thought we see how you are doing, but maybe is better if we not come.’

‘No, no, not at all. It’s very kind of you to give up your free time.’

Scully waved a beckoning hand to Lucy who was deep in conversation with Wanlaya.

Lucy ambled across, appendage still firmly attached. The women were formally introduced and conversation flowed effortlessly, without a single, awkward silence, the conviviality jollied along by the Russians’ status as pilots/stewardesses.

Drinks were ordered as Olga’s and Natasha’s remaining window of alcohol intake for active pilots shrank from two hours to one. No one gave a second thought to drink-drive regulations.

Scully was anxious to turn the conversation to cornstarch, but could think of no way of detaching Lucy and Wanlaya from the Russian pair.

Fate rode to the rescue in the shape of a phone call from a Daily Mail reporter who had got straight through to Visit Vatayanon.

Visit had been warned repeatedly about the wiles of the British media; warnings that had been emphasised to such a degree that he felt reluctant to speak to them at all.

The questions were not unsettling, concentrating mainly on Nam Horm's facilities and how it had come to be chosen, but Visit felt his street-wise daughter needed to be on hand in case the questions became too penetrative or there were cultural/ linguistic snags.

Lucy immediately volunteered to act as extra back-up on the understanding that any really tricky questions would be referred to Scully who had a 360 degree take on the whole project.

Scully was at last left alone with the Russian pair and immediately launched into his own intensive questioning.

'We have a real problem at the moment,' he told them, speaking urgently.

'Many of the 27 still cannot shit and some are feeling unwell. I need to know how much cornstarch was put into that compote. The hidden laxative you slipped them before landing seems to have had no effect.'

Natasha answered unhesitatingly. 'I put eight tablespoons into hot apple juice, nothing more. Is according to plan. The effects should go by now.' Olga's face took on the pallor of wood ash.

'YOU put in the cornstarch!!' she almost screamed. 'That was my job. I also put in the cornstarch.'

Scully's head collapsed into his hands. 'Sweet Jesus! So anyone who ate the compote has overdosed on cornstarch?'

The Russians shrugged simultaneously, Olga trying to put some positive spin on the situation.

'Ludo, it does not mean they all have same amount of

cornstarch. Maybe some have a little compote, others more. I remember some compote bowls come back only half finished. They would have eaten according to plan,' she smiled.

Scully felt a strong urge to tip a bowl of something other than compote over her head.

'That's not the point, Olga. The fact is there are old English people staying at this place who might die tonight – burst a blood vessel, have a heart attack or something – because they can't shit.

'And they can't shit because you two got their meals wrong.' The Russians felt hurt. Scully felt desperate.

'Is there anything, anything at all, you know of that can be done to help them? Modern or traditional medicine – something ancient you might have heard, but not more laxative? That risks dehydration.'

Natasha spoke. 'I remember my grandmother was many times angry because my grandfather spend too much time in one outside toilet when everybody else waiting.

'He always had difficulty with the shit, she'd say. People get so crazy they would just go and make the shit in the forest, like bears.'

Scully's eyes rolled. 'So, how does that help us, Natasha?'

'Well, my grandma spend hours massaging his belly to help the shit come out – with good result. But she again gets angry when he is so drunk that he does not allow her near his belly, calling her a witch and cursing.

'If she could not work on his belly, it is again forest for everyone else next day.'

Scully felt like giving Natasha a bear hug, but the return of Lucy and Wanlaya brought the conversation to a halt.

A few more drinks and the Russians headed back to the airport where they were to spend the night sleeping aboard the Tupolev in readiness for an early morning departure.

Sergey Chuikov had considered a hotel room for the night an unnecessary extravagance. The plane now had plenty of makeshift beds for the crew to choose from, he'd argued with perfect logic. No one dissented.

***

'You want the carers to do what?' Wanlaya queried, unsure that she'd fully understood Scully's request. Lucy zeroed in:

'What he's saying, Wanlaya, is that many of the residents are finding it hard to have a crap after the flight and that a belly massage might help.'

Lucy was impatient at Scully's waffle. 'Just tell it as it is, Ludo, Wanlaya's a woman of the world. She 's not wrapped in cotton wool.'

Scully was taken aback at Lucy's directness towards the Thai; not a hint of embarrassment. The easy chemistry between the two was something he'd only seen in families or among very old friends.

'The thing is, do you think the carers would mind massaging the guests that way?' Scully probed, still unsure of his ground. 'Unless, of course, you have other answers.' Wanlaya was perplexed.

'I'm sure they'll be happy to help in any way they can. Some will be more experienced than others, of course, but a belly massage should be a very simple thing. I think it's a good idea. Why do you think our carers would mind?'

'Well, it's just that the men will be lying on their backs and their bellies are near other bits.'

'So?'

'Well, Wanlaya, the girls are, as you know, very pretty … and … and … even though they're old enough to be the girls' granddads, even great granddads, the men might get an … an …'

'Oh, for heaven's sake, Ludo, just spit it out,' Lucy broke in.

'An erection is what he's trying to say. What is it with Englishmen when it comes to talking about sex? Their brains seize up if another woman's around.'

Wanlaya laughed reassuringly. 'Yes, I think the girls will be aware of how men's bodies work, Mr Ludo. I believe they are made the same way in the West as in Thailand.'

Embarrassed, Scully looked for a way to steer the conversation back to massage.

'Right, so you think belly massage is a good idea for constipation, then? Are you familiar with it?'

'We're familiar with lots of things here, Mr Ludo, much of it grounded in Chinese medicine, dating back thousands of years.'

Scully felt a sense of relief. Although the subject had been ticklish, at least the answer seemed to be getting the thumbs up.

'How did you know about belly massage, Mr Ludo?' Wanlaya probed.

'Oh, it was probably something I heard as a child. Maybe from my grandparents.'

Wanlaya fixed Scully with a steady stare as she got up to leave, the faintest trace of a smile on her lips.

'I'll make arrangements for the massages. The men will have to strip down to their underpants, but if they find that too embarrassing, we can ask the carers to do the massages under the bed sheets.

'And if the men really are worried that the carers are too pretty, I can fly down to Muslim Malaysia and find out whether there are any spare burkas I can borrow.'

With that, Wanlaya turned on her heel, leaving Scully to what she felt sure would be the less than tender mercies of Lucy.

'You made a complete fool of yourself there, Ludo,' she hissed as soon as Wanlaya was out of earshot.

'What is it with you these days?'

Scully shook his head, groping for any half-decent riposte. 'Burkas, eh! As if. But I've learnt something new today.'

'Oh, yeah, and what's that, Ludo?'

'These people can do a good line in piss-taking.'

9

Helping Hands

Word spread quickly and the following morning 19 old Lancashire men, clad only in underpants, lay on their beds, waiting for their carers' attentions.

Scully was almost certain that two of the men had filled their bedpans effortlessly during the flight, but said nothing. If their lives were going to be brightened by a massage, what the hell.

He did however notice, with mild trepidation, that some of the underpants were already encasing unseemly bulges, before a hand had been laid on anyone.

The arrival of the girls, mostly clad in cool, flimsy tops and tight jeans, oil and towels in hand, generated a low rumble of appreciation.

Some of the carers were amused by Scully's deep interest in how the massages were going, surprised to see his head pop round the door every few minutes.

The 'patients,' however, were not amused, resenting the 'invasion' of their privacy. Shouts of 'We're all over 18' and 'Just sod off and leave us alone' peppered the otherwise romantic tropical evening.

The more thoughtful grilled Scully, questioning why he was even bothering to check up on them and whether he had no home to go to. Scully muttered something about ensuring everyone had settled in nicely and recovered from the flight.

Unconvinced, Lipton, who had been gently lifted from his wheelchair, opted for crudity: 'You some sort of perv or what?' he bellowed.

'Just leave us alone, Ludo. Leave us to the girls. Maybe

he's jealous, eh lads' he added, loud enough to generate the odd cackle from adjoining rooms.

Scully was forced to retreat, slinking off to the bar for a quiet beer and a chance to gather his thoughts. The peace was occasionally interrupted by greetings from people who he dimly recognised, their faces blurring into an international kaleidoscope of accents, colours, ages and gender.

Of Lucy, Wanlaya and the regular staff there was not a sign, only a couple of unfamiliar faces handling reception. He assumed that most were still deeply involved in the behind-the-scenes logistics of settling everyone in, and that the girls had somehow managed to squeeze in their early evening swim, which had become something of a ritual.

His mind flitted back to the massages, and he wondered whether Wanlaya and Lucy occasionally massaged each other – or at least helped in the application of sun cream

Lost in thought, a scream suddenly shattered his reverie, instantly upping Scully's pulse rate.

The sound of running feet and some sobbing could be heard from the direction of the main corridor. A tear-stained carer appeared, babbling furiously to reception in Thai. All three headed back down the corridor at breakneck speed, not stopping to say anything to Scully.

Fearing the worst, he ran after them, into the room of Albert 'Bert' Hancock.

He was greeted by the sight of an 82-year-old man, stretched out on the bed, his underpants valiantly restraining what appeared to be an advanced state of arousal.

So much of the undergarment fabric had been dragged southwards by the erection that pubic hair and some penis root could be spotted.

Hancock had made no attempt at covering up, nor would he ever do so. His colour, temperature and open, staring eyes signalled the end. Vain attempts were made at resurrection, but only the erection survived, briefly outlasting its owner.

None of the quartet seemed aware that engorgement of the male organ could continue beyond death, and they alternated between pounding Hancock's chest and giving the kiss of life.

Frantic phone calls had meanwhile been made and soon the sound of an ambulance siren could be heard in the distance.

Scully, now joined by Lucy and Visit's entire family, was crestfallen. Attempts to establish exactly what had happened were hard to extract from the still sobbing carer, but Wanlaya seemed to have pieced the bits together.

The carer had been massaging Hancock for about an hour. He'd seemed perfectly happy, in fact a little too happy, as his arousal became increasingly evident, accompanied by breathing that grew heavier by the minute.

She'd wanted to pause the massage, but Hancock had insisted it was 'doing the trick' and pressed her to continue no matter what, all the time trying to manoeuvre his groin so that it made contact with her hand.

The girl insisted she had not actually touched his genitals and that he'd simply let out a final, desperate groan. No one gave voice to their thoughts, but opinion was divided on whether it was the sexual arousal or frustration at non-consummation that had brought on his last mortal moment.

Only Scully was privy to the certain knowledge that constipation was indirectly responsible. He had played a leading role in a sequence of events that had killed a man.

The one bit of consoling news came from Joe Dean who told Scully that at least the massages had had a positive effect on some of the men.

'Loos were going like the clappers, but the bloody pong was terrible,' he said.

As he phoned Ratledge, visions of likely headlines dominated Scully's mind. They'd all have a field day if word of Hancock's 'condition' and circumstances got out.

Raising his eyes heavenwards, he lamented bitterly on the whimsical nature of life. Why, of all the 27, did it have to be someone named Hancock; a gold-plated gift to every headline writer in the country.

In answer, the restless spirit of his mother took up temporary residence in his head. 'Oh, Ludo, what are you getting yourself into?' He was not sure he knew any longer. The ground beneath his feet again felt rubbery.

Regaining some focus, he knew that the name of the game now would be damage limitation. Finally, Ratledge answered the phone.

***

The elected Mayor of Wigburn was on his way back up the political grease pole, and nothing, but nothing, would stand in his way.

Scully's account of what had happened had been heard in stony silence, but the monologue puzzled Ratledge.

The death, the circumstances and its potential repercussions were all crystal clear, but he could not understand Scully's seeming obsession with the bowel movements of the others. He wondered whether some mental disorder was gestating.

'Ludo, why are you going on and on about constipation? Hancock couldn't crap, he had a massage, felt a bit fruity, and died. I'm sorry about it, the timing's rotten, but that's life. Constipation comes and goes, like diarrhoea. That's also life. They'll all crap in the end. It's what we all do eventually.'

'Aaaah, but you don't understand, Arnie,' Scully persisted.

'What don't I understand, Ludo?'

'Elvis and Catherine the Great died on the loo because they couldn't have a proper dump. It killed 'em, Arnie.'

'Ludo, I'm not interested in Catherine the whatever or Elvis's bowel movements. It's their fucking problem – or was. You were dead right to ring me about Hancock, but can you give constipation a rest. Just forget the crap problems of others.'

Scully said nothing. 'Now, can we get on with what matters. The papers will be all over this once they get wind of it, and we need to be ready. Give me a ring in the morning and meanwhile do whatever you can to keep a lid on it. There must be no bollocks dropped.'

Ratledge's increased assertiveness was not lost on Scully. Both knew that the loss of a major PR client had hit Scully hard and tipped the balance of power between the two.

Scully had said nothing to Ratledge about the loss and assumed his former boss was unaware of the misfortune, not suspecting for a moment he was its architect. He simply assumed Ratledge could smell dithering in Scully's conversation.

Showing Ratledge the slightest weakness was never a good idea and Scully immediately moved to re-balance the scales.

'I don't drop bollocks, Arnie, as you well know, and I don't need talking to like that.'

'I see … well maybe you'll like this bit of talk. Lots of councils, some junior ministers and shadow ministers, charities and quangos in the care business have been pestering me to death, asking how it was all set up.

'They're querying whether the idea could be extended to all parts of Thailand and to other – these are their words – "caring, economically attractive countries in the Far East."

'They want me and my team to act as consultants, Ludo. Did you hear that, "consultants," on a basic fee, plus bonuses and a percentage of takings for each care home successfully established.'

Scully allowed himself a restrained 'wow.'

'I've already got the lawyers setting up a private consultancy company, ARCO, and as you've been an asset to the whole enterprise I've pencilled you in as a fellow director.

'This is potentially colossal, Ludo, and could make you

millions in a relatively short time, instead of pissing about for peanuts at that agency of yours.'

Scully's face turned blood red. 'I didn't get involved with this for the money, Arnie, as you well know. Not everything in this world's about money. I just wanted to help old people enjoy their last few years … find some way out of the nightmare for them. And I acted because of my mother, nothing else, and you know it.'

Ratledge came close to despair. 'For God's sake, Ludo, no one's questioning your motives. But what's wrong in doing good and making money at the same time?

'If you object to the money, donate it to some old people's charity, a kids home or some sanctuary for journalists who've gone fucking bonkers.

'But don't let it stand in the way of a real opportunity to make a difference in the world; it's your final chance to make a mark, and I'm not talking about the bleedin' currency.'

The attempted joke lowered the temperature, Scully responding in kind. 'There's no mark any longer. The Germans use the Euro, Arnie, you should know that.'

Both men paused, each in their own way frazzled. Ratledge took a deep breath and returned to the fray, tacking to fatherly mode:

'Look, Ludo, I'm telling you this as an old comrade. I know you don't like the word, but just hear me out.

'Lots of old comrades have ended up on the scrapheap, like Joe Dean, going through a living hell in Haven until we saved him. None of us is getting any younger, and I certainly don't want to see you ending up like that.

'Just for once in your life, think of yourself … and Lucy. It'll not turn you into a selfish bastard like me.'

Scully was momentarily nonplussed by Ratledge's unheard of self-criticism.

'Let's not blow this one … we've hit the right idea at the right time … we're the flavour of the month … let's get out there and do the business.

'One thing's absolutely certain if we don't.' Ratledge had, as ever, saved his killer punch till last. Ludo obligingly walked into it.

'And what's that?'

'If we don't do it, some serious rip-off merchants will.

'And how would you feel about that? They'd be devising schemes to cream off every penny they could from these foreign projects; our idea – hijacked by money-grubbers who couldn't care less about old people.

'The wheel could so easily turn full circle if we don't keep a grip on it all.'

Scully felt battered, but still retained enough consciousness to recognise when a knock-out blow had been delivered.

'OK, Arnie, fair point,' he conceded. 'I need to think; there are things I've got to straighten out urgently. I'll cobble together a press release which I'll e-mail across, just in case the worst happens and the Hancock stuff gets out.'

Ratledge risked an 'OK, comrade' and ended the conversation. Receiver safely replaced, he vented his innermost thoughts.

'What a prat. How can so much brainpower and stupidity inhabit a single skull? Beats me.'

***

'Hancock's hard hour,' screamed *The Sun*; 'Expat's last stand,' mourned the *Mirror*; 'Hard Thai-ms,' mocked the *Daily Star*. The red tops were in fully cry, having sucked up every detail of massage night at Nam Horm (or 'Horn' as *Loaded* later dubbed it).

Ratledge and Scully immediately concluded someone had blabbed and it had to be an inside job at the resort. Even the name of Hancock's masseuse was given.

Nothing was left to the imagination in the reports, and the cartoonists were let off the leash, their artwork allowed to run as rampant as Wigburn's ex-pats were said to have been.

Relatives in the UK had been door stepped incessantly, as journalists trawled for damaging quotes. More seriously, middle-brow papers questioned how old people who had been removed from alleged sex abuse in the UK, now apparently found themselves victims again; only this time, on the other side of the world.

'Maybe this entire enterprise ought to have been subjected to far greater scrutiny,' came the wail from the *Mail*.

Ratledge knew he was treading a fine line and that fickle public opinion could swiftly tip in either direction. Oddly, there was support from two very different ends of the social spectrum: Relatives of the 27, now 26; and the quality papers.

The Times had largely stuck to its guns, defending the Thai experiment as it had done since the story first broke. This time, however, it hedged its support with heavy scepticism directed at the official version of events as described in Scully's Press release.

'It stretches human credulity beyond breaking point to ask anyone to believe that 19 out of 27 residents at Nam Horm suddenly contracted severe constipation, requiring the immediate attentions of a bevy of nubile Thai ladies,' *The Times* leader argued.

'That credibility gap enters the realms of fantasy when we are told that all 19, mostly in their 80s and 90s, and newly arrived in Thailand after an exhausting plane journey, were ordered to strip down to their undergarments and then massaged on their tummies as they lay on their beds. And all to relieve constipation.

'Does the Far East's much-admired medical knowledge not extend to laxatives?

'Not that we accept for one moment the likelihood that 19 people suddenly discovered that they shared an acute inability to defecate.

'Unless, of course, the Russian plane that transported them laced their borscht with concrete mix.'

Having comprehensively shredded Scully's release, *The Times* switched to sympathetic mode, bordering on sexual advocacy.

'Let's not be prissy about all this,' the editorial continued. 'Throughout British history, from princes to paupers, people have breathed their last while in the act of procreation.

'Although there is, as yet, no evidence that events reached such a climax (and we use the word advisedly), from all accounts the mood music at Nam Horm seemed to be facilitating something of a similar nature.

'Perhaps we should all take a step back, look into our hearts and ask in what precise circumstances we would prefer to shuffle off this "mortal coil."

'Who among us would not elect for the Hancock option, as an alternative to lingering, pain-wracked, dribbling decay; all independent thought, intellectual inquiry and sensual longing cauterised by the insidious inanity of day-time television?'

Key among the relatives, was Hancock's one surviving blood relation – a slightly younger cousin – who weighed in positively, giving *The Times* important grassroots cover. Most of the papers subsequently picked up her quote.

'Obviously someone needs to find out exactly what happened to Bert,' Maureen Hancock had told *The Times*, 'but if it is what it looks like, so what. He was always one for the ladies was Bert, and if we're honest about it, wouldn't we all like to go out that way. And I'm not just talking about men.'

Her sentiments found a ready echo in most of Wigburn. Combined with *The Times'* position, it gave the red tops encouragement to jump off the fence in later editions, and throw most of their weight behind the Thai venture, albeit with caveats.

The middlebrow papers looked decidedly isolated. Social historians noted – and not for the first time in British history – that toffs and toilers had found common cause against the rest.

Ratledge felt that the pendulum was swinging back in his favour, remembering how *The Times* decades ago had been instrumental in saving some of the Rolling Stones from long jail sentences for drug offences; a stance that had major repercussions on Britain's social development.

Maybe this too was a pivotal moment in the country's uncertain direction. Any lingering doubts were comprehensively swept away the following day.

Scant column inches were devoted to the constipation angle, as the focus switched to brashly supportive stories, celebrating how in spite of everything – failure to land the 2018 World Cup football venue, lousy weather, economic hardship – the 'miracle' of Lancashire's lusty octogenarians and nonagenarians had 'RAISED' everyone's spirits.

Some of the tone verged on the belligerent, with The Sunday Sport setting its sights on 'politically correct sourpusses.'

'No doubt the Guardianista killjoys will bang on about Third World sexual exploitation. Well, let them tell that to Maureen Hancock whose cousin died with a smile on his face. She says she wouldn't mind going out the same way. And good luck to her.

'The PC brigade speak for no one but themselves. And certainly not for the Thai stunners who were said to be only too happy to HAND out creature comforts. Nudge, nudge, w**k, w**k.'

Ratledge cringed at the crudity of the lower end support, but knew he had to grab whatever was on offer.

More penetrating was a *Daily Telegraph* column by Dominic Broadbent that, like *The Times*, struck an historical theme, but in greater detail, tapping into a long-neglected reservoir of patriotic sentiment.

'We all accept that the virile glory days of roast beef, good English ale and ships setting sail for undiscovered lands are dead and gone forever,' Broadbent wrote.

'It was an age of empire building when lusty Englishmen girded their loins for the great beyond, many destined never to return.

'Well, Bert Hancock WILL be returning to these shores, having made the most important voyage of discovery of all: About himself. He discovered the essence of life that spurs most of us on had not died simply because he was old. It just needed re-awakening.

'I'm sure he would forgive us for saying that millions of elderly people who meekly accepted that they were "past it," will today be given new heart, quietly rejoicing that there was life in the old dog yet and drawing the necessary conclusions.

'The fact of the matter is that Hancock sent a last message to us all: Not to go gently into that good night. And nor should we.'

'Jesus,' Ratledge thought, 'the man only had a stiffy. Truly, when it comes to spinning the bullshit, British journalists are in a class of their own!'

***

Mention of Hancock's return had Ratledge on the phone to Scully instantly. The body itself could become heavy with symbolism, providing priceless photo ops at the funeral.

The man had acquired something approaching hero status, particularly among the old, as an irrational collective hysteria seemed to overwhelm the nation.

The same mantra was repeated endlessly in pubs, clubs, bars, cafes and duly recycled by the media: 'That's the way I wanna go out.'

Rumour had it that sixties rockers, The Spadge, were reforming to cut a new single, hijacking the mantra for their title.

'Ludo, they've gone absolutely crackers here,' Ratledge gushed.

'It's completely crazy. I've seen nowt like it since Diana died. The papers are turning Hancock into a bloody hero.

'How about your end?'

'It seems to be going fine here, Arnie. We reckon there are only about four now who have still not had a crap, and the girls reckon there are signs that they'll produce tonight.'

Ratledge came close to bursting a blood vessel.

'LUDO, FORGET THE FUCKING BOWELS. NO ONE WANTS TO KNOW. THE STORY'S MOVED ON. IT'S NOW ALL ABOUT SEX. GEDDIT??? SEX, SEX, SEX IN OLD AGE. WHAT'S HAPPENED TO YOUR NEWS INSTINCTS? THE PRESS RELEASE MADE US LOOK LIKE IDIOTS. FORGET ANYTHING TO DO WITH SHIT. FORGET CONSTIPATION. JUST FORGET BOWELS. PERIOD. UNDERSTOOD?'

10

Crossed Words

Ratledge's voice had carried across the whole of the seventh floor, and brought Faulkner running into his office.

'It's OK, Eileen, just take your lunch break.'

'I've already taken one.'

'WELL GO TO THE POWDER ROOM OR SOMETHING. JUST GET OUT OF HERE,' Ratledge bellowed, almost out of control.

Faulkner ran out the office in tears and straight to the nearest pub. 'He's shouted at me for the last time,' she vowed.

Gulping three double vodkas in quick succession she tottered into an electronics store and bought herself a pocket-sized tape recorder, complete with phone attachment. Swamped by vengeful thoughts, she headed back to the office.

Scully, chastened by Ratledge's outburst, gave him a factual run-down on the Samui situation:

No one had been able to winkle out the resort's spy; KKSA and the resort itself were being continually plagued by hacks, some specially flown out from Britain. Others, mainly locals, were acting as stringers for news outfits abroad.

Nam Horm and KKSA managements had been less than pleased at all the attention, but reasoned that in a few days all would calm down.

'What worries me long term is KKSA,' Scully warned. 'I'm sure I'll be able to handle things at the resort, but I think KKSA will turn out to be the weak link. I suspect one of their girls could be the mole.'

'I need to know more about this outfit,' Ratledge said.

'Has anyone done a real number on them, looked at them in depth?'

'Yeah, I heard some Asian youth mag started probing; they were concerned that only good-looking girls and boys were being recruited and then hired out for any old jobs.

'They thought the whole idea of just recruiting stunners was a bit iffy.'

'So what did they find?'

'Well, they ran a couple of quite revealing in-depth pieces, I was told – and then they just dropped it like hot shit. Oops, sorry, Arnie.

'I've not yet read the pieces, but I think you should be able to Google them.

'I think the mag's called Youth in Asia, something like that.'

'Right, now what about shipping Hancock's corpse back to Britain? What sort of time scale are we looking at?'

'Well, the mechanics of it shouldn't be too difficult. It's in a nearby mortuary. Just transport dates, some paper work and there'll probably be a preliminary inquest. The case has attracted so much publicity, it's just the Thais covering their arses.'

'But that could take months,' said Ratledge, deflated. 'Will this always be the case when there are deaths?'

'Well, I'm glad you raised the subject, Arnie. I want to talk to you about this whole death business. I've heard that In the States and in Belgium they're discussing a new, green way of disposing of bodies.'

'Go on Ludo, I'll make some notes, but before I forget what's the name of that mag again? I'll write it down.'

'I'm not 100 per cent sure but I think it was Youth in Asia.'

After much drunken fiddling, Faulkner finally clicked on her tape at the precise moment Scully uttered the words 'it was Youth in Asia.'

She'd heard none of the previous conversation, but knew that if Ratledge had wanted her out of the way, he would most probably be having one of those interminable conversations with Thailand that he never liked other people to hear. Her befuddled brain thought she'd heard 'euthanasia.'

'I'm gonna check out Youth in Asia or what ever it's called as soon as this call's over, Ludo. Now tell me more about this green body disposal. You know, this could bring the environmental lot on board. They're always screaming about stuff. They could be useful allies.'

Faulkner, suddenly stone-cold sober, double checked that her tape was running smoothly. It was. Bolt upright, she listened with growing horror.

'Well, instead of cremation, which generates a lot of smoke pollution, what they do is drop the bodies into some special solution – the method's called resomation. Look it up in the dictionary,' Scully added helpfully.

'What they're left with is some gunge-type liquid which is bunged in a container for relatives. You know, a bit like an urn. The secret is in the stuff the corpses are submerged in. It's some sort of acid-based liquid. I hate to use the term, Arnie, you know how much I hate the Nazis, but the stuff could technically be called a final solution.

'Please don't ever repeat those words outside of this conversation.'

'Of course not, Ludo, I'm not mad. Incidentally, how many bodies at a time could this stuff dispose of?'

'I've not a clue. I suppose it all depends on the size of the containers, the vats, whatever, and I've no idea how they would tell who's who.

'Anyway, as I say, it's only in its early stages yet, but it's certainly something we should keep an eye on. If this project gets really big, it could smooth things out for us.'

'Plenty to weigh up there. Thanks, Ludo. Sorry I was angry earlier. But I'm glad to hear you're not talking shit anymore.' Both men chuckled.

'This is serious stuff. I'll give you a buzz tomorrow. I'm now gonna see what I can find out about Youth in Asia or whatever it's called.'

***

For five full minutes Faulkner sat rooted to her chair, believing she had just eavesdropped on a plan to cull the economically burdensome elderly and dispose of their bodies.

All the pieces suddenly slotted into place: Extreme sexual excitement, bringing on death; environmental friendly body disposal; and the whole thing cheered on by a sex-obsessed media that had lost its moral compass.

A truly diabolical plot that had readily won the economic establishment's seal of approval – right down to the Taxpayers Alliance.

Britain and the world must be alerted to what was afoot. She was working for a monster in human form, a man whose evil intent, if brought to fruition, would make mass murderer Harold Shipman seem like a minor felon.

Ratledge had to be stopped at all costs and the first step was safe removal of the tape from the Town Hall.

Without saying a word to Ratledge, Faulkner packed her little bag with the precious evidence and headed home.

Alone in her bedroom, another vodka in trembling hand, she weighed the options. The police were the obvious first port of call, but could they be trusted to act? The chairman of the police authority was a close friend of Ratledge, and attempts might be made to discredit the tape as a forgery.

Faulkner was aware that her drinking had not gone unnoticed in the Town Hall, and colleagues she could trust were few and far between. Many of them, jealous of her position, would be only too ready to wield the knife.

Rushing home without letting Ratledge know had not been a sensible move. That could also be used against her.

And then there was her pension to think about. Ratledge had hinted that he would not stand in the way of her early retirement, once the council finances had been strengthened.

She had long suspected he would be glad to see the back of her, but the tape could – at the very least – complicate the situation. He might suspect she was the bugger.

Yes, it had been a stupid move to have rushed out of the Town Hall on the very day of the damning conversation. It would all be on CCTV. She poured herself another vodka.

Then there was the mood in the country to consider. Very pro-Ratledge at the moment – she would be swimming against the tide of support, echoed by most of the Press. Most, but not all. No, not all.

There was that journalist Ratledge hated with a passion; worked for the *Daily Express* ... Wallis, that was his name ... Charlie Wallis. The hatred between the two was mutual. He would be a safe pair of hands and know how to use the tape to maximum advantage.

But timing, as with everything, timing was crucial. With that thought firmly fixed in her now contentedly pickled brain, Faulkner's head slumped onto her chest, the vodka glass slipping to the floor.

A disturbed sleep ensued, largely dominated by dead bodies immersed in boiling vats of pineapple juice.

***

'Is the coconut juice to Mr Ludo's liking,' the waiter inquired as Scully and Lucy settled down for what promised to be a relaxed working dinner with Visit's family.

All agreed that the past few days had been chaotic and tense, but generally speaking the remaining 26 residents had settled in contentedly, forming relationships with their carers that were quite obviously warm and perhaps in some cases a little more.

The girls had worked hard to get the men interested in

some light yoga, and for the really brave, a spot of gentle Tai Chi. Whenever possible, the men were encouraged to use the pool, its positive health effects repeatedly emphasised.

'I know it's still only the beginning, but I'm seeing signs that this whole thing could prove a real winner,' Scully observed, slurring his words slightly from the effects of some earlier whiskies. Visit nodded his agreement.

He reminded Scully that when the dust had settled, the next stage would be to transfer another batch of elderly from some care home in Wigburn or further afield.

'Only when Nam Horm is entirely devoted to the care of your elderly – and no more holidaymakers – will I rest happily,' Visit said.

'Don't worry, my boss is already working on that. All we have to do is ensure that there are no more silly scandals – and that deaths are seen as in the natural order of things.'

No one was quite sure what Scully was driving at, so Lucy stepped in.

'I think the exercise and the swimming is a brilliant idea. That, combined with the climate and the healthy food here' … Visit nodded his appreciation … 'will extend lives, I'm sure.'

Wanlaya, ever the business lady, said, 'It would be interesting to start keeping statistics, comparing the longevity rates of those who move here, with those from the same locality who remain in UK care homes.

'Those statistics would make excellent publicity for future expansion of the enterprise.'

'That's brilliant, Wanlaya,' Lucy responded, with all the enthusiasm of a star-struck teenager addressing her favourite pop star.

'And it wouldn't be just the number of months or years added to life, but the quality of that extra time that we'd need to identify and emphasise,' Lucy added. Scully looked thoughtful.

'You two seem quite relaxed about being in this for the long haul, but it's more complicated than that. It all sounds fine at the moment, sitting here, speculating on what might be, but it could overwhelm us all.

'Besides, we still have commitments in the UK. We need to talk about that as well.'

'Ignore him, Wanlaya. Ludo can be a really wet blanket at times,' said Lucy.

'Well, as you know, Lucy, we don't have wet blankets here – but sometimes wet sheets,' Wanlaya said in a just audible aside.

Lucy blushed as the rest of the Vatayanon family feigned not to hear, but Scully's face hardened.

'I'm serious, Lucy. This isn't some lotus-eating escape we're talking about. It's much bigger than that and, like it or not, there is still our life in Britain.'

Silence fell and Visit's eyes shifted from Lucy to Wanlaya and back again. His attention had been diverted from Scully's words by an unmistakable frisson he was detecting in his daughter's relationship with Lucy.

For years, both he and his wife had longed for grandchildren, but the younger daughter, Sureerat, had very little chance of attracting a man – any man, in fact, who possessed eyesight.

Friends and the wider family had marvelled at how two sisters could be so utterly different in appearance.

It wasn't simply a case of Sureerat picking the short straw. Wanlaya had so thoroughly scooped the genetic beauty pool, there had been no second straw available.

All hopes had rested on Wanlaya to breed the next generation, but there had been few boyfriends, and those she'd had were very short term.

Wanlaya's girlfriends had been far more plentiful and for some time her parents wondered whether their daughter's interest lay more with her own sex.

At the very least, they entertained the hope that their daughter could be bi-sexual. A grandchild by natural means would then still be a possibility. Both parents had shuddered at any of the other options.

Visit's eyes shifted back to Scully and the seed of an idea began taking root. Scully felt something and stared back, shifting a little uncomfortably in his seat.

He couldn't understand why Nam Horm's owner was eyeballing him so intensely and acted as he normally did in such situations, smiling an innocent and friendly smile.

Visit rested his elbow on the table and allowed himself a gentle smile back. One question troubled him:

Was Scully a man of intelligence and talent? Or an idiot in disguise? Much would hinge on the answer.

'I'm sure we all have nothing to worry about, Mr Ludo,' Visit purred. 'Everything will be fine in the end.'

Scully felt a little more at ease. Maybe this was, after all, just an evening to enjoy, relax for once and let business be discussed in a more laid-back fashion.

He ordered another round of drinks, requesting that this time his coconut juice be livened up with a little dark rum.

***

Joe Dean had been the first to spot the approaching danger, and immediately alerted fellow swimmers. Frail arms and legs churned the water as they frantically made for the pool side, some helped by their carers.

An 'oil slick' that seemed to come from nowhere was spreading outwards, threatening to engulf anyone in its path. Within seconds its diameter had expanded to three metres, and at its evil-looking centre there appeared to be a wispy black coconut.

It was in fact the bobbing head of the normally grey-haired Phil Malden. 'Get out of there, Phil,' Dean shouted. 'There's been an oil spill or something and you're dead centre of it.'

His old pal appeared to take no notice, blithely splashing around in the darkening water around his head. Malden's insouciance prompted Dean to take a closer look from the pool side. The spreading slick appeared to originate at Malden's head; not a victim, he was the problem's source.

'What the hell have you got on your head, Phil?' No reply came.

Dean was unaware that as time wore on, Malden had become seriously infatuated with his regular carer. Throwing caution to the wind and ignoring all warnings about old fools' Thais, he had decided to roll back the years.

Fellow residents knew it was for real when he even made strenuous efforts to control his flatulence.

Malden thought that dying his hair black could knock at least 10 years off his age, but he needed to be certain. A trial run was called for.

Boot polish would be an ideal test. If it didn't suit, he would simply wash it out, he reasoned. It never occurred to him that the pool might do that.

Crestfallen, face streaked black, he left the pool without a word, heading straight to his room. He had desperately wanted to surprise his carer, who would not be on duty for another hour. Instead, he had made himself a figure of fun. As he sat on the bed, staring at his own reflection, tears mingled with the black trickles.

Hacking coughs – nurtured in dank Lancashire's heavy-industry days – had slowly given way to sweeter sounds over the weeks.

Bird songs gained ascendancy, drowning out the morning fight for breath that had reduced many of the listening carers to their own tears. For the men it had been a novel experience, witnessing carers who really did care.

Exercise, diet and air quality were making a significant impact, and for those who included swimming in their regime, progress was even more marked.

Malden's escapade closed the pool for several days, forcing Visit to spend money on a thorough clean-up. There was some tension over the incident, and fresh guidelines on pool use were issued.

Nam Horm's owner was bewildered why any man should want to plaster his hair with black boot polish, especially one in his eighties. It was beyond his increasingly stretched boundaries of human understanding.

Wanlaya thought it might be senile dementia. Scully explained as best he could, having finally winkled the reasons out of Malden. 'No, Wanlaya, more like penile dementia.'

Father and daughter exchanged glances, not knowing whether to be shocked, or even offended, at Scully's unchacteristically brusque earthiness.

Wanlaya broke the ice with a nervous laugh that soon infected her father. Sanuk had again ridden to the rescue. Wanlaya's re-assessment of Scully took yet another turn.

***

'They seem to have got over the pool business,' Scully said as Lucy casually rubbed herself dry after a much-needed shower.

'Who'd you talk to, Visit?'

'Yep, and Wanlaya. I thought she was with you.'

'Yes, we went for a good long dip in the sea. Absolutely glorious. It felt a bit sticky after, though. You know, the salt. You should have a dip, Ludo. You always seem to be sorting out something or other.'

'Well, you know how it is. Teething troubles, as ever. I just put the Malden nonsense down to a bit of penile dementia and that seemed to defuse things.'

'Still finding the words, eh, Ludo!'

Lucy slipped into a raw silk dressing gown, left open at the waist. Scully sat on the bed, noticing that the effects of the waxing were already starting to wear off, as a dark stubble struggled to re-emerge.

'Not be long before you're back with Wanlaya's waxer,' he suggested, eyes digesting the lips of paradise that could lay any man low.

Scully's third mention of Wanlaya within two minutes did not escape Lucy.

'What do you really think of W-a-n-l-a-y-a?' Lucy probed, the name deliberately drawn out. 'I mean *really* think of her.'

'Well, I'm impressed with her business and diplomatic skills, she seems to have a sharp brain – and she's not without humour.'

'Come on, you know what I mean. You're a man. What do you think of her as a woman?'

Scully fidgeted a little, the air conditioning doing little to cool his increasing heat. The mere phrasing of the question seemed to add to Lucy's excitement.

'Well, she's very pretty, has a nice little figure, petite. Errr, desirable really. You know, like you.'

'I bet you'd love to screw her, eh Ludo? Be honest. Wouldn't you just?'

Lucy moved towards Scully, maintaining her monologue through shorter, rapid breaths.

'Imagine it, Ludo. Getting her little bottom into those undersize jodhpurs you brought from England, the stitching unpicked at strategic points … giving her a strict spanking … making her wetter and wetter … then doing it with her.'

In a state of raw, unstoppable lust, Lucy dragged Scully's shorts below his knees in one movement, sat astride him and began a ride of unbridled ecstasy.

Scully had no doubt who was in the driving seat, and thought Hancock was about to get company as his heart pounded out a wild drumbeat of total abandon. And he could not have cared less as his petit mort aped its big brother.

Lucy's climaxes were punctuated by a stream of precise instructions on how a 'scrumptious tart...' should be consumed ... 'eat her all up now ... like a good boy ... leave no crumbs...'

Both bodies bathed in sweat, heaving, recovering, the golden-glow moments, Scully struggled to come to terms with what he'd just heard.

'My God, Lucy, that was out of this world. She's a real turn-on for you, eh?'

'Well, I wouldn't say she was a passion killer for you, either. It felt like I was riding a...'

'So the smaller size jodhpurs were for Wanlaya, then?' Scully interrupted.

'Yes, she'd ... errr ... she'd seen me in mine and just fancied a pair.' Scully felt too other-worldly to press the point, but did.

'Hang on, we only use 'em for sex, how could she see you in yours?'

'Maybe she saw some pictures of me in my riding days – we often look at snaps. I can't remember the details. Anyway who cares.'

Scully let it drop, resting his head between Lucy's breasts, listening with interest as both hearts slowly nudged their way back to earth.

'It's amazing, though, how talk of her turns us both on,' mused Scully as he slid out of bed and rummaged for a beer. Lucy readily agreed.

'Yes, she's got a sort of bewitching quality. It's very powerful, even for me and I'm a woman.'

'I know what you mean,' Scully said. 'Real beauty can rouse the beast in us all.'

'You know, looking at some of those carers, I can understand what happened to Hancock. What do you think really goes on with the girls, Ludo?'

'I know what goes on, but say nowt, not even to Wanlaya.'

'My lips are sealed.'

'Well, I had it from the horse's mouth, Joe Dean, that old union guy. He seems to have slotted in as some kind of unofficial spokesman for the men, and keeps his ear to the ground. I've found him fairly reliable, a different generation – and a different breed – to the Ratledges of this world.

'Anyway, he says there's some sort of understanding between the men and the girls and it seems to be working quite well. The constipation problem's over, but the men – all of them, even those who can hardly bloody walk – now want to be in on the massages.

'They've developed a real taste for it. Joe says the amount of oil they go through would probably keep someone's central heating ticking over in the UK.'

'Are they having sex with the girls?' Lucy asked.

'Well, it depends what you mean by sex. If you're talking about what we've just had, no way. We'd have the hearses queuing round the block for half of 'em.'

'So what does happen?'

'Well, it seems that if they get really aroused, they get the hand job, the old "happy end" massages as the parlours call them.'

' 'Like Hancock?' Lucy pressed.

'Well no one's quite sure what he got. We'll have to wait to see what the inquest comes up with. He had a stiffy all right, but some think it was the frustration of not getting "relieved" that killed him.'

'Poor sod.'

'The girls share your sympathy, Lucy. At least that's what Dean tells me. They think it's less of a risk to give the randy old buggers a bit of gentle, caring relief. That's it in a nutshell – or nuts shell – and everyone just seems to get on with it.

'They operate on a sort of "don't ask, don't tell" basis and, you know what, it seems to work.'

'Don't the girls get pestered for something a little more, at least by the fitter men?'

'Tell me about it. Joe wouldn't name names, but hinted that a couple of the old sods have even had the "sandwich" job; you know, slithering around starkers between a couple of oiled-up girls. Jammy buggers!'

'Aha, I smell envy?'

'Naah, but it can't be bad at their age, tucking into a bit of that. Speaking of age, Joe thinks that Dan Williams, he's the "daddy" of the lot at 95, is getting a bit of oral.'

'Isn't that going a bit far?'

'What do you suggest? A "nil by mouth" hospital sign?

'It's his arthritis, it limits what he can do,' Scully explained. 'The others say they often hear him cry out in pain. In fact his shouts get so loud, he can sometimes be heard at both ends of the block.

'His carer, Pu, is very understanding, though. I'm told they're quite close. She's proud to be taking care of the oldest of them all. Dan's also got a few bob, and that never does any harm out here.'

'And that's it?'

'Yep, I think so. Anything more than that, and we're getting into deeper territory – the girls' wider interests. Shenanigans higher up the sex chain come at a price – marriage, or something like it.

'And, you know, Lucy, that doesn't seem to put the men off. Joe says that at least four of them are already talking wedding bells.'

'Don't you mean "balls." Jesus, Ludo, men's brains really are in their bollocks.'

'Do you think they care? They're in a beautiful setting, great food, each sleep could be their last. What have they got to lose?' Lucy stayed silent.

'Do you know that there's even jealousy among some of the men, fancying someone else's carer. A couple of 85-year-olds came within a whisker of thumping each other.

'Think about it, 85-year-olds fighting over someone young enough to be their great, great, grand-daughter.'

'Don't you find that a bit seedy, Ludo?'

'No, I find it inspirational. Anthony Quinn fathered a child in his eighties and most people applauded him as a bit of a Jack-the-lad. If it's OK for the rich and famous to do it, Lucy, why not old working class men?'

'Aha, the old communist lives,' smiled Lucy.

'More the old lecher,' Scully corrected.

***

The belligerent 85-year-olds turned out to be Lipton and Malden, as Scully suspected. Nothing had mellowed the bad blood between the pair, and now it had flourished anew in a teenage-type quest for love's favours.

It was as though the past 70 years had never happened and they were again spotty youths, competing for the same maidenly hand.

That hand belonged to Lipton's carer, Thitaree Chatkupt, who on a beauty scale of one to 10, would have broken the mechanism.

Although still besotted by his own carer, Malden now coveted Lipton's even more, and was determined to prove himself the worthier of the warring pair, setting himself up as Thitaree's protector.

She needed no protection from the largely wheelchair-bound Lipton, who since his arrival in Thailand had made some modest progress against crippling rheumatism. With great effort, he could now stand for brief periods and take some faltering steps.

To Malden, none of this was of the slightest concern as his thoughts became increasingly occupied with the object of his desire. Protection, sought or not, would be given.

All was fair in love and war, and with the true warrior's resolve, he determined to win this battle. This time, genuine hair dye was applied.

Malden was soon put to the test, courtesy of Lipton's love for red-hot Thai curries. No matter how spiced the served-up dish, extra chillies were always demanded.

Thitaree was concerned about the health effects. 'Enough, no more, you die,' she pleaded as Lipton demanded more chillies for his curried prawns.

Malden, on one of his self-appointed corridor patrols, stopped outside Lipton's room as voices were raised.

'No, please, Mr Sam, no more prik, not good for you.'

'I want it, it's my right, and I'm gonna have it.'

'No, enough prik. Stop please.'

The sound of breaking crockery brought Sir Lancelot bursting through the door, face contorted in rage, words spilling from his mouth in a sentence that never got completed.

'You dirty, filthy, raping bastard, take your hands off her or I'll …'

Thitaree shrank back in horror at the intrusion while Lipton tried to swivel his wheelchair around, hampered by the plastic tray that limited his arm movements.

'What are you doing, you lunatic. Get out of my room,' he bellowed, struggling to grab a wheel and failing. Malden took in the scene:

On the tray was a bowl of what looked suspiciously like red curry and a separate container of steaming rice.

A knocked-over glass was dripping some liquid on the floor where another bowl lay in pieces, its little red contents scattered among the debris.

No one seemed to be in a state of undress or sexual arousal.

'What were you trying to do to her?' Malden demanded. 'You were trying to force yourself on her, weren't you? You disgusting pig.'

Lipton finally managed to reach the emergency cord and

pulled hard.

'You ARE mad. I was trying to do nothing to her, ask her. We were just arguing over a bit of food. Isn't that right, Thitaree?'

Thitaree's limited English prevented her from following the conversation. Lipton tried to simplify his message with the aid of gestures.

'You, me, we fight' … he clenched his fists … 'over prik.' He pointed to the little, red chilli peppers scattered over the floor.

'I want more prik, you say no. I try to get prik. Bowl fall. Whooosh.'

Thitaree understood. 'Yes. You want prik too much. Bad for you. I am care for you. I say no.'

Malden put his head in both hands as a care supervisor, fearing the worst, burst into the room. A swift exchange of Thai between the two girls, in which the word prik featured prominently, left the supervisor bemused.

'It's not good you make alarm because bowl of …' she pointed to the floor … 'chilli,' Malden supplied the missing English word … 'is broken. That is not for alarm. Only make alarm if something very bad. Thitaree can sweep up prik. Not big problem.'

Malden tried to shoulder the blame in best pidgin English. 'I am sorry. I thought there was very bad fight. I did not understand. Mr Sam and Thitaree get afraid because I rush in room. I will not do again. I am very sorry.'

As Malden slunk out of the room, ending his 'patrol' prematurely, he thought it might be useful for the residents to be schooled in at least a few basic Thai words, maybe even phrases. He'd suggest it to Joe.

Malden already had a head start, with the word for chilli, the first bit of Thai he'd mastered, branded on his brain for whatever life remained.

***

The question of Hancock's body was devouring huge chunks of time as the wheels of Thai bureaucracy laboured at a barely detectable pace, drawing in the lawyers.

The lack of urgency from a people largely admired for their industry and enterprise frustrated Scully and Lucy, but slowly, without really noticing, both were beginning to adjust to the Thai way and pace of doing things.

Scully could see his UK business contracting by the week. Loss of the prestigious Sebastian cosmetic-surgery account had created a snowball effect among other clients.

Now, only two staff remained, and he was seriously toying with the idea of selling up, while he still had a business to sell.

After much debate, he'd finally agreed to join Ratledge's consultancy and, in between smoothing out problems at Nam Horm, found himself spending more and more time checking out similar resorts that might prove equally suitable.

Reluctantly, he'd admitted to himself that Ratledge had been right all along.

The Thai experiment had been ground breaking and business for the consultancy had mushroomed as local authorities, hard-pressed by unavoidable cuts, sought expertise and guidance on how to slash care costs by exporting the elderly.

The work was not something Scully intended to do for the rest of his life. He still couldn't quite shake off a mild distaste at the hard commercial aspect of what was essentially a social problem, but Lucy had no qualms.

'If market forces are acting to solve the problem, what the hell's wrong with that? Like your Russian friends are forever pointing out – "what matters is what works."' It had now become Lucy's mantra, too.

Scully wondered where it was all going. His partner's

sights were more prosaic:

'Who knows, Ludo. In a few years the Japanese might invent robots to look after the elderly. It could be their next big thing, but for once can we just focus on the here and now and seize our moment.'

'You see things very short-term, don't you, Lucy?'

'No. I just see things as they are. That's what concerns me.' Scully remained lukewarm.

'Look, Ludo, your business seems to be going down the pan. Decisions need to be made. I really think this is an opportunity to clean up ...' Scully winced at the term ... 'and we need to grab it.

'For years you've talked about buying a place here with a private airstrip, getting a plane or two, taking up tourists, doing a bit of writing in between, enjoying the sun, the food, the swimming. Well, it's all knocking on your door, Ludo.

'The way that consultancy's growing, in a couple of years we should have the money to live the dream, instead of just dreaming it. What is it? Why is it at times like this you seem to slip into a sort of paralysis?'

Scully never got to answer. The bedside phone rang. A care supervisor wondered whether he could help out with a small problem. Her English was not quite up to it and, yes, it was Lipton and Malden again.

'You did what, Phil?' Scully doubted that he'd heard correctly. Lipton had been stretched out on a sun-lounger next to the pool and Malden had suddenly been seized by a severe coughing bout as he passed behind.

Out of his mouth had shot a gobbet of phlegm. It had followed a looping trajectory and landed almost dead centre on the head of Lipton who was blissfully unaware of the viscous visitor he was now hosting.

'I could have just left it there, Ludo, and no one would ever have known it was me, but I did the decent thing and this is the thanks I get.'

The "decent thing" was a clumsy attempt by Malden to remove the gobbet by hand without offering up any detailed explanation to Lipton.

'I just said there's something on your head, Sam, tried to wipe it off and he went absolutely barmy.'

Lipton had a different take: 'What I think is that this bastard coughed into his hand and tried to wipe it on my head?'

'Why the hell would I want to wipe it on your head?' Malden shouted, quickly apologising to the gathering knot of carers for raising his voice.

'Why, I'll tell you why. Because with the Thais there's no greater public insult than touching someone's head.

'I've been reading up about this and they believe the spirit, the soul, it's called the khwan – not that an ignoramus like you would know anything about it – lives in the head.

'And you touched it with your filthy phlegm. You wanted to humiliate me in front of her,' he said, thumb pointing in Thitaree's direction.

'Everyone knows you're after her, you're a menace, a bloody nutcase.'

As the carers spoke animatedly among themselves, Scully did his best to restore peace. Thitaree helped, gently wiping Lipton's head – but not before clasping hands together in the Buddhist wei, as convention demanded – and offering Malden a fresh towel for his hands.

A modicum of quiet restored, Scully, head shaking in disbelief, made for the bungalow to put Lucy right about his thinking.

For the second time that day, he never got the chance. Only this time the interruption was of a different magnitude, threatening catastrophe.

***

Ratledge was on the phone. He and Scully were at the centre

of a media storm claiming that the whole Thai project was part of a subtle euthanasia plot in which bodies were to be dissolved.

The *Daily Express* broke the 'exclusive' story under the headline 'Final Solution.' As both men grappled for answers, one mile to the south of the Town Hall, a vengeful, satisfied woman devoured every line of the story.

Eileen Faulkner had been up at the crack of dawn to get her *Express* that morning. Four days earlier she had finally been given her early retirement wish.

Even by Faulkner's standards it was a little early for a drink. But as she drank in the lurid report, relishing every word, she allowed herself a special treat and poured an extra large Pertsovka, pepper-flavoured Russian vodka that had caught her eye in the off licence. The habitual bullshitter who served her claimed it was Stalin's favourite, not that she cared.

It was Ratledge who claimed her full attention as his puffy face stared out from the front page. Faulkner raised her glass. 'Here's to you, Arnie. You'll shout no more at me – or anyone.'

Ratledge and Scully were hardly off the phone as they went into crisis mode. Vociferous denials of any underhand euthanasia plots were countered by a media that smelled blood.

A tape existed that clearly mentioned euthanasia and a new system for body disposal. The evidence was overwhelming. Scully and Ratledge were dumbfounded.

Yes, they had mentioned in passing there was a revolutionary, eco-friendly method for body disposal that Belgium and some US states were considering, but euthanasia, never. Both hated the idea.

They were already in touch with their lawyers and unless retractions were issued, there would be blood – legal and financial blood – spilled. The papers were having none of it.

Ratledge and Scully could do what they liked. There was the tape. End of story. End of careers.

Scully and Ratledge dredged every backwater of their memories. They had never discussed euthanasia, so how could the Press be so certain.

It was Scully who made the breakthrough, asking Ratledge if anything unusual had happened on the day they discussed resomation.

Ratledge leafed through his official diary and noted that Faulkner had left early without permission or notification. If she'd been the bugger, both reasoned, it must have been something startling she'd heard to make her head for the hills so suddenly.

And now this stuff was all over the papers before the ink was even dry on her retirement. The answer had to be on that day.

'Think, think, think, Arnie, what else did we discuss on that day?' Scully urged.

'Well, I certainly remember you talking shit most of the time, Ludo. Still going on about bloody constipation, but nothing about euthanasia. Even a deaf as a doorpost half-wit couldn't confuse the two.'

'Anything else, Arnie, anything at all?' Ratledge was blank. 'All I remember was that after our conversation I tried digging up that stuff about KKSA.

'You said a magazine had done some in-depth pieces about the outfit. I couldn't find a site for the mag … what was it called … Youth … Youth in As … Oh fuck … oh fuck … fuck … fuck.'

Simultaneously, both heads drooped into hands. A few seconds elapsed before communication was resumed. Scully spoke first.

'You really couldn't make this up, Arnie. They've confused Youth in Asia for euthanasia.'

'But that's impossible, Ludo. It was perfectly clear we

were talking about a magazine. That's what that bit of our conversation was about. It doesn't make sense.'

'Agreed, unless … unless … whoever bugged us didn't hear the full conversation … only snatches.'

'Well, that's their problem. The point is we've identified the source of this euthanasia nonsense and can blow them out the water.'

'I'd like to think that, Arnie, but aren't we forgetting something?' Ratledge was unnerved by Scully's tone.

'What, exactly?'

'Well, you said you couldn't find any trace of the magazine on the net.'

'So?'

'It might not exist.'

'What do you mean "It might not exist?" You gave me the name over the fucking phone, remember? How else would I have known about it?'

'No, Arnie, what I said was that I thought it was called "Youth in Asia," but I wasn't quite sure. I said it needs checking out.'

'So what are you saying, Ludo?'

'Well, just think it through. If we claim that 'euthanasia' was mistaken for the title of a non-existent mag, who'd believe us? We'd come across as the biggest pair of lying tossers on the planet. Didn't you come up with anything at all in your search, Arnie?'

'Just a punk rock band in New Jersey called Youth in Asia and a magazine called *Today's Youth Asia*.'

'That sounds promising.'

'Yes, it does, apart from the fact that it's based in Katmandu, in the foothills of the Himalayas, 100 miles from Mount Everest.

'Now I wouldn't say my Nepalese is up to much, but when I started phoning and asking them about KKSA and the employment of beautiful young people I got the impression from their jabber that they thought a nutter was on the blower.'

'If no such mag exists, we're screwed, Arnie. Unless we can come up with a tape of our full conversation. Maybe you should have done what Nixon did in the White House and had every conversation you ever made at the Town Hall recorded.'

'I don't think that would have been very wise, Ludo, knowing what's gone off here over the years.'

'Wise or not, only a full tape will sort this mess out.'

11

Moments of truth

Three days after the 'euthanasia' exclusive, a second Nam Horm resident died, giving the story a timely set of 'fresh legs,' as grateful journalists described it.

George Aldiss, a former postman, had a semi-watery end, unintentionally helped along by his carer.

Aldiss had never learnt to swim and Porntip, his carer, had offered to fill that void as the ex-mailman entered his 89th year.

Like most of the others, Aldiss had formed a strong, intimate relationship with his carer and made a point of telling anyone who cared to listen how 'expert' her massages were, adding the usual nods and winks and remarking on Porntip's exceptionally strong hands.

No one, least of all Aldiss, attached any significance to this unusual strength, until moments before his death.

Aldiss had made real progress in the pool and was able to float unaided, managing up to half a dozen strokes on a good day. Nothing, however, could have prepared him for his final day of life.

As he clambered out the pool, assisted by Porntip, his hand slipped from his carer's arm, and ensnared itself in the side of the cutaway swimsuit.

The material, unable to stand the weight of a man's body, ripped almost entirely in half, revealing a small but perfectly formed set of male genitalia.

Witnesses claimed that the shock propelled Aldiss straight back into the pool where he could be seen ingesting large quantities of water before slipping under for the last time.

Frantic attempts at pumping out his lungs proved fruitless and within 24 hours he had joined Hancock in the mortuary.

Involvement of a 'ladyboy' added piquancy to the more salacious end of the press, with the *Daily Star* going for 'Last post as ex-mailman meets ex-male woman.'

For Ratledge and Scully the timing and circumstances could not have been worse. The pendulum was swinging yet again and now the whole enterprise felt under threat.

Ominously, the relaxed approach of commentators seemed to be in short supply. Potential care-home sites in Thailand and beyond – and the staff they would be employing – all needed greater scrutiny, the papers urged.

Health and care professionals, and the politicians, were urged to examine the entire concept afresh. What added to the sense of gloom, was that even those who had been strong supporters of the project, were now asking more searching and considered questions.

Underpinning everything was the whiff of euthanasia that still hung about. Although the word could not be linked in any way to Aldiss's death, it padded around in the background like mournful mood music, words from the tape skilfully worked into most of the Press reports.

The injustice of it all enraged Scully. Shedding his trademark laid-back approach, he tore into the 'hypocrisy' of fellow journalists, politicians and the UK care-home industry. His ferocity alarmed Ratledge, rekindling mixed memories of the strike days.

Both Lucy and Wanlaya manned extra phones as Scully prepared to tackle Britain's press, radio and TV head on with a series of non-stop statements and interviews that men half his age would have blanched at.

With the broadcast media, he insisted that whenever possible interviews should be live, so that his words could not be edited out and twisted at the time. Those black arts would be employed later when the interviews were re-broadcast, he told anyone who cared to listen, bitterness and cynicism in his voice.

Wanlaya looked frightened, realising what was at stake. 'Don't worry,' Lucy assured. 'I've seen him like this before. He doesn't often really stir himself, but when he does he's unrecognisable.'

Wanlaya was not convinced. 'But it's not enough to be angry, Lucy. One wrong word and there could be a terrible cost to us all.'

'That's true, but please believe me. He'll be well armed with his favourite weapons – facts.' Wanlaya still looked concerned.

***

Two minutes into the live interview with Radio 4's Today Programme, the word Scully had been waiting to sink his teeth into surfaced from the interviewer.

'So, you want to talk about euthanasia, eh? I'll tell you about euthanasia ... practised on 1,800 dementia sufferers in UK care homes each year.'

'Where's your evidence for that, Mr Scully?'

'*Daily Telegraph* report. You need to do your homework before making unfounded accusations against me or Arnie Ratledge.'

'Are you telling me that British care homes effectively put to death 1,800 demented people a year, Mr Scully? That's a very serious allegation. Aren't you just trying to divert attention from your own flirtation with euthanasia?'

Scully was at boiling point, but kept himself in check. 'I presume radio journalists don't limit themselves to talk and can actually read.'

'No need for the insults, Mr Scully. Can we just stay with the issue.'

'Well, I'm going to read you a short quote from the

Telegraph's Medical Editor, discussing antipsychotics, a liquid cosh. Writing about dementia, she says, and I quote word for word:

'"An estimated 144,000 sufferers are prescribed antipsychotics to keep them quiet in care homes, causing around 1,800 deaths a year." End quote. If that isn't euthanasia, you tell me what is.'

'But just because one journalist makes these claims doesn't make it all true.'

'"One journalist?"

'She was following up a letter to the *Telegraph* signed by 45 organisations and respected individuals, including a professor from the Royal College of GPs; the Junior Minister for Care Services; and an eminent member of the Royal College of Psychiatrists. They are so concerned they've formed the Dementia Action Alliance.

'There are 750,000 people with the condition in Britain, and estimates are that the figure could grow to a million in15 years. How many of those will ultimately be put on the liquid cosh and killed early?'

'We'll be talking to other agencies later, Mr Scully, who I'm sure will have a different perspective on this issue. Meanwhile, thank you Ludo Scully, in Thailand.'

Scully tried for the last word: 'I hope that includes the Government which is on record as saying that its four dementia priorities include reduction of the chemical cosh and improving the quality of life in care homes. Those homes could learn a lot from Nam Horm, where there are no coshes and quality care is excellent.'

'Yes, Mr Scully. Thank you for the advert. I'm sure the two deaths have already made our listeners fully aware of Nam Horm. Goodbye.'

Apart from Today's kiss-off line, Scully was pleased with the way the interview had gone and was soon in his natural element, jousting with other broadcasters. Plugs for Nam

Horm were made early in subsequent interviews, ensuring ample time to counter any anti comments.

Ratledge, himself fielding a barrage of questions, largely took his stance from Scully's e-mailed press releases which covered all the main arguments. A complex web of speaker, phone, Net and recording equipment meant that the two men were in a position to monitor how each other was performing.

Also monitoring was Visit who had additional communication equipment rigged up. He too sensed that a crossroads had been reached and listened with a mixture of awe and fascination at the gladiatorial nature of British journalism.

Not only could the future of Nam Horm hinge on this man's performance, but he was also curious to learn whether Scully was of worthy genetic stock. The right stuff.

Moments of truth were piling up.

Sustained by endless cups of green tea, crispy fried prawns, rice and the highly nourishing pad pak ruam, a favoured dish of mixed vegetables, Scully coped impressively, focussed and utterly determined.

Lucy and Wanlaya did little to hide their admiration, offering words of encouragement and praise as the hours ticked by.

Inevitably, fatigue set in at about midnight, still only 5pm in Britain. The most crucial hours were yet to unfold as agenda-setting early evening TV and radio news bulletins got into their stride.

Scully switched to toe-curlingly-strong double espressos to keep tiredness at bay, but a new problem piled on the pressure. The intensity of his concentration had seriously stiffened his neck muscles. Lucy suggested an answer.

'Wanlaya is an excellent masseuse, Ludo. I'm sure she'd be able to sort out your neck and shoulders.'

'Would you mind, Wanlaya?' Scully asked tentatively.

‘I would consider it a great honour … and a pleasure, Mr Ludo.’

Scully felt a warmth at how she’d elongated the word ‘pleasure.’ Both women smiled and a jolt of fresh energy coursed through his body.

‘Right, who’s next for shaving,’ he asked as the phones rang and Wanlaya slipped out to fetch oil and towels. A long evening and night stretched ahead.

***

An hour passed before Wanlaya returned. She had been hijacked by her father for a long and detailed chat, and her face was serious.

‘Mr Ludo I must tell you that my father thinks …’

‘Yes, Wanlaya, what is it …’

‘He thinks that …’ She paused again, prolonging the agony …

‘He thinks that you...are wonderful and have done a magnificent job defending the resort … and the honour of Thailand.’

Scully and Lucy fell on Wanlaya with a vengeance.

‘Do you know what a wind-up merchant is, Wanlaya?’ they asked as they seized her hands and feet. Grinning from ear to ear, the Thai girl shook her head.

‘Well, it’s you, and they get thrown into pools while fully dressed.’ Shouts and protests ignored, they struggled to man-handle Wanlaya out the door. Yet another phone call interrupted her watery fate.

Some quotes for the *Daily Express* duly delivered, Scully & Lucy agreed to postpone the Thai girl’s punishment as she revealed more of what her father had said.

‘He cannot thank you enough, Mr Ludo. His personal mobile has not stopped ringing. I was there while he took some of the calls, from business acquaintances, friends and even some politicians. These people rang in and asked him to pass on their thanks to you.'

'What particularly did they like, Wanlaya?' Scully queried, keen to build on the success.

'The way you exposed the hidden euthanasia in your own country and contrasted that with the Thai attitude to old people. We thought that was such a kind and good thing to do.'

'I did it because it was true, Wanlaya.'

Lucy nodded good-naturedly, adding: 'But that's not going to save you from a ducking later, Wanlaya. We've not forgotten.'

Screams of delight rang out as this time Lucy and Scully made pretend grabs at the Thai's impossibly dainty hands and feet. Lucy suddenly adopted a mockingly stern tone:

'You might, just might, escape the ducking if you do a thoroughly professional massage job on Ludo.'

More phones rang as Scully discarded his shirt and Wanlaya rubbed oil into his knotted neck and shoulders.

The evening melted into night as Wanlaya continued working her magic on Scully, expressing concern at how tense his torso was. She kneaded, pulled and pummeled, resting only a few minutes every hour.

Scully felt as though he'd been through a mangle, yet the tick of the clock was preventing the full benefits from working through.

The early hours of the morning, 4am and 5am, when the body is at its most tired, would be his crucial testing time. They corresponded to the UK's main evening TV bulletins, 9pm and 10pm, and Scully knew that being available for live interviews would be vital.

It could win the respect of the interviewers, who would probably not be able to resist mentioning that their 'prey' had given up his shuteye to talk to them live. That would probably gain the admiration of viewers, too.

Whatever the cost, it was worth a gamble. This was war.

As the crucial hours drew nearer, Scully's upper torso still tensed up, despite Wanlaya's best efforts. A battle was being fought between body and mind and the outcome uncertain.

A further worry for Scully was whether Lucy and Wanlaya would have the commitment and stamina to see the night through.

When he explained his fears, there was not a moment's hesitation. Their courage moved Scully and he thanked them generously.

The massage suddenly stopped and both women went into a huddled conversation.

Without uttering another word, the door of what had become a makeshift studio was locked, Wanlaya and Lucy kissed each other – it looked like fully on the mouth, but Scully couldn't be sure. Wanlaya resumed her neck and shoulder massage, and Lucy sank to her knees in front of Scully's chair.

She commanded, rather than asked, that for the next few minutes, if the phone rang it would go onto the answer machine. The phones stayed silent, the only sound disturbing the quiet was the gentle unzipping of Scully's jeans.

Wanlaya never broke her massage rhythm as her eyes feasted on the live show below. A few weak, initial 'buts' from Scully, his thumb motioning towards Wanlaya, were swiftly silenced by Lucy with a single wave of her hand and a furiously hissed, 'for once, just go with the flow.'

And Scully obeyed, head swimming in ecstasy as he let himself bathe in the knowledge that a true Thai beauty was massaging his upper body, watching his 'wife' fellate him. And – as the full-length mirror testified – watching in some heat.

The thought was too much; the explosion instantaneous; control or delay out the question.

Wanlaya, eyes popping, now dug painfully into his flesh. For all Scully cared, it could have been red-hot needles.

Finally, he slumped back, gasping his thanks and apologising for being so sexually selfish. Lucy and Wanlaya were breathing heavily, but Lucy managed words of re-assurance:

'Don't worry, Ludo, there'll be a pay-back.' Wanlaya said nothing.

Scully felt a sense of relaxation so deep that he was ready to take on not just the bulletins at nine and ten, but even Newsnight at 10.30.

'Bring 'em all on,' he muttered, before sinking into a 15-minute power nap shrilly interrupted by a phone call.

***

By common consent, the night had been a near total success, but the euthanasia mud still incubated worms of doubt in the public mind.

Something more would need to be done to restore confidence in the whole project. Scully was not sure what and had toyed with the idea of letting Joe Dean speak to the media as a voice at the coalface.

It was a high-risk gamble that he'd discussed with Ratledge, who shared his nervousness.

Although elated by the interviews, Scully's thoughts had been clouded by the 'public' sex session with Lucy and he now felt mildly embarrassed whenever Wanlaya was in their company. Lucy was dismissive.

It had been a 'vital' bit of fun that had brought results. 'Sometimes, Ludo,' she chided, 'I think that behind that sexy exterior, there's a puritan trying to get out.

'Sex doesn't have to be a deadly serious business. It can be fun, recreational … like being kids again. I've been thinking about it a lot recently.'

'I know what you're trying to say, Lucy. So where does all that sense of fun go, what happens to us?'

'We grow up, Ludo, whatever that is. The child dies.

Whatever's fun, spontaneous, gets squeezed like a lemon. Only it's not lemon juice that trickles out – it's us, our essence. And it's so bloody sad.'

Lucy paused and looked at Ludo full face. 'And that's the reason I'm now going along with this whole project so wholeheartedly. I've been re-assessing.' Scully looked puzzled.

'These old people, Ludo, what do you think they are, now, at this stage of their lives?'

Scully waited.

'They're back to being kids, Ludo, that's what they are. Nature plays the supreme sick joke. All of us start life utterly helpless, and that's the way many of us go out. But it doesn't happen in a vacuum.

'Along with the returned vulnerability, the innocence also comes back and we end up asking the same question: "Did any of it really matter?"'

'What matter?'

'Whatever life-long guilt trip we've endured – and for many that means sex. And, if we're honest, Ludo, most of us will die regretting not having had more.

'Blame parents, blame grandparents, blame religion, blame politicians, blame control-freaks who make a living messing with people's heads; countless lives, needlessly frustrated by the killjoys of this earth.

'But the elderly at this place are seeing the light late on – very late on – and grabbing what they can as they enter the final stretch. And here's the best bit: They're doing it because they've returned to being spontaneous, fun-loving, enjoy-the-moment kids.

'They've reclaimed sex as innocent fun. And if they don't do it successfully, they're prepared to die in the attempt.'

'So we're no better than animals, eh Lucy?'

'Well I don't know of any animals that top themselves, get pissed or pop pills because they're so sexually frustrated.

Look, it's simple. People's lives are blighted because their natural desires are stifled. And some only realise it later in life; almost too late – if ever.'

Scully sensed a big moment. He rose to pour a couple of whiskies, forcing himself to ask the question he feared being answered.

'Do you include yourself in that category, Lucy?'

'Yes.'

'It's Wanlaya, isn't it?'

'Yes, but it isn't just her. It's someone else as well.'

'Who?'

'Well, you actually.

'I crave the both of you. Sometimes individually, sometimes together. I've thought about this long and hard, Ludo, and that's what I want. I cannot run away from the person I am.

'You, Ludo, you're a rarity. You might not think so, but you understand a woman's needs very well.

'You're not a woman, though. Wanlaya is, and her level of understanding – the jealous would call it "depraved" – speaks to me in a way no man ever could.'

Rubber returned under Scully's feet. Only this time it felt soft as latex. Now the foundation's foundations were shifting. Mixed butterflies in the pit of the stomach. Threatening *and* thrilling. Next day, next week, next month, what, if anything, still solid, the same, predictable?

'Am I getting this right? You two have been having an affair?'

'Yes.'

'How long?

'Months.'

'And now you want to bring me on board like the proverbial spare prick – or should that be dildo?'

'Oh, Ludo, Ludo. Don't cheapen us – or yourself – with the old, stupid cliches.'

'Don't "Ludo" me, Lucy. You've deceived me for months and now you're asking me to make it official; share you with another person.

'Just answer me this: How would you feel if I suddenly asked you to share me with someone else?'

Lucy spoke. 'What would we all have done if we were in our early teens? At sleepovers?'

'Well, we're not teens and we don't do sleepovers.'

'But that's the point. Age is just an artificial time construct. Why should it constrain us?'

Scully sank deep into thought. 'You really do think it's all child's play, don't you Lucy? Do you realise what's at stake. We're not just talking some kinky escapade like the other night.

'Ever considered the green-eyed monster … how you'd feel if I spent nights with Wanlaya … and you, left in your bed, alone, wondering? And how would Wanlaya feel about it all? Have you even considered her, I mean really thought it all through?'

'More than that, Ludo. We've had sex while fantasising about you. That should tell you something.'

Without another word, Scully left the bungalow, ignoring Lucy's demands to know where he was going.

He strolled along the beach, jealousy and carnality struggling for supremacy in a crowded head. Whether he bowed to Lucy's wishes or not, either option risked losing her to Wanlaya at some stage.

But nothing in life could ever be certain. As Lucy always argued, 'enjoy the moment, Ludo, just go with the flow.'

With that single thought uppermost, Ludo Scully wasn't quite free, but on the way. What the hell! It's not every day that paradise is offered; for however long.

Heading back to the bungalow, he worried that he might have overplayed the 'reluctant bride' bit a little. On the other hand, appearing too accepting would have risked Lucy cooling to the idea. Reflecting heavily, he concluded that he had struck the right note.

For once in his life he was not emerging from a barrel of breasts sucking his thumb.

***

Sucking – along with suspected suffocation – gave Nam Horm its third death in four weeks, claiming Dan Williams on his 96th birthday.

The number itself was deemed highly significant, paving the way for the resort's first direct involvement with the police.

Williams had attached great importance to his big day, loudly observing that 96 reversed was 69, and something 'extra special' might be served up.

After some minor persuasion, the ever-obliging Pu agreed that, yes, a full 69 would be on the day's menu.

A big man in every sense, his carer could not know that Williams' tongue was of a size and dexterity that had delivered huge satisfaction over the years – and she was to be no exception.

Williams, a go-getting city broker in his early life, lost no time in getting down to business. Halfway through the 'meal for two,' his tongue working its penetrative magic, screams of delight escaped from Pu's overfull mouth.

Nothing escaped from Williams' mouth as strong, young thighs fatally tightened their vice-like grip on a head nearly 80 years older.

Detectives and pathologists could not decide whether the sex killed Williams or he'd been suffocated.

The situation was not helped by a number of harsh, red weals across Williams' behind. An ancient schoolboy's uniform, complete with peaked cap, short trousers, socks, tie, shirt and blazer deepened the mystery.

Unknown to anyone, corporal punishment had secretly

inserted itself into Nam Horm, dished out twice a week to the oldest 'schoolboy' on the face of the planet, and no one had suspected a thing.

Every Tuesday and Friday night, Pu, playing the role of headmaster or headmistress, according to mood, would swish her cane menacingly as Williams raised his hand to confess imagined misdemeanours.

Grinningly dementedly from under his cap, Williams owned up to homework cheating, smoking, peeping, penile activity with liver, dead chickens – anything that popped into his endlessly creative head.

Pu, unfamiliar with British public school traditions and numbed by the sight of a 95-year-old squeezed into a 13-year-old's uniform, at first assumed Williams was mad and resisted the charades.

'Why you dress like that, Mr Dan?' she'd protested.

'You papa, not child.'

'No, I am very naughty child who needs to be caned on my bum,' Williams urged.

'Why you want me hit you? You are good man, not bad man.'

'No, Pu, I have been very naughty boy who must be punished. You must hit me on my bum.'

'Maybe you think bad spirit live in bum. Not true, Mr Dan.'

'Yes, is true. Bad spirit lives in my little boy's bum, Pu.'

'I have little bum, not you. You have man's bum.'

'Just cane me, goddamit,' Williams exploded in exasperation. 'Jesus, you can't get the staff these days,' he muttered, almost giving up on the whole idea.

Finally, after days of sensitive negotiations, eased by large tips, Pu relented and settled down to a rota of oral and caning – the true source of the shouts of pain heard by others and falsely blamed on arthritis.

Despite repeated requests, PU found she could not carry

out cane and oral simultaneously. The sight of a 95-year-old schoolboy made it mission impossible for her Thai sense of humour. Laughing with something large in her mouth would not be a good idea.

There were, however, other ticklish requests, calling for great tact and delicacy, that she satisfied.

On visits home, curious parents had noticed Pu stuffing bits of her school-age brother's soiled uniform and underwear into her case.

Initial explanations that she was simply making use of Nam Horm's laundry facilities did not wash entirely. A highly inventive half-truth was also necessary:

Dan Williams missed his schooldays so much that the mere sight of such clothing brought back fond memories, she told her bemused parents.

But they had to be genuine 'in use' items. Newly bought school wear would not look right.

'Mr Dan's old school clothing – now so threadbare that it could not even be washed for fear of disintegration – gave him very little happiness,' she said, smiling gently.

Her brother's soiled clothing – always returned laundry-fresh – filled a vacuum and made 'Mr Dan full of joy. The English are very sentimental,' Pu added.

Had she dropped the 'senti,' Pu would have been on more accurate ground:

Williams had been driven sexually mental at a succession of public schools, picking up enough perversions for a psychoanalysts' conference.

Chief among these was sniffing soiled underwear or uniforms while developing a taste for the cane. Boys' or girls' clothing mattered not. Either would do.

It was his schooldays' legacy, bequeathed by seniors and staff who forced him to sniff their most intimate items while handing out a thrashing.

Many were the hours Pu gazed in wonder as she

administered the cane, Williams' head lost in the heady delights of her young brother's underpants or her own knickers.

Slowly she absorbed the lesson that the great country of England might be somewhat diminished these days, but it could still turn out an erudite and articulate elite who were sexually barking.

***

Although Williams' marks of cane were too old to be an immediate cause of death, pathologists were divided on whether they could have been a contributory factor.

Ratledge was divided about nothing:

'What the hell's a 96-year-old doing licking the pussy of an 18-year-old, for Christ's sake?' he quizzed Scully.

'Have they all gone completely insane out there?'

Scully couldn't give a meaningful answer beyond the significance of 96 and Thai 'special skills.'

'What special skills? He died during a 69-er, maybe couldn't get enough air. End of story.'

'Well, that's just it, Arnie. Air.'

'What are you on about, Ludo?'

Scully sighed. The next bit would not be easy.

'It's their fannies, Arnie. They're not normal.'

'Whaddya mean, not normal? They shag, they give birth. Millions of Thais are living proof.'

'No, no, you don't understand. It's what they do with their fannies. I've seen it with my own eyes in pubs and bars.'

'Seen what?

'Ping- pong balls and all that. They can shoot 'em out.'

'So what. Everyone's heard about that nonsense. What are you telling me? Williams choked on a fucking ping-pong ball?'

'No, Arnie. It's the air. They shoot the balls out by compressing air in their fannies. I suppose it's a bit like us gearing up for a mega-fart.'

'And?'

'Well, here's the really crazy bit. The ping-pong balls are just a by-product of intense fanny exercises.'

'Where's all this going, Ludo? You're giving me a blinding headache.'

'The exercises are all about making their fannies into … well...like vacuum cleaners, so that cocks are sucked in. Why do you think westerners can't keep away from Thailand. Just imagine a sort of reverse fart.'

'Whatever, Ludo.'

'No, it's absolutely true, Arnie. I've seen 'em smoke fags and cigars, drawing air and smoke into their pussies. It's my guess – only a guess, mind – that his carer got carried away and sucked air from Dan's lungs at a key moment.

'If she'd pushed air out, like with the ping-pong balls, she'd have given him the kiss of life and he'd probably still be alive.'

Ratledge was now passed the stage of intelligent listening.

'Ludo, hear this and hear this straight. The conspiracy theorists are back out the woodwork and this time they mean business.

'Their euthanasia bollocks is gaining traction and some even believe we're working hand-in-glove with the Government, softening up the population for culling the old with extreme sex.'

'That's crazy, Arnie.'

'Crazy or not, more and more are buying into it. We have to do something – and quick. Have you had a word with Joe Dean yet?

'No.'

'You're gonna have to. The men themselves need to speak out, saying they're happy, well treated … and … and … well, accidents happen. It's getting serious here.'

***

Joe Dean did not want to feature in any broadcast interviews. His heart-racing bouts of verbal jousting were over, but he had no objection to Scully quoting him.

Relationships at Nam Horm were very much on Dean's mind and Lucy's child analogy found a ready echo.

'You should pay more attention to that missus of yours, Ludo, she seems to have got it right. Yes, we're all into our second childhood and having the time of our lives, even those who've been diagnosed with … well, you name it.

'But there's one big difference of course … when you're a kid you think you'll live forever … at our age every day could be our last … so what the hell does it matter what we get up to.'

'That's dangerous thinking, Joe.'

'Aye, I know. There are still plenty in Britain who, given half a chance, would write us off as dirty old men for even looking at carers this age. They'd love us to go the way of Haven.'

'Well, you'll always get that.'

'Lecherous old European men exploiting young Asian girls … claims of abuse … the PC brigade would be dancing in the streets, Ludo.'

'I can't see anything like that brewing, Joe. Anyway, the vast majority of punters for Thai girls are Asian – many, in fact, Thais.'

'Maybe you don't know this world as well as you think, Ludo. All it takes is some crafty allegation … a department you're supposed to be expert in, according to Ratledge.'

Scully gave Dean a hard stare: 'What do you mean, "crafty," Joe?'

'Let's have a bit of honesty here, Ludo. Yes, Haven was a rotten place and deserved what it got. But not all the staff were bad, and some did their best, despite working in lousy conditions.

'Don't get me wrong, I was more than happy to get out and come here, but the thing is, we did lay it on a bit.'

'Hang on, Joe, you've just admitted the place was rotten. Yeah, we laid it on, but once the media smells blood, that's the way it is. I'm sorry innocent staff got caught up in it all, but the home got what it deserved.'

Dean feared he might have said too much. Ratledge had told him and Malden that no one, including Scully, must know how hyped the allegations were; hyped to the level of invention. Surgical masks had not been worn by staff, and there was no hose-pipe, unless a length of flexible pipe leading to a shower head could be deemed a hose by anyone outside of Ratledge's imagination.

Ratledge had frightened Dean and Malden with warnings that disclosure could result in both men being brought back to Britain to face legal action. Dean rowed back a little:

'That Care Quality Commission, which supposed to keep tabs on care-home abuse – malnutrition, dehydration, deep pressure sores, urine-soaked carpets, that sort of thing – maybe that would have been the route to go, Ludo.'

'Yes, but how many of them actually get closed down, Joe? *Private Eye* investigated it all and exposed it as a farce.'

'You're right, Ludo, very few. But somehow what happened at Haven turned into a feeding frenzy. Everything seemed to be rushed along.'

'I know, Joe. Arnie was in trouble, saw an opportunity to make a comeback and we are where we are. You know what he's like.'

'And that's what bothers me, Ludo. His path to fame and fortune has always been via useful idiots like you and me on the left. He could just as easily have been a ranter of the right.

'They're all bullshitters, claiming to protect one lot of people from some other lot and spouting garbage. You know, when I was a young lad I was made to feel guilty for doing a fucking crossword. An old socialist I respected used to bollock me for it.

'"A waste of brain power, comrade," he'd rant, wagging his finger while he quietly feathered his nest. He was another Benny.'

'Benny?'

Dean smiled.

'That's my private nickname for Arnie. Benilyn, you must have heard of it. Loosens phlegm, helps you cough it up?'

Scully nodded, idly wondering why phlegm was entering his life again so soon after the Malden incident.'

'Benilyn's an expectorant. Geddit?'

Scully looked blank. Dean looked disappointed.

'I thought you were sharper than that, Ludo.

'Every time Arnie speaks you can ... "expect a rant" ... sounds like "expectorant" ... Benilyn ... and so ... Benny.

'God, I don't know why I bother sometimes.'

'Sorry, Joe, my mind was on phlegm. So why do we fall for it every time?'

'They're very good readers of people, Ludo. They know our weak spots. Arnie told me how you're guilt ridden over your mother's care-home death, so who better to wind up over care homes.

Scully smiled, staring at the floor. 'There's truth in what you say, Joe. I still feel guilty about what I did to my best mate, Harold, as a kid.

'Like Ratledge, I could also be very persuasive, even when speaking pure crap. I convinced Harold to fight me. I'd have an air pistol and he'd have five elastic bands strung between the struts of chairs.'

'Was he retarded?'

'No. I just stressed that he had five weapons to my one. I let him wear his glasses so he didn't get shot in the eye accidentally. I wouldn't wear any.

'"But you don't wear glasses anyway," Harold protested. That's just the point, I said. You're going into this battle with more protection than me. If one of your pellets hits me in the eye, I might end up with worse eyesight than you. With a name like Harold, eyes were a sensitive subject.'

'How the hell did it end?'

'I hit him with a lead pellet in the leg. Tears and yelps, but no lasting damage, thankfully.'

'Come on, Ludo, you were a kid at the time. We all do daft things.'

'Yes, but I knew it was wrong and still went ahead. Same during the strike. I knew, deep down, that something wasn't right, but I upped the persuasiveness – the propaganda – to win at any price.

'All those men and women who lost their jobs, communities ruined, drugs rife. It didn't have to happen. There was a compromise out there somewhere.'

'Come on, it's time to let go, old lad.'

Scully's smile turned sad.

'Funny, I was in my own way beginning to do just that … let go … when Arnie rang me here, at Nam Horm. I had a sort of premonition that I should put the phone down. I'm beginning to wish I had.'

'Well, I'm bloody glad you didn't...I wouldn't be here having the time of my life.'

'I don't know, Joe. There are some nasty buggers out there. Care-home business is very big, worth billions. What's to stop the so-called professionals with the real financial muscle from stepping in?

'We could be back to square one in terms of abusive care – only this time in the sun and away from prying western eyes.'

'Well, no one knows what's round the corner, Ludo. All we can do is seize the moment, get stuck in and enjoy the time we have.'

'Yes, that's what Lucy keeps saying.'

Scully stepped into the warm, night air and swatted an unfortunate mosquito dining on his arm a fraction of a second too long. No one could guarantee anything; nothing certain. Others just did a better job of living with the fact. And life might still offer sweet compensation.

The regular evening jet from Singapore crossed the star-studded sky, prompting idle dreams of joy-riding tourists in open-top aircraft, while on earth four arms waited to welcome 'their' pilot back home.

12

Tape Worms

Highly sensitised to the slightest variations in political temperature, Ratledge's suspicions were confirmed by feedback from the new offices of Arco, his consultancy company.

Organisations – mainly councils, but even some reputable care homes keen to spread their wings – were beginning to peel away.

Where advice and guidance had once been eagerly sought, now the phones rang mainly to say 'unexpected' snags were putting plans on hold.

Embryonic networks embracing administration, finance, insurance, health, overseas staffing and air transport (Scully had strongly advised dropping Troika, without going into detail), now languished in a no-man's land as key decision makers hesitated.

Ratledge was in no doubt that the mere mention of the word 'euthanasia' had spooked the powers in the land. Organised religion now joined the fray.

Already upset at Nam Horm's 'loose morals,' the 'euthanasia' target was too tempting to ignore, and high-minded statements about the sanctity of life did the rounds.

Stanley Vincent brought Ratledge back to earth, entering his office with a sheaf of council papers to sign.

Ratledge got through them in a blur, the signature seemingly increasing in size with each document. Normally such occasions were silent affairs, but Vincent spoke.

'I don't know whether anyone's ever told you, Arnie, but it's often said that the bigger the signature, the greater the ego.'

Ratledge stopped in mid-signature, surprised by his finance officer's effrontery. He had no doubts that Vincent hated him, but he had always been deferential – not to him personally, he knew that – but to the office he held.

'When I want your opinion on my signature or my psychological make-up, I'll ask for it, Stanley. In the meantime, please keep your views about me to yourself.'

'You mean the same way you keep your views about me to yourself, Arnie?'

Ratledge looked stunned. The man he always described as DC – the 'dried cod' – was apparently in revolt. 'Is something eating you, Stanley?'

'Yes there is, actually. You. I don't like the way you talk about me and I think it's about time you showed me a little respect.'

Ratledge's eyes narrowed. 'What do you mean, the way I talk about you? How would you know?' Vincent came close to a smile.

'Have you been spying on me? Have you been listening in on me? Hang on, are you the one that bugged me, you bastard?'

Ratledge stood up, face puce, fists clenched. 'Oh, I taped you all right, Arnie, but you should thank me for it.'

'What the fuck are you talking about, you … you...'

'Go on, say it, Arnie, DC, "dried cod," how you described me to Ludo Scully.'

'You mean you've listened to my Thai calls?'

'Yes, listened in and taped every one – and not just the Thai calls.'

Ratledge grabbed Vincent by the lapels. 'Your dried cod's arse is within an ace of going through that fucking window.'

'For a so-called leader of men, you're really not that bright are you, Arnie? No wonder the strike was lost.'

'What?'

'I wasn't the person who released that euthanasia tape. Whoever did, obviously started recording you half way through your conversation with Scully – or doctored the tape.

'I've got the whole conversation and it's perfectly clear you and Scully are talking about a publication. The tape kills stone dead any idiotic suspicion of euthanasia; it's your saviour, Arnie, and it's safely locked away with other interesting items.

'Now I suggest you remove your hands from my lapels, calm yourself down and pour us both a couple of drinks. Your special reserve malt, if you please. Then we can both sit down and discuss terms.'

'Are you blackmailing me?'

'No, of course not. That's a despicable thought. Blackmail is a threat to release damaging information about someone.

'This is something completely different. It's about releasing positive information on someone. I suppose the correct term would be "whitemail." Yes, that sounds about right. Wouldn't you agree. Arnie?'

Ratledge sank into his leather chair, drummed his fingers on the desk and waited, vainly, for Vincent to say more.

'How long have you been taping me?'

'Ever since you started taking an interest in this care home business. I wasn't going to shoulder any more blame for you, if it all went wrong. Those days are gone forever.'

'I trusted you!'

'Trusted me? You've never trusted anyone, Arnie.

'At heart, you think the rest of the world is down at your level. And that's why you treat them like dirt. Alone in bed at night – when you can't pay someone enough money to sleep with you – the truth has to dawn that you're a scheming slime ball.'

Ratledge rose.

'Go on, Arnie, have a go. Let's see what happens. I have

enough hate for you to …' Ratledge resumed his seat.

'So no punch-up, then?

'Speaking of which, I should mention there's also a tape of you arranging the £20,000 pay-off for that guy who lost Scully his most important client. It's filed under The Punch Affair. If Scully ever found out and got his hands on you …'

Ratledge eyed Vincent intently, taking deep breaths in a determined effort to control his racing pulse, trying to understand how 'the dried cod' could possibly have outsmarted him.

'What's Scully got to do with all this?' he demanded, all pretence at civility stripped from the conversation.

Vincent was lifted by Ratledge's agitation, and he hoped the stress might lead to some medical problem, nothing too serious until the conclusion of business.

'Quite a lot really. I only met Scully a handful of times, but I liked him. In fact I felt quite sorry for him.'

'He does all right,' Ratledge interrupted. Vincent brushed the intervention aside.

'Well I think his life's been messed up by politics. More precisely, your rabble-rousing tripe. But that's what you do, isn't it, Arnie? You wreck lives.'

'What would you know about it all. You're just a glorified clerk who learned to add up.'

Vincent felt murderous, but remained in the driving seat, steering the conversation.

'And all for what, Arnie? Your power? Your wealth? Last I heard you were worth millions. Wonder what those strikers would think.'

Ratledge said nothing and tugged irritably at his shirt collar.

'But that's only monetary value, Arnie. Truth be told, as a person you're worthless.'

'I've had enough of this crap. Piss off out this office.'

'Oh, I don't think so. If you want that tape, you'll hear

me out. You see, I always made it my business to have a few beers with Ludo whenever he flew across. He felt like the son I always wished I'd had. A decent lad, not just another rung up your ladder.'

'Cut the sermon and just tell me what you want,' Ratledge snarled.

Shaking his head, Vincent paused to top up his own glass, cheekily offering some to Ratledge who gloweringly waved it away.

'You always were a pig-ignorant listener, Arnie. I'll tell you exactly what I want when I'm ready.'

The fresh shot of whisky had added a purplish hue to Vincent's face and now there was only contempt in his eyes.

'The last time Ludo flew over he told me he was thinking about selling his PR business. I kept quiet about what you'd done to him, although the temptation to tell was enormous. I felt like a shit for keeping my mouth shut.

'And now, Arnie, guess what. It's pay-back time.'

'Oh, is that right, Stanley? And what exactly do you propose to do? I'm quaking in my shoes.'

'In return for the tapes, you are going to encourage Ludo to put his business up for sale. He expects to get around £150,000, at best. But you're going to pay him £500,000.'

'You're stark, raving mad.'

'You think so, do you, Arnie? You seem to be forgetting that you're talking to someone who knows a bit about money and what it does to people.'

'OK, just to humour you for a minute, what makes you think Ludo would want half a million?'

'Why did you want your millions?'

'I'm not saying I've got that much, but just suppose I have, I'm down in your books as greedy, right?'

'Right.'

'So for me that would be in character. But obviously you don't know Ludo as well as you think you do. He's not really interested in money. Just enough to have a roof over his head, eat, drink and a pretty woman by his side.

'That's Ludo made happy. The bare necessities. Frankly, I could never understand it.'

'No, and you never will, Arnie. But there's one thing you're forgetting.'

'Yeah and what's that?'

'Everyone's got a dream. You know he's a pilot, of course?'

'So, what of it?'

'Well, if you'd ever taken the trouble to really know the man, you might have uncovered a little fancy he's been entertaining for years.' Ratledge feigned a yawn.

'We were on a North East Coast pub crawl, heading towards Scotland. For some crazy reason, he wanted to find the exact pub where the Geordie accent turned Scottish.

'I was driving and sober, he steadily got more drunk, sometimes insisting I double back so that the twang in some pub could be re-checked. In fact he nearly got thumped, hopelessly mimicking a Glaswegian accent to test the response.

'Each stop equalled a drink, until he'd had so much that everything spilled out.'

Ratledge again signalled boredom with a second manufactured yawn.

'He told me that after the strike all he'd wanted to do was buy a private airstrip somewhere, a couple of cheap, second-hand planes and take passengers up for short joyrides. But his dream faded with time as cost estimates rose.

'Funny how life works out, but it's your care-home project that's re-awakened his dream.

'"You know, Stan," he said, "I reckon I could do it on Samui for about half a million; now wouldn't that be something. Flying tourists around the island.

'"I don't really believe I'll ever see a half a million, but if this care-home business were truly to take off, who knows.

Don't get me wrong, Stan, I didn't get involved for the money, but I suppose we've all got our dreams …"

'Well, Arnie, he is going to see that half million and it's coming straight out of your pocket!'

'And what will you do if I tell you to fuck off?'

'Destroy the euthanasia tape, naturally, and as an added bonus, let Ludo have the other tape, the one in which you effectively set about destroying his business.'

'Got you, you bastard. That's blackmail.'

'Fine, Arnie, give the police a ring. I'll even repeat what I've said in front of them. Again, you're not thinking clearly.

'Ask yourself, who's got most to lose if it all comes out in court? And who, potentially, has got most to gain if the full "euthanasia" tape is released? A lot of money could be at stake. You'd be gambling half a million against an added fortune.

'On the other hand, release of the second tape could cost you more than money. Ludo's a nice, gentle lad, but like all of us, he's got a temper. I know how I'd react if someone deliberately sabotaged my business.

'As I say, Arnie, there could be more than money at stake here. I should weigh the odds very, very carefully. This is no game of poker, no bluffing, all cards are on the table.'

'And you want nothing for yourself?'

'No money, not a penny, Arnie. Just a signed piece of paper saying that the state of Wigburn's finances is in no way my fault and that throughout the Iceland crisis and the chastity-belt nonsense I acted on your instructions, even when you chose to ignore my professional advice.

'I think that will do. I'm off for a bite now, Arnie. I'll be back in an hour. I expect an answer by then – or to be in the company of the local constabulary.

'Just one more thing. Moving large sums of money around is a tricky business these days. The terrorists have made it awkward for everyone. But I've worked out a plan to deal with that.'

'Yes, I'll bet you have,' Ratledge half muttered as Vincent placed his glass on the edge of the huge desk, deliberately ignoring the coaster, and made for the door.

Ratledge stared at the mockingly placed tumbler as the door closed. 'I never thought the bastard had it in him.'

The sound of smashed glass was just audible to Stanley Vincent as he smiled his way to the lift, a man reborn.

***

'I've a condition of my own,' Ratledge announced when Vincent returned, 10 minutes late.

'Thought you might.'

'Our working relationship is finished. I want you to leave – early retirement, voluntary redundancy – whatever grounds you like, but I want you out of here ASAP. The terms will be generous.'

'I'm ahead of you, Arnie. Why do you think I asked for that piece of paper? I've no wish to be in your company a moment longer than absolutely necessary. I want to rejoin the human race.'

'So what genius plans have you come up with for moving the … the …'

'Go on, spit it out, Arnie, the money.'

'Well, I'm waiting.'

'Oh, dear, my glass seems to be missing, Arnie. Fetch me another one, there's a good chap.'

'Don't push your fucking luck, sunshine.'

'Such bad manners.'

Ratledge could hear his own heart pounding as he reached into a glass-fronted cabinet and slammed a whisky tumbler down on the desk.

Vincent poured himself a modest measure, leisurely, and this time declined to offer Ratledge any. Finally he spoke.

'Once Scully's business goes on the market – without any

price specified – just a Price-on-Application tag, a newly-formed front company, with no trace back to you, will put in a bid.

'This company will be presented as an aggressive foreign-based outfit, keen to break into the lucrative British PR market and wanting to acquire an established firm with connections in the cosmetics industry.'

'Ludo's not a complete financial idiot,' Ratledge said. 'He'll still wonder why he's being offered way over the odds.'

'I was coming to that.

'The cosmetics industry is worth billions and fiercely competitive. You should read your *Financial Times* more closely. With a bit of subtlety and finesse it shouldn't be too difficult to give Ludo the impression that the acquisition is part of a bigger battle in the industry, but cloaked in secrecy.

'You know the game, Arnie. Or are you just trying to talk the half million down?' Ratledge said nothing.

'The company needs to be set up now – and I'm not bothered which one of your foreign accounts you use. The funds must be in place and ready for transfer the moment Ludo's company's sold.'

'Who said anything about foreign accounts?'

'You really know nothing about your old staff, Arnie. Who the hell do you think told me? The only mystery is why your staff never blew you out the water years ago.'

Ratledge again sized up his finance officer. 'All bullshit, of course, Stanley, but no doubt you've got some fancy theory.'

'Misplaced loyalty, I would guess, Arnie. Confusing you with the union membership; and you still exploit it, via left-wing idiots, mostly in the media. A genuine human tragedy.'

Both men remained silent.

'There's work to be done,' Vincent announced, and without another word left Ratledge's office, business concluded. Three hours later Scully rang, rounding off a very bad day indeed for Wigburn's Mayor.

The Readers, Mick and Eric, were no more. Nam Horm had recorded its first double death in circumstances that defied any rational assessment.

Ratledge picked at his left nostril furiously, a lifelong nervous habit acquired when confronting bad or disturbing news. This time he drew blood.

***

The Readers had presented an unusual problem for Nam Horm. Both seemed oblivious to the beauty of their carers, showing them not the faintest romantic interest.

This was not good news for the girls who could see no pot of gold during, or at the end of, Mick and Eric's lives. Their beauty was being needlessly squandered on morons.

For all The Readers cared, a couple of chimps could have been looking after them.

Depressed and bored, the carers, Phalasuk and Bunrakham, suffered in silence each day, listening to the constant chants as Mick and Eric charged through some book's pages.

It was Eric's carer, the unfortunately-named Phalasuk, who first noticed that the pair's insane competitiveness was not limited to meaningless reading.

Two dart boards had been installed which, at the shout of 'Go!' each Reader tried to race round. As with the reading, finishing first was all that mattered; skill, of no concern whatever.

No real aim was taken, just flurry after furious flurry of darts, sometimes all three at once, thrown wildly at the board in the vague direction of 1, 2 and so on.

The more darts thrown, the greater the chance of getting round the board first, they reasoned, although, in truth, the capacity to reason had long since died in both men.

'All that matters is coming first in everything,' Phalasuk noted, sowing seeds for the oddest sex story in the history of Nam Horm, Koh Samui and possibly the whole of Thailand.

Mick and Eric had gradually been persuaded that an innocent massage was good for their health, but both wanted their individual carer to finish first.

Slowly, very slowly, a little friskiness crept in as the carers took tiny risks, hands brushing against genitalia. Initial, blank responses set the girls wondering whether both men were asexual.

The breakthrough, when it came, was both startling and yet utterly predictable as the girls' hands wandered.

'Hey, Mick, me willy's gone bigger,' Eric shouted through the open, adjoining door.

'That's nowt. Mine went bigger about two minutes ago,' Mick shot back.

Progress from then on was rapid, with Eric and Mick racing each other through the stages of 'asleep,' 'awake,' 'bigger,' still soft,' 'hard,' 'right hard,' and finally, 'bloody hell, there's some sticky stuff coming out.'

It was difficult to tell who was more relieved – Readers or carers.

After that, the massages followed a simpler pattern, with 'sticky stuff' the only acceptable finishing line. As an exercise in logic, it was unchallengeable: The winner always came first.

And, as with the book pages, progress reports were fine:

'I've just got to bigger, Mick, where are you?'

'That's nowt, Eric, I'm already at right hard.'

Bitter arguments over dead heats were at one stage resolved by having a third carer, positioned exactly half way through the adjoining door, adjudicating.

Word filtered through to Visit Vatayanon who immediately banned the use of extra carers for 'our two very strange guests.' It would add to staffing costs unnecessarily.

It was his last act before taking himself off to a sanatorium for a week of much-needed rest and reflection. He would never set eyes on the Readers again.

Eric, desperate to get to 'sticky stuff' first after losing three 'bouts' in succession, made a supreme effort that cost him a catastrophic brain haemorrhage, dying within the hour.

Phalasuk was distraught. Mick was devastated and could see no purpose in life without his long-time competitor.

That evening he washed down a bottle of Aspirin with a pint of whisky, leaving a note with a simple request:

'If Eric's body is being sent back to Britain, could someone please ensure I go with him – and my body's unloaded first!' Tears of mixed emotions overcame Nam Horm.

With Scully's full account of the deaths still ringing in his ears, Ratledge went into his office toilet to wipe off the dry nose blood staining his tie and shirt. The wash basin mirror reflected a lost man.

Yes, The Readers had been seriously unhinged, the result of some wartime trauma when they raced each other to a bomb shelter, Scully had found out.

But how could that translate into a deadly sexual competition? Could Thai women be so desirable they made old men court death in their battle to demonstrate superior virility.

Ratledge remembered his own bouts of 'cock-fighting,' when it was 'game on' to see who could pee highest in the school lavatories. Starting from a modest base, he never won.

Defeat also stared him in the face during winter when school pals competed to see who could pee their entire first names in the snow. Lucky bastards named Ian or Roy always won. With a name like Arnold, he had no chance. Life could be so unfair, but at least it was innocent stuff. This was of a different order.

'Jesus, that's five dead in under seven weeks,' he told himself.

'At this rate there'll be no one left in about six months.'

***

In the offices of the *Wigburn Sentinel*, Editor Ken Corner had also done his sums.

An 'import' from Yorkshire, forever bitter at his ex-Sheffield paper's decision not to send a reporter to Russia to cover the first Briton in space – Sheffielder Helen Sharman – he now feared that once again he was running a local paper that was about to miss the big one.

Corner had pleaded with his bosses to send an undercover man to Nam Horm, someone who could pass off as a resident and get the real inside story.

The prudish owners resisted, claiming it would be too expensive and complicated, and anyway it would all be a little distasteful, sordid even, for the *Sentinel*.

Corner neared despair, arguing that Nam Horm, keen to recoup lost revenue from the deaths, would surely be looking for replacement residents; a perfect opportunity to slip someone under the wire.

He'd even fashioned a plausible three-part cover story:

*The reporter could pose as someone administering his own Personal Care Budget, and therefore free to choose how the cash was spent.

*Being from Wigburn, he'd obviously taken a special interest in Nam Horm, and as he was holidaying in Thailand, he'd like to give it a try. The juiciest bit of the bait was left till last:

*If he liked it, he wouldn't even bother going back to Britain. Relatives, who helped him administer his budget, could sort out all the paper work and send on his personal possessions. And, as a goodwill gesture, he would even pay two months' care costs in advance.

Reluctantly, the owners agreed that Corner had come up with a workable plan, before falling back on the argument that it was all a waste of time because there was no reporter old enough to carry it off.

And then someone, Corner thought it was the managing

editor, muttered the name Horace Hides.

Corner pounced. 'Hides, of course, yes, our invisible man.'

***

Horace Humphrey Hides was 78, but could easily pass for 98, such was his take on life or, more accurately, death.

Since retiring early with a serious heart condition, he came into the *Sentinel* building one day a week, updating obituaries in a tiny, musty office that had glimpsed neither word processor nor computer.

A phone and an ancient typewriter was its only nod to communications technology.

Young reporters, kept in ignorance, would occasionally wonder at the gentle tap, tap, tap of the typewriter, usually on a Monday, and speculate about ghosts and old hacks.

Very few people actually saw Hides in the flesh – what was left of it.

First in and last out, he simply beavered away, making sure that no notable Wigburner, and the bar was set exceptionally low – successful flower-arrangers, egg-and-spoon-race victors – would die without the *Sentinel* recording the smallest details of their lives.

Hides had been doing this for as long as anyone could remember after coming down from the dizzy heights of cheque presentations, dog trials and inquests; the perfect companion-in-waiting for the dead.

Hides had not been keen, his wife even less so, but four days later, pockets stuffed with cash, he climbed aboard a Thai-bound Jumbo, Corner's detailed briefing still ringing in his ears.

His foreign horizons were at last stretching beyond the usual fortnight in Belgium's Blankenberg.

***

Ratledge, still very much focussed on sex and death, empathised with Scully's decision to sell his business, taking care not to overdo the fake 'concern.' In moments of great delicacy, it was important there was not the faintest whiff of rat.

The line about not stating a price was smoothly delivered – and swallowed:

'It's up to you, of course, Ludo, but if I were in your position, I'd just sniff out the market. You never know what's out there. When they make contact, get them to post a written bid, and see what happens.'

'I suppose you're right, Arnie,' Scully conceded. 'It can't do any harm.'

'No it can't, Ludo,' he said, his words out of kilter with his dominant thought:

'You're getting half a million pounds of my money, you prick. I might as well at least get maximum kudos out of it.'

Days later, when the offer emerged, Lucy and Scully stared in disbelief, eyes glued to the impressively-headed notepaper. Both suspected a sick hoax.

Straining to control the tremble in his voice, Scully rang the Luxembourg number, seeking verbal confirmation.

'Yes, Mr Scully, we confirm our offer, but we must insist on the greatest confidentiality. The beauty industry is a world of intense competition, and I'm sure you will respect our wishes.'

'Of course, Mr Barnes, I understand. I will have the necessary papers prepared and we should be able to complete the sale by the end of the month.'

'Yes, that's important. We live in a fast moving environment and time is money.'

Part-time actor, general gofer and petty criminal Alan Barnes (AKA Lawrie Hunt), had played his part to perfection and followed Ratledge's instructions to a t.

He did think his £5,000 payment was a little stingy,

though. Still, mustn't grumble.

After all, he'd hardly made a dent in the £5,000 from Ratledge's last, far simpler, commission – delivering £20,000 to that Crowther bloke for nobbling the same Luscu PR company that he was now making an inflated £500,000 offer for.

The business world, eh! Who would ever understand it?

'Well, Lucy, this changes everything,' Scully said. 'If it all goes through, I'm going to buy that airstrip and we can live as we want to.'

'I need to talk to you, Ludo.'

'Yeah, sure, but first I've got to ring Arnie. You know, he gave me some really good advice. He didn't have to do that. Maybe he's not such a sod after all.'

'Aaaah, Ludo, Ludo, you always want to see the best in people...'

'Is that such a bad thing?'

'No, I suppose not, but it gets you hurt, love.'

Ratledge milked Scully's appreciation and feigned surprise at the speed and size of the offer. Each day that went by was costing him political capital, as the euthanasia tag dogged all his attempts to expand the care-home project. A rapid conclusion was judged very much in his interests.

'I know we've had our differences in the past, comrade ...' he now felt secure enough to resurrect the sacred word at will ... 'but I wouldn't tell you wrong, Ludo.

'I don't know much about the PR business, but if, as you say, that represents a shedload, you'd be crackers not to take it. And you'd still be able to do your work for me.'

'Well, the point is, Arnie, I'm planning to branch out if it all goes through. Obviously I'll still do some work for you, and tie up loose ends like the body business. Hancock must be like a block of bloody ice by now. The lawyers and bureaucrats are clogging everything up at the moment, and plod's getting involved. Complications we could do without.

'Anyway, the fact is I'm feeling like a bit of a shit. Your advice about not naming a price was crucial. Without that, I wouldn't be able to follow a dream I've always had: Flying tourists around the island, joyrides, that sort of stuff.'

'I understand, Ludo. We can still work together while you get it all off the ground. And I'm sure there'll be plenty for us to do in the future, if the lawyers and bureaucrats over there are anything to go by. Just let's see how it all pans out, eh!

'Listen, there are no hard feelings – sometimes, as the cowboys say, a man's gotta do …'

'Thanks, Arnie. You know, I can't understand why the bureaucrats are dragging their feet over the deaths. The only ones benefitting are the lawyers.'

'There's your answer. The more paperwork, the better for them. There'll be some backhanders flying around.'

'You really think that, Arnie?'

'I do. Look, Ludo, this death business needs sorting double quick. It's costing a fortune, driving me bonkers, and the media just won't let go. Can't you at least get some ugly women in so there are no more deaths. Give KKSA's lot a holiday or something … a wank holiday.'

'I think not, Arnie. Old they might be, but there'd be a fucking riot if we tried to take their carers away. This Wigburn lot are really something else.'

13

Lift off

'Unbelievable, Lucy. Couldn't believe I was talking to the same man. It was as though he'd had some sort of epiphany. Even cracked a joke.'

'Long overdue, after everything you've done for him, Ludo. You don't value yourself enough; that's always been your problem.'

'Yeah, maybe not. Anyway, you wanted to talk.'

Lucy seated herself on the floor, semi-cross-legged, in what Scully took to be a half-baked Yoga position

'If this offer is genuine and you get your airstrip, what would happen between us?'

'What do you mean?'

'I think you know what I'm talking about, Ludo, our living arrangements.'

'Obviously there'd be a house near the strip, and that's where we'd live.'

'But say it was on the other side of the island – you know what state the roads are in – how would I get to see … to see … Wanlaya?'

'You're jumping the gun a bit, aren't you. I've agreed nothing about sharing you with anyone. I told you I'd think about it, nothing more. You talk about me not valuing myself enough. Is it any wonder?'

Lucy corrected, 'It wasn't just you who said he'd think about it. It was to be both of us, remember.'

'OK, so?'

'You're probably not going to like this, Ludo, but you mentioned jealousy, the green-eyed monster, and you were right to warn about it.'

Lucy blinked nervously. Scully feared the worst.

'You guessed correctly that I would be the problem, Ludo, not you. I've thought about it again and again. The idea of you and Wanlaya together – the two people I love and long for – without me, would be too much to bear.

'I would go crazy. Sometimes I think you know me better than I know myself.'

'So that kills all that then, Lucy?' Scully said, the taste of thumb choking his words.

'Well, no, actually it doesn't.'

'How do you mean?'

'The only way through – and I'm sure you'll call me the world's most selfish bitch – is for a special arrangement: Every permutation – except you and Wanlaya alone.'

'Jesus, Lucy, what are you asking? To give up part of you … a part of your life … in fact, a chunk of my own life?'

Lucy stayed focussed:

'But in return you get a part of someone else's life. The mere thought of her enjoying uninhibited sessions with both of us has Wanlaya breathing heavily.'

'Come on, Lucy, save the carrots for donkeys.'

'No, I'm serious. Yes, she prefers women, but she has a powerful itch to enjoy the both of us together. And it's not just the sex. She thinks you're witty, funny, clever and basically a kind man – although a little strange.

'Oddly, she often says how much her father likes you.'

'I find that hard to believe,' Ludo said, his brain feverishly calculating the remaining coupling permutations as he mentally gave himself a thorough kicking for ever planting the seed of Lucy's jealousy.

'No, Ludo, she says her old man's genuine about it.'

Scully spoke with great care, desperate not to blast a second hole in his foot. He feigned weariness.

'I don't think I'll ever really understand these people,

Lucy. In fact, I'm not sure I'll ever understand anyone on this planet.'

'Maybe, but whatever you do, don't underestimate Wanlaya. Behind all that innocent, butter-in-mouth exterior, her language skills and razor-sharp business brain, beats a sexual heat that could melt the Polar ice cap; she's a one-girl, global-warming threat, only this one's absolutely genuine.'

'So what if I refuse, what then? Do you prefer her to me? Am I getting an ultimatum here?'

'No, but what I'm asking is this. If it all goes through and you get your airstrip, but we end up on the other side of the island, then I'd like to see Wanlaya at least a couple of times a week.

'One day she travels to where we are, next, I travel to hers. Of course the ideal solution would be a house for the three of us near the airstrip.

'That would be a wonderful life, sharing the chores, growing our own fruit and veg, helping with the flight administration ... but of course Wanlaya's father would never agree to her leaving the family business.'

'Oh I don't know, Lucy, with the powers of persuasion you two have, I get the feeling the old man would agree to disembowel himself if you both worked on him.'

Lucy laughed. Scully maintained his serious air, exercising extreme caution. Overdoing it this time could blow forever the prospect of an occasional *menage a trois* that might just work.

'I still need time to think,' he said, but very softly.

***

Horace Hides could not believe the heat coming at him from all directions.

The air temperature in Bangkok had been suffocating, but now a different kind of heat stirred as he walked the capital's gaudy streets alone.

Women, and others he was not quite sure about, showered him with invitations to join them, sparking feelings of unease and deeply-buried longings.

In the dim and distant past, a polite cough had signalled his peak of ardour during husbandly duties. This belonged to a different world.

Against his better judgment, Hides finally allowed himself to be half frog-marched through the doors of a sex club by two smiling ladies.

Paying for endless rounds of drinks as they massaged his boney thighs, Hides was treated to a swift lesson in multi-tasking.

Girls on stage peeled bananas, painted pictures, wrote letters and performed conjuring tricks from the same sort of place his head had emerged 78 years ago.

Top billing was given to a slightly older performer who pulled a string of razors from her vagina, using them to fashion a perfect aircraft out of paper. Origami at its most original. Cheered on by the crowd, she glided her creation into Hides' lap.

Hides bolted for the club door, face crimson, and headed straight for the airport, boarding the first available flight to Koh Samui.

The short hop gave him time to reflect on what he had seen, and he prayed there was nothing similar at Nam Horm.

There had, however, been one entertainment – relegated to a corner of the club as a background sideshow – that he could live with if practised at Nam Horm: The Sandwich.

The image was still fresh: Two young girls, oiled and naked, rubbing themselves along the entire length of a nude man, one on each side. Rude, of course, but quite interesting in its own way.

The sandwich rekindled the unfamiliar heat and his pacemaker rebelled – disturbing the rhythm of the pace and risking an early meeting with his 'Maker.'

***

Visit Vatayanon, desperately keen to replace the dead, readily accepted Hides' cover story.

Within three days of being on the island, he was sleeping in the late Eric's bed, looked after by Phalasuk who had just learned her now silent Reader had left her nothing.

She resolved that would not be the case with Horace Hides and immediately set about pleasing him.

Gentle, affectionate care graduated to real friendship and then more as Hides effectively forgot about his undercover mission and began to live life instead of death.

Corner's calls to send stories were deflected with a terse, 'still investigating' which, technically, was true.

But the investigation was into himself and all the delights he'd missed in what he now considered a wasted life.

Repeated heart murmurs grew into grumbles and then shouts as his sexual awakening graduated from cuddles and hand relief to an ever-expanding menu.

The longed-for big one, the 'sandwich,' finally became possible only after Phalasuk persuaded Bunrakham to give it a go. She, too, was bitter that her dead Reader had left her nothing.

Date chosen, a whole evening was set aside. Hours earlier, Hides, suspecting he might not survive, sensibly drafted the most important obituary of his life: His own.

The primary destination was to be the *Sentinel*, but fearing censorship, copies were made for the news desks of every national paper in Britain.

Instructions to Phalasuk were clear: If he croaked on the sandwich, the prepared envelopes were to be posted immediately, and she would be well rewarded. Phalasuk needed no other incentive.

The obit opened:

'Long-serving *Wigburn Sentinel* reporter Horace Hides,

who has died at the age of 78 while working undercover in Thailand, was a man who believed he had found his true calling late in life.

'Eyes opened by the fleshpots of the Far East, he memorably suggested to the Nam Horm care home he was investigating that they erect a sign over the front entrance, reading:

GIVE US YOUR OLD AND YOUR SICK
AND WE'LL STIFFEN THEIR DICK

'He never did complete his investigation into the home where a spate of Expat deaths generated wide concern in the UK.

'Hides, who leaves a wife, Victoria – the couple were childless – was known for his shy, retiring nature, a reputation he came to regret, according to acquaintances at Nam Horm.

'"Thailand opened his eyes and unzipped his trousers to what might have been," one fellow resident remembered.

"He bitterly regretted not living a more adventurous sex life."

'Shortly before his death, Hides attacked UK Government adviser Martin Green for raising the issue of assisted deaths for elderly dementia patients.

'"It's not help to die that the elderly need, but help to live in a fashion and style they want," he wrote in a letter to the Bangkok Post.

'"It might shorten life, but whether it's sex, booze, parachuting, biking or whatever, the old should have the right to choose the pace and circumstances in which they live out their final years."

'The circumstances of Hides' death, understood to have involved some sexual activity, are still under investigation.

'**NOTE FOR SENTINEL EDITOR ONLY: My full obit is in the second drawer down in the fawn filing cabinet in my office. It needs amending to record that on August 11 last* *year I came second in the All-comers Lancashire leek-growing competition. I intended an update but other matters intervened.*

'Horace Humphrey Hides.'

***

Hides' final evening on earth had not got off to a promising start. At 7pm on the dot, Phalasuk and Bunrakham entered his room, bathrobes concealing olive bodies glistening with coconut oil.

Both girls understood the vital role packaging played in any sandwich and wore the flimsiest of briefs, topped by gossamer-thin bras restraining small but cheekily engaging breasts.

At six minutes past 7, as Hides was feverishly undoing his second bra, reception rang. Victoria Hides was calling from England and needed to speak to her husband urgently.

'What's going on, Horace?' she demanded.

'Nothing, dear,' he assured through short, shallow breaths as the hooks finally gave way, revealing nipples erect enough to stab with.

'Nothing? You've been out there for weeks and no one's had a word out of you. Your office doesn't tell me anything. Are you in some sort of trouble?'

'Not at all, I'm in the pink.'

'Well you don't sound it to me.'

'What do you mean?' Hides gasped as his free hand gently tugged down Phalasuk's panties, revealing pink to complement the olive.

'You sound like you're having trouble breathing.'

'It's just the heat ... nothing ... I'm trying to grab a sandwich ... can I ring you back ...'

'Sandwich? Well, I hope you're not having butter. You know how bad it is for you. Gives you heartburn and wind.'

'It's not butter ... aaah ... aaah ... for heaven's sake ... aaah ... it's oil ...' Hides managed.

'Horace, I'm worried, you don't sound right to me.'

'Phwoar … I'm struggling with the … oooh … sandwich packaging …' he said, making his third one-handed attempt to pull Bunrakham's briefs down.

'All this trouble for a sandwich. What's in it? Caviar?'

'Meat.'

'What meat?'

'Thai meat. How should I know.'

'Well what colour is it?'

Bunrakham's briefs snapped, along with Hides' patience.

'Olive; pink in the middle. And I'm now gonna tuck in. Goodbye.'

They were the last words Hides ever spoke to his wife of 55 years, slamming the phone down and disconnecting it.

For the next half hour loud cries of 'Yes, do it … squeeze me like a pip … on the bottom … aaaah … turn round … no, not you, you … slide right down … oh yes … nipples there … rub, keep rubbing … good girl … get it all, all out … whoah … so slippy … more coming … lovely tight bottoms … aaargh …' rang through the corridors of Nam Horm.

The 30 minutes up, Hides was dead, sporting the biggest smile yet witnessed on a resident's face.

To a man, fellow guests wanted to have whatever he'd been having, although an ultra-envious Malden thought the smile was more to do with early rigor mortis.

Phalasuk and Bunrakham, having chalked up three deaths in as many weeks, wondered where their careers were heading.

The *Sentinel* carried a highly-filleted version of the obituary, the national papers were less censorious, with only the *Sunday Sport* publishing Hides' words in full.

His enraged widow threatened to sue, and Corner promptly resigned at the humiliation of his own paper being scooped by the *Sport*.

***

Ratledge and Scully marvelled at the ease with which a reporter had penetrated the resort. It did not bode well; neither did the body count.

'This is getting bloody ridiculous, Ludo.'

Scully agreed. 'You know, Arnie, The *Telegraph* claims that the troops In Afghanistan have a greater chance of short-term survival than Nam Horm residents.'

'It's not just that, Ludo. It's these costs I keep going on about. We're not responsible for Hides, of course, but the endless rows over the deaths of our five are sending the bills sky high.

'The corpses are caught like piggies in the middle and now relatives are demanding we fly them out to Thailand to see their dear departed.

'I think they just want a free holiday, but it's all eating into the cost benefits of the whole bloody idea.'

'I'm really sorry to hear that, Arnie. I just don't know what the answer is.'

'When people die why can't bodies just fucking disappear? I mean they're no bleeding use anymore, are they, Ludo, apart from organ donations, and who wants a spare part from an octogenarian?'

'Maybe another octogenarian?'

'For fuck's sake, Ludo!'

***

Having half a million pounds paid into a bank account does peculiar things to normal men. To men who are already peculiar, it does even odder things.

Scully pored over the printed fund transfer staring back at him. No doubt about it, there was the figure '5' followed by five zeros. He mused that all it would take is for the '5' to be absent and then he would have nothing.

Yes, the '5' was important, a bit like the 'not' in a 'not guilty' court verdict.

His head started to throb a little and he paced the bungalow, waiting for Lucy to return from whatever she was up to with Wanlaya.

He urgently needed another human being to confirm that those six digits were as they seemed. For the umpteenth time, he moved the piece of paper around the room, this time placing it on his bedside table.

Yet again he checked that it wasn't showing half a million Thai baht, which would be a paltry £10,000. He walked to the bathroom, again peered in the mirror to marvel at what a genuine half millionaire looked like, returned to the piece of paper and shook his head repeatedly.

What would Marx have said? Probably, 'you can stand lunch today!'

The thought, plus the sound of Lucy's key in the door, jerked him out of his gentle descent into absurdity; too many monkeys were screeching around his skull.

Lucy looked flushed; it peeped through her ever-deepening tan. 'A good time with Wanlaya, then?' Scully asked distractedly, eyes still riveted on the piece of paper. She threw herself on the bed.

'She's amazing, Ludo, I can't believe how she knows all this stuff, where it comes from. It's not just physical; she gets right inside your innermost thoughts, blowing the cobwebs away, utterly uninhibited … freedom … freedom … freedom.'

Scully looked at her; the piece of paper; her; the piece of paper. Which would triumph? In such a mood, little he could say would have major impact, but half a million quid must be noteworthy.

'The half million's in the bank, safe and sound, it's arrived. We are now, officially, half millionaires.'

Lucy was pleased, but not ecstatic; only so much ecstasy could be handled in a single day.

'That's wonderful, Ludo, I'm so glad.'

The muted response was a jolt to Scully. Lucy barely glanced at the piece of paper.

'Well, I suppose this means you'll go ahead with your flying club plans.'

'Our flying club plans,' Scully corrected. Lucy pondered how much to reveal.

'I told Wanlaya that it looked like you'd sold your business for a lot of money.'

'You didn't say how much, did you? You know what it's like here. If they think you're rolling in it, prices for everything can suddenly shoot up.'

'No, of course not. All I said was that you were thinking of starting a flying business for tourists, and if you did, you'd make sure that any Nam Horm loose ends would be looked after.'

'What was her reaction?'

'She thought it would be really "cool" to live with an active pilot and his wife.'

'You mean you've already suggested she moves in with us, before I've agreed, before I've bought an airstrip … before we've even got a house?'

'Ludo, Ludo, I was only going through possible scenarios; nothing's even been discussed with her father yet. You do get yourself worked up over nothing.

'Now be a good half millionaire and take your very hungry lady for a long drawn-out meal of Thai specialities. Then, if you're not too tired, I can introduce you to other Thai specialities.

'Palates can get jaded in either department, love, but with imagination, all is possible.'

'Will we be alone, or can we expect company?'

'No, Wanlaya will not be with us. Not tonight.'

***

Stanley Vincent had not trusted Ratledge to the last, insisting on access to bank codes and passwords that ensured Scully's old business had been sold and the half million transferred.

Only at that point had the tapes been handed over, but not before Vincent had done a little transferring of his own. The words on the tapes, as promised, had not been doctored or altered in any way. Vincent had kept to the letter of their agreement, but modified its spirit by giving Ratledge copies of the originals.

The copies were identical to the masters in every department – except one. Three additional, audible clicks were added to the 'euthanasia' tape.

They obscured none of the dialogue, signified nothing, and to the outside observer would have served no purpose whatsoever.

The added clicks were made by an old non-working radio that Vincent simply switched on and off during the copy taping of the original recording.

The sole purpose was to invite suspicion that the tape had been tampered with when it came under scrutiny – as it inevitably would. Ratledge had queried the clicks with Vincent, but not in any great detail. His eagerness to focus on the words swamped all else.

Vincent confessed to Ratledge that he'd been responsible for the poor mobile reception that dogged the Mayor's Thai calls. Some crude jamming equipment had worked fine.

This had forced Ratledge and Scully to communicate via the council landline, making bugging far easier, although the equipment Vincent had used for that had been a little dated. Hence the clicks.

Ratledge accepted the explanation. The media were harder to convince.

To Ratledge's frustration, the clicks became the story as speculation mounted that the new tape could be an elaborate hoax to 'bury' the euthanasia angle for good.

This was in line with what Vincent had planned and hoped for. As the months went by, he observed with growing satisfaction the ebbing away of Ratledge's political capital as, like a man in quicksand, the more he struggled against the suspicions, the more he was sucked under.

And adding immeasurably to his problems, no credible Youth in Asia magazine was ever unearthed by any journalist.

Ratledge's frustration grew exponentially as 'respected' organisations now jumped on 'his' bandwagon, switching care for the elderly to a host of agreeable, far-flung locations – at a fraction of the private and public cost.

Germany was quick to follow the British lead, and there was much hilarity over the possibility of octogenarians carrying the flame of beach-towel battles on to the sands of South East Asia.

Other Western European countries, headed by the Scandinavians, got in on the act, while across the Atlantic, the mushrooming Government debt and demographic problems of the USA led to the setting up of a special Congressional committee to examine the whole issue.

It had all become so much bigger than Ratledge whose Arco consultancy was simply being steamrollered out of the picture.

The one area of comfort for Wigburn's Mayor was that no one else had solved the growing problem of costly death complications, and the sudden explosion in numbers of 'devastated' bereaved.

Both Ratledge and Scully had noted with increasing cynicism how grieving relatives from across Europe – people who could not have cared less when their 'beloved' rotted in domestic care homes – were miraculously discovering a new sense of loss when offered a free flight to view the body in some tropical paradise.

With even the best international legal brains stumped for a comprehensive answer to death's many challenges, occasional one-off bilateral agreements were concluded. But costs were horrendous as lawyers made hay over complex technicalities while corpses gathered ice in exotic lands. There had to be an answer somewhere, Wigburn's Mayor felt.

But for now, Ratledge was like someone trapped in a time warp, largely reduced to making speeches about the whole care-home idea being his – and, maddeningly, no, he did not believe in euthanasia.

As his influence and putative empire shrank, with just Nam Horm and two much smaller Samui-based care homes under his control, he was left to dwell on what might have been.

There was the odd phone call to Scully, but they became less frequent. His 'boy' was enjoying himself up in the air, although still deeply enmeshed with the five corpses back on earth.

Poking the coals of a fire in the vast living room of his mansion, Ratledge thought he saw Scully's face dancing in the flames. 'Well, you branched out just in time,' he muttered.

'You, spending half a million pounds of MY FUCKING MONEY, you won't have a clue. Head in the clouds, as ever. You need your feet on the ground, sorting out deaths and bloody relatives with some new idea. Pilot. Pillock.'

***

Ratledge might have felt differently had he been a fly in the cockpit of Scully's Cessna 172 at that very moment. Grass airstrip, a house and the first of two aircraft in his possession, Scully was in business and the joy rides already underway.

Although he'd successfully converted his Private Pilot's Licence to a commercial rating, for the flight on that day, it mattered not.

It was a freebie for Moo, a particularly helpful employee at Nam Horm who had been kindness itself to both Lucy and Scully over the years.

Moo had never flown in any aircraft and Scully was fulfilling a long-standing promise to take him up at the first opportunity.

The problem was the opportunity fell at 8.15am one Monday morning, at the same time Ratledge, unable to sleep, settled into his 1.15am, fireside whisky.

Fifteen minutes later as Ratledge imagined the face of Scully in the flames, his former 'comrade' fell fast asleep at the plane's controls.

Scully, eyes on cheeks after a night of the most satisfying, inhibition-free sex with Lucy and Wanlaya, had been urged by both women to cancel the flight, but a promise was a promise and there was no way he was going to let Moo down.

At 8.30am, just as the plane straightened out over the Gulf of Thailand, exhaustion won the battle of wills with Scully. In a highly illegal move, he asked Moo to put his hands on the dual control joystick.

'Keep the needle on that heading,' he instructed, pointing to some numbers.

'If you need to go left, turn the stick gently to the left; right, turn the stick to the right. Don't worry about the (rudder) pedals.

'One very important thing to remember, very, very important, is don't let this aircraft speed indicator (ASI) get below 60. Very dangerous. We can fall out of the sky. Push the stick forward to go faster, pull stick back to go slower.

'Don't worry about engine speed, I've set it, that's a different sort of speed. Got all that?' Moo nodded, smiling, evidently assuming it was all just a normal part of flying.

'Good man, you're a natural. Now I'm just going to close my eyes and rest my head on the side here. Any problem and you must tell me immediately.'

Moo beamed at the sense of responsibility he was assuming. Within seconds Scully was fast asleep and was within a whisker of it being his last.

He woke with a jolt, horrified to see the Cessna in a gentle left bank towards the water.

He grabbed control from his still beaming 'co-pilot' and calculated he had been asleep for two minutes, and that a further two would have killed them both.

The shock still reverberated as he landed back at the airstrip, 25 knots in excess of touchdown speed. After two significant runway bounces, the plane finally stuck. Through it all, Moo still smiled, assuming it was all part of the great adventure of flying.

'Thank you very much, Mr Ludo, that was very nice.'

'Oh, you're welcome, you're welcome, Moo.'

He declined to ask why he'd not woken him. The man had been through enough. Truly, truly, ignorance could be such sweet bliss.

Lucy and Wanlaya had come to the airstrip, happy, glowing, confident; carefree, apart from concern at Scully's fitness to fly.

'That was a bit of bouncy, bouncy,' Lucy said as Wanlaya spoke in Thai to the still beaming Moo.

'You mean the flight or last night?' Lucy grinned, almost shyly.

'Seriously, though, Ludo, we were worried about you.'

'Yeah, you were probably right to,' Scully said, adding. 'We need to plan our … err … social life with a little more thought.'

***

The 'social' arrangements for all three had been a compromise, the central feature of which was essentially a six-month trial *menage*.

For both Lucy and Scully, the big surprise factor had been the lack of opposition from Wanlaya's family.

Scully felt that something more was in play, but couldn't work out what. Lucy decided she could not care less.

As she never tired of saying, for the first time in her life she felt like a woman completely fulfilled in every dimension – mental, physical, spiritual – and with not a financial care in the world.

The after-sex glow was every bit as important as the carnality itself. The three-way sessions opened minds to depths of discussion in which no subject was taboo.

It was their own mini enlightenment. Liberated from the enslavement of unrequited lust, it freed up oceans of space for inquiry, intellectual challenge, creativity – and endless humour.

Lucy wanted life to live forever, learn Thai, help the less fortunate, spread the joy around. Life could be truly free … liberating … and she felt a generosity deep enough to embrace the earth.

But not a generosity that could ever extend to Scully and Wanlaya embracing each other – alone.

To her joy, Scully had eventually agreed to that one condition. In self-sacrificing fashion, he'd even supplied Lucy with the ammunition to win the argument.

'If I were bisexual,' he'd said to her one evening, 'and we all enjoyed threesomes, I'm sure I could never extend the arrangement to you spending nights alone with my male partner.

'So, yes, I agree to your condition. I understand where you're coming from.'

Lucy almost cried, 'You really are a rarity, Ludo. You're always willing to see the other side. I think that's why I love you so much.'

'Let's not get too carried away, though, Lucy,' Scully had cautioned.

'These things can easily go wrong – zip off in any direction. I mean, just look at Nam Horm now.

'The old lads are having a beano all right, but there have been the six deaths, near fights over the carers, and, would you believe, I've even been asked to act as best man at two weddings next month. What do I do? Act like a father, giving a couple of 88-year-olds away?'

'No, silly, the father of the bride does that sort of thing!'

***

The six months had seemed a reasonable period to assess the *menage*. They were now into their third month and the carefully laid out ground rules had worked well.

The cooking was shared good-naturedly, and the general tidying up delegated to a cleaner who came in twice a week. The state of the beds often prompted puzzled frowns.

By common consent, any young, pretty cleaners would not be engaged. Temptation was to be put in no one's way.

The unshakeable bedrock of the agreement was that no one else would be involved in their sex lives – for emotional, physical and, above all, health reasons.

The moment that was broken, the *menage* would end. And the ground rules – effectively, the threesome's constitution – could only be altered by unanimous agreement.

Even the nature and use of sex toys and aids had been dealt with in fine detail. To Scully's delight and astonishment, nothing had been banned:

A mouth-watering array of vibrators, creams, gels, whips, face masks, chains, dildos, cuffs – and every variety of clothing in a range of materials, including his beloved jodhpurs – was to be available.

Some of the proceedings would be filmed for later delectation, adding an extra frisson to whatever was going on next door when either Wanlaya or Scully spent every third night alone.

All agreed that restriction of the special 'sweeties,' the threesomes, increased the sexual tension and ultimate enjoyment enormously.

It was apparent that real brainpower had gone into

the planning. And that included the ticklish subject of contraception.

Wanlaya's concern that Ludo's enjoyment should not be hindered by sheaths had won the admiration of both Scully and Lucy. That's why, she'd argued, it was so important that none of them had sexual contact with any other partner.

Both women agreed, without reservation, that they would take care of the contraception.

On the threesome nights, Scully was always overjoyed to empty his seed into Wanlaya, keenly egged on by Lucy whose lower lips were lovingly savoured by the Thai girl.

Twice a week Wanlaya would visit her parents, ostensibly to check on how the resort and its wildly happy residents were doing. Her parents' first concern, however, was to question whether she was 'late' that month.

By the fourth month of the *menage*, she appeared to be late, but no definitive test had yet been conducted. Lucy thought she could detect a slight weight gain. Wanlaya smiled.

'It's these delicious green curries, you're always cooking, Lucy. You're outdoing the Thais. They seem creamier and … I don't know … sort of thicker than the ones I cook up.'

Wanlaya was sitting across from Scully, playing footsie under the table. Lucy came round to her, put a gentle arm around the Thai girl's shoulders and kissed her on the cheek.

'It's a secret English ingredient, my love. It's called cornstarch.' Ludo Scully, possible father-to-be and unknowing sperm donor, came close to choking on a prawn.

'Shellfish bastard!' he muttered to no one in particular.

Meanwhile, at Manchester Airport, an expensively chartered cargo plane was about to unload six coffins flown in from Thailand.

Ludo Scully had been painstaking and determined, finally hammering out an agreement that put legal questions on the back burner, to be settled in the British courts.

It was a one-off arrangement that allowed all six bodies to

come home, the *Sentinel*'s man piggy-backing a ride.

The coffins were labeled with the first name of each man and had been loaded in alphabetical order.

Albert, Dan, Eric, George, Horace and Mick.

Last on, meant first off.

Reader Mick had been granted his dying wish.

Acknowledgements

My grateful thanks to my literary agent, Sonia Land, whose creative suggestions, support and unwavering belief in me was inspirational. Thanks are also due to Bill Rogers for his invaluable help in explaining the complexities of the book industry.

My deep appreciation to my long-suffering wife Leena for her rock-like support, putting up with the many mood swings that all debut authors must surely go through. Finally, a word for my daughter, Tanya, who survived a major road accident, yet still found the strength to guide me through many Internet thickets. Her contribution was heroic.

8524676R00163

Printed in Great Britain
by Amazon.co.uk, Ltd.,
Marston Gate.